Imogene's Grand Fiasco

Imogene's Grand Fiasco

The Misadventures of Imogene Taylor

David Putnam

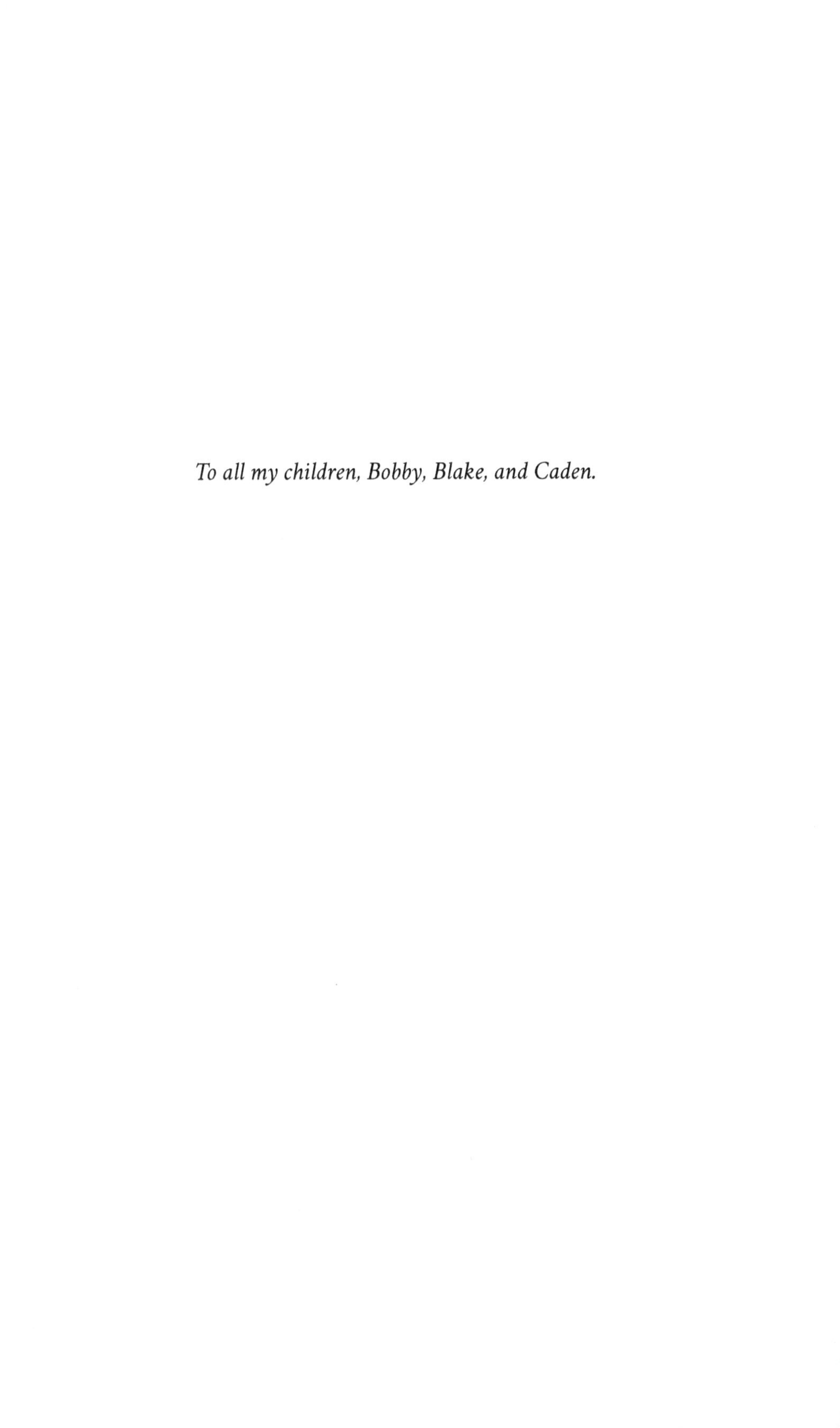

To all my children, Bobby, Blake, and Caden.

Chapter One

While Imogene waited for her name to be called, she winked and surreptitiously waved at the shy, towheaded little girl who peeked from around her mom. The mom, a speed freak who twitched and scratched at unseen bugs and couldn't remain still in the chair, hardly acknowledged her daughter's presence.

The little girl was too thin, scruffy, with a dirt-smudged face. In her mind, Imogene named her Sophie.

Two…no, it was three decades ago, Imogene's hope for her own granddaughter died along with Joyce, their only child. Never gonna happen now, that window closed. Shattered actually. And Imogene, seventy-five, headed all too quickly toward eighty.

The place looked and had the feel of a filthy Department of Motor Vehicles waiting room. Only these were not folks in need of registering a vehicle or taking a driver's test. Like Imogene, they all waited for an audience with a parole agent who had the absolute right to impinge upon their freedoms by violating their parole and sending them back to the Big House. The Joint. The Clink. The Cooler.

Imogene smiled at Sophie, raised one finger, and moved it up and down in an indiscreet wave. From three seats over, Sophie smiled back and hid behind her twitchy mom. Imogene opened her black clutch purse, pulled out a piece of saltwater taffy wrapped in white waxed paper. She held it out as a child would in a petting zoo, trying to coax a shy kid goat. Sophie stood up straight at the sight of the candy. She looked at her mom, whose attention was anywhere except on her daughter, then back at Imogene, not knowing what to do. Sneak over, snatch the candy, risk mom's wrath, or play it safe and stay put. One of many small choices now that, as she grew older, would turn into more important, larger choices.

Sophie's expression shifted to sorrow, choosing not to take the risk of a slap upside the head. She stuck her thumb into her mouth and again leaned against her mom's leg. A child three years old shouldn't be sucking her thumb.

Imogene casually dropped the candy to the floor and kicked it over. The candy slid right up to Sophie, who bent and snatched it up. She turned her back to her mom, unwrapped it, and turned around, a lump in her cheek and a huge smile on her lips.

Her mom wouldn't pass the drug test or the parole agent's scrutiny. She would, without a doubt, be violated and sent in on a ninety-day violation to get sober. Sophie would be handed over to Child Protective Services. The child should never have been brought to a parole office in the first place. It broke Imogene's heart, the senseless emotional pain that awaited Sophie. She didn't have chance one to make a life for herself. Destined to follow in her mom's footsteps. A senseless waste of life.

Imogene shifted on a molded plastic chair in that crowded windowless room, the walls a putrid green, faded from too many years of inattention. The state could at least spring for some art, maybe some of those inspirational posters. Criminently, this was 1973.

The room reeked of body odor and despair.

She clutched her purse close to her chest. The new dress and black orthopedic shoes might not have been a smart choice. She stood out, or hoped she stood out from the rest of the crowd in their soiled and tattered clothing, sporting black ink tattoos only obtainable in the state prison system.

Oh, please, please call her name.

The new clothes might not have been a good idea, flagging her as a victim in a pond filled with class A predators. She arrived early, not wanting to be late. This punctuality exposed her to a longer vulnerable period in the pond.

One other fellow also didn't match the cast of ne'er-do-wells and miscreants. A cowboy of sorts who sat across the room, dressed in tired and worn-out dungarees, though recently cleaned. He kept his black cowboy hat down low on his forehead to shield any possible expressions. He wore a long-sleeved, small-checked shirt with snaps instead of buttons. The skin on his hands and face, tanned and wrinkled, looked like the old dried-apple dolls. His white hair hung down to his collar and matched his gunfighter mustache that stood out stark against brown skin. Around his neck hung a black bolo tie with a thumb-sized lump of real turquoise.

His gray eyes clung to Imogene in an impolite manner, as if she'd been chosen as his next victim, a vulnerable doe amongst the degenerate bucks. Or that, too, could be overheated imagination.

She looked away from him and wished for the umpteenth time for her name to be called. Her nicotine addiction tried hard to overpower a conviction to stay the course and instead give in, hurry outside, and light up a Marlboro, one of a two-pack-day habit.

The receptionist, a large woman similar in size, shape, and color to a walrus, sat behind a thick Plexiglas window, one marred with smudges and etched with gang insignia. She communicated through a little metal-covered speaker. If anyone needed to give the woman documents, they slid them into a stainless-steel metal tray that extended then retracted. Everyone brought papers already signed by their superiors, their masters, really. People who controlled their lives. Employers, workers at halfway houses, and law enforcement agencies that meted out the laminated cards for convicted narcotic offenders and degenerate perverts.

Each time the drawer clanked, Imogene jumped in the chair. The Plexiglas and the drawer further segregated folks on the outside looking in and further confirmed their position in society as nothing more than animals in a zoo. Maybe that was true. Criminal statistics she read while on the inside stated that six percent of the population comprised "abnormal maladjusted people," who should be kept away from "the normal and vulnerable groups within a well-adjusted society."

Imogene took offense to those words when she first discovered them, read every word over three times. Now, looking at the collection of the county's worst congregating in one place, maybe the theory was correct. But based on the number of people coming and going through the door, maybe that six percentage number should be a tad higher.

Sitting in that molded blue plastic chair on the wrong side of the glass left her with only one conclusion: that she would never again attain the status of the normal and socially adjusted.

When Imogene checked in, she used that same drawer to submit her document signed by Micheal Higginbothom, the owner of Dentco, where she had worked for a little over two years. Higginbothom fired her two weeks prior after the fiasco that involved his girlfriend, Suz Davis, who was arrested and held for a short time for killing three men in Imogene's living room. Higginbothom blamed Imogene for the entire unfortunate incident.

Imogene still needed the proof of employment. After being fired she merely forged his name to the card and trundled her big butt over to the parole office in San Bernardino. After this meeting, she would show up at Dentco like nothing ever happened, sit on her tall stool, and run the store. All the while, hoping the souls of those three dead men grew tired of haunting her and moved on to wherever they were supposed to go. Purgatory, in Hell's little half acre. That's what Wayne used to call it.

She fidgeted. If this new person at the San Bernardino office called Higginbothom to confirm her employment, that would be it. Done, finite, c'est la vie, the big adios for Imogene.

The metallic speaker embedded in the Plexiglas spoke, crackled, really, "Imogene Taylor?"

She stood and paused. Her back ached from sitting in the same position for an hour and a half. Sitting shoulder to shoulder with the "others." Her worn-out knees rattled and ached as if filled with broken glass. In a civilized world, a seventy-five-year-old woman shouldn't be subjected to this sort of tyranny.

At that moment, after two long weeks of silence, Ange finally spoke into her ear. *Hold your head up, girl, throw those shoulders back. You're no kinda slouch. You're frickin' Imogene Taylor, killer of men. And I've said it before and I'll say it again, men are nothing but ugly, cheap, two-timing bastards who deserve a good killin'. Kill 'em all and let God sort 'em out. Right, E? Right?*

Imogene smiled, happy for the return of a long-time friend. Even though it was only a voice in her head. Emotional support in any form came as welcome relief.

The door next to the Plexiglas window buzzed as Imogene approached. The knob, sticky from thousands of other degenerates who came before. Those who moved through the door, unsure if they would ever again step back out on the freedom side. Their nervous flop sweat mixed with dirt composed the gummy substance on the knob.

Inside, she walked down the short hall and stopped when it opened to a huge cubicle farm spanning at least a hundred and fifty feet in each direction. A perfect rectangle. A constant hum rose from all the talking, in person and on the phone.

Damn, girl, how many of those idgits out in the real world are on parole?

More important, how was anyone to know which way to proceed? The state needed to put up street signs with addresses. Down a ways, off to the left, was a kitchenette with a sink, refrigerator, table, and chairs, and of all things, a microwave oven. Something rarely seen, a new invention that had not yet filtered down to the common man.

Next to the break area sat a detention cage. One made of common chain link fencing on all sides and on top, with a gate used to toss in the animals. A holding pen before the unfortunates caught "the chain" to Chino. One of those unfortunates, a woman, sat on the wooden bench inside the confinement, crying. She wore a dirty yellow tank top and cutoff shorts. Dried dirt smears covered her arms and legs as if she might live under a bridge like a troll. When she looked up and caught Imogene's eye, tears had left streaks down her dirty cheeks. Imogene looked away. Of course, it just had to be a woman. A stone-cold reminder of the stakes involved for herself. To get tossed back in the joint at Imogene's age equaled a death sentence.

She steeled herself and forced her feet to walk the short distance to the cage. On the kitchenette counter sat a box of fresh donuts. All cake left. Most of the tastier raised donuts already picked over. She opened the refrigerator, took out an ice-cold can of Pepsi, ignoring the sign that read, "Pop, $.50.

Don't be a sneak-thief convict." She picked out a chocolate cake with pink frosting and a white cake donut with white frosting and coconut sprinkles.

Now the difficult part. The dangerous part. The cage key attached to a long piece of wood hung on the wall by a hook. She looked around first and then made her move. She grabbed the key and opened the cage gate.

The poor ne'er-do-well looked up from the bench, dejected and forlorn, resigned to her fate. Her eyes lit up for a moment at the prospect of a reprieve.

Imogene set the meager offering on the floor, quickly backed out, and relocked the gate before the gal bum-rushed her to get out. Back in CIW, fresh sugary treats came with a heavy bounty.

A tall black man's head rose up above the cubicle farm. If he had done it seconds earlier, he would've caught her. Thrown her in alongside the poor wretch. "Imogene Taylor, take a right, go over two rows, then count down to eleven. Get a move on, I'm running behind schedule."

Whoa, baby girl, did you see that handsome hunk of man devil? You're the luckiest wench I ever saw.

"Right. You call this lucky. I call it a sharp stick in the eye."

She had to tone down the replies to Ange or risk the label, "a headcase," something that would shift her life into a whole 'nother dimension of hate and discontentment. They'd toss her butt into the Booby Hatch. Then forget about her. She would drop into the classic "Haldol drool," and forever live in a straitjacket in a room with padded walls.

Imogene followed the directions given and arrived at a cubicle filled with filing cabinets and stacks of skewed files on the floor two feet tall. A beat-up desk and chair, worn and tattered, matched a harried occupant. No free space remained, hardly any room left to swing a dead cat. Not without hitting a piece of governmental property, which included the dude.

"Sit."

Don't do it, Imogene. Keep standing 'til this dickwad masquerading as a black Adonis says it nicely. Asks you to "please sit." Talks to you like a lady of your true status.

Imogene ignored Ange and sat. Sometimes Ange prompted Imogene to do things that would get her tossed back in the joint. Even so, having Ange back took away a whole lot of pressure. It meant Imogene wasn't alone.

Stuck with gray masking tape to the side of the cubicle wall was a desk monument that would normally sit on an uncluttered desk. It read, "James Humphries, Parole Agent." She eased into the chair alongside the desk with her purse in her lap. Too close to the man who held sway over the remainder of her life.

Humphries never looked up from the file and continued to write. He used his left hand that had a solid gold wedding band on the appropriate finger. Left-handed people meant a thinker, someone creative. He wore a dress shirt and a matching tie over a used pair of denim pants with razor-sharp, ironed creases. Who ironed denim? What foolishness.

On the wall below the name monument hung pictures of his family at play in a park. Two children, a boy and girl, ages eight and ten. No wife anywhere in sight.

This man wasn't an ogre, he just acted like one. Exposed day in and day out to the miscreants that populated the lobby. Who wouldn't be? You worked around unscrupulous recidivists long enough; they rubbed off on you. How could you not take it home like a virus? Spread around the affliction, infecting your loved ones.

The slow, meticulous way he wrote put him behind on his schedule. He had no one else to blame. A clock on the desk next to her shoulder and ear ticked too loudly. A countdown to her time left breathing free air. And don't let anyone tell you different, free air was sweet by comparison.

The narrow red hand swept around the numbers. After a time, her eyes locked on that red second hand and mesmerized all thoughts.

For the past two years, after being released from CIW, Chino Institute for Women, and given her tail, Nancy Do-right had been her parole agent. Nancy preferred meeting "out in the field," at Dentco, or designated times and places in coffee houses and the like. For the first time, after sitting in the lobby, Imogene understood why.

What happened to Nancy? Imogene didn't like the woman, but at least understood her. To understand where Nancy stood on important issues mattered a great deal.

Two days after the shootout in Imogene's living room, a card came in the mail requesting her presence at the San Bernardino parole office. The card also said a new parole officer had been assigned. For twelve days, she fretted and argued with herself, fighting back and forth: stay or take it on the lam to Mexico.

Humphries grunted and closed the file. He looked up with mahogany brown eyes that stared straight through her and on into the next cubicle. Sweet baby Jesus, he could read her every thought.

She squirmed under the pressure, the vulnerability. "Ah...did I do something wrong?"

"I don't know, did you? Take off that sun bonnet, those white gloves, and sunglasses. You're not fooling anyone."

E, this guy's a total horse's ass. Go on, get up and just walk away. Do it right now. You don't need this kind of heartache. You're a self-made woman. And more important, a killer of men ta boot. Doesn't he realize that? Come on, let's get the hell outta here.

Imogene didn't care for him answering her question with a question. Using interrogation 101 techniques. She read up on how cops worked, the justice system, forensics, courtroom procedure, rules of evidence, and the like. All during those ten years she wasted back in C-block.

"Of course not. And you took me away from my job. Now my boss is angry. By your silly rules, I'm supposed to remain *gainfully* employed. You're making that very difficult."

He gave the stare again. "Would you like it better if I put you in that cage you saw on your way in, let you catch the chain back to where you belong?"

Her face flushed hot as she held back a blinding rage. How dare he threaten her? She hated anyone with that kind of power held over her head. A guillotine blade about to drop, his itchy hand on the lever.

She took in a deep cleansing breath. "Of course not. I'm here. How can I help you?"

He swiveled in his chair to face her and leaned back.

"Help me? You need to change that attitude, Missy, and think about helping yourself. Hand me that hatpin. It could be used as a deadly weapon."

"Oh, for goodness sakes. Really?" She handed the pin over.

He slid a thick file off the stack and opened it. "Hmm. Seventy-five years old, did ten years for killing your husband. Shot him in the forehead and claimed you thought he was an intruder. Jury didn't buy it. Been out for two. Stayed clean until two weeks ago when three men died in your living room from GSW, gunshot wounds." He leaned forward. "That, little Missy, is why you're sitting at my desk. Right here, right now, I decide if you had anything to do with those killings."

"Not really."

"What?"

"Well, there is a thing called due process. If you decide to violate my parole, send me back, your report first goes before a parole board who then decides my fate. Not you."

His jaw muscle bulged as he ground his teeth.

He waited a beat to regain the stolen momentum. "I read all the police reports. They say your neighbor, Susan Davis, pulled the trigger and did all the shooting. I ran a background on her. She's clean as a Safeway chicken. Not so much as a parking ticket. And you want me to believe, when you have priors for murder, that she's the one who pulled the trigger? Gunned them down in cold blood? Killed three men?"

"Two. One of those men, the gun-thug who worked for Giancana, shot dead my neighbor Bernard Lowery. He was the third dead man. Bernard was."

Sweat broke out on Imogene's forehead and ran down into her eyes. This turd had to love this grilling, got his jollies out of it. "If I may interject, you also have some other facts skewed."

He held out his hand, "Please, enlighten me."

Imogene *had* been the one to pull the trigger. She shot first or she would've been killed right along with Suz and John Catskill. Suz copped out to doing the deed in order to shield Imogene from criminal proceedings. Friends like Suz didn't come along every day. And now that was all ruined she wouldn't come over or answer her phone.

Imogene said. "One of the deceased happened to be a mafia kingpin named Giancana, known as the Cigar. The feds were trying their best to get a piece of him. He was extorting all the stores in the Cherry Center strip mall. He killed a friend of ours, Ibrahim the owner of Cherry Liquor. And you seem to have forgotten, all three men in my living room had guns and were trying to kill *us*. The DA ruled it self-defense."

Humphries pointed a finger at her. "When you paroled, you signed an agreement that said you understand you are not to associate or fraternize with ex-cons. You are not to be around any firearms. That's enough right there to violate your parole and send you back."

"Then why don't you do it? What's stopping you?"

Sometimes her mouth overloaded her butt, wrote a check her butt couldn't cover. This was the wrong place, wrong time for it.

She couldn't pull the words back and wanted to in the worst way. She cringed and held her breath.

But wait. Something wasn't quite right. Something—

He didn't explode like he should've. That was it.

Something was up.

"Oh," she said, "I know what's going on here."

He said nothing.

Lem, her friend in the Secret Service, took a hand in her parole status. He must've thrown in his two-cents worth and that amounted to just enough influence to let the crap roll off her like a fried egg in a Teflon pan.

A slow grin wormed out and into her expression. Slithered across her teeth. "I know why you just pulled back those sharpened canines. Because you can't do anything. Your hands are tied."

His expression suddenly shifted to pure anger. She had poked the beast.

She pressed the issue and shouldn't have. "Someone higher than your pay grade whispered in your ear. Didn't they, Chuckles? Hah."

Humphries jumped out at her, grabbed her by the throat in a vice-grip hand that immediately clamped off air. He squeezed while he moved in close to whisper in her ear. His breath foul, the same as if he'd stopped at a deli for lunch and ordered a turd sandwich. "This is your one and only get-out-of-jail-free card. You understand? Left up to me I'd have already thrown your sorry ass back in the can. You don't fool me, lady. Not for one second. From here on out, you so much as jaywalk. I'll be there to stick a fork in ya, because you'll be done."

She struggled for breath. Her hand, all on its own, snaked over and grabbed the hatpin he'd laid atop a file. Pure and simple survival instinct and nothing more. She raised it, ready to stab him in the arm to get him off.

"Go ahead, lady, do it. Please do it."

They stared at each other for another long, interminable beat. Two.

Bright stars flashed in her vision. She couldn't go much longer before darkness sauntered in and closed down all the lights, called it a day.

Still, she waited him out.

He abruptly let go and sat back.

She gasped and bent over, her lungs a bellow sucking in air too fast. She stood before her body said it was a good idea. Picked up the bonnet, put it on, and pinned it. Picked up the white gloves and slowly put them on. All the while staring at him, letting him know she wasn't afraid, wasn't impressed by his misogynistic tendencies.

She straightened her dress. "You ever touch me again and it'll be your last conscious act." She turned and walked away.

He followed along, his anger not allowing him to do anything else. "You will be here every Wednesday, same time. If you are one minute late, you're done. You hear me, capital DEE, capital UN."

Imogene didn't look back, kept going. She raised her white-gloved hand and wiggled her fingers. "Have a nice day, Agent Humphries. You just made mine."

Chapter Two

Outside, standing by the little red AMC Gremlin, Imogene put her head back, closed her eyes, let the sun warm her face. Freedom. Warmth. Comfortable. Prior to walking into the parole office, no possible scenario she could think of allowed for her to come back out. No parolee walked away from three dead in a shootout. Lem was owed big time.

She finished reveling. Survival instinct prodded yet again to take another look around the parking lot. Giancana's people promised a blood feud-grudge to the death. A gunned-down made-man never sets well with those people. Especially not when done by an old woman. In fact, in the books, the news articles, the rumor-fueled anecdotes, in the history of the mob, a woman had never gunned down two men from the Nostra Familia. No way could those idgits let it stand. They would come for her. It wasn't a matter of if, it was a matter of when.

Her invisible tail precluded her from carrying any type of weapon or risk a violation and getting thrown back in the can. Not a pretty choice; spend the remaining life in C-Block with her friend Ange, or wait until a button man rolls up quiet as a mouse and rams a shiv between her ribs. Or pumps a lead pill into the back of her head. Ugh. She shivered.

She unlocked and opened the car door, reached under the seat, and retrieved a stolen .380 automatic. One obtained from Odette, a nice, ill-adjusted heroin addict who worked at Dentco. Imogene put the gun in her purse and took one last look around the parking lot. She watched the two entrances for a couple of minutes.

Two kinds of cars entered and left: derelict wrecks with skeevy parolees, or spectacular cars with glittery paint jobs and shiny chrome owned by street gang members. Nothing else stood out. No rental cars. No thugs with previously broken noses leaning against cars with their arms folded across their chests, wearing cheap gold around their necks and on their fingers, gleaming in the bright Southern California sun.

She got in, took in another lungful of free air. She reached to turn the ignition key. Her hand began to shake just as the full ramifications of the dodged prison threat took hold. Her hands fumbled in her purse and shook as she got out a Marlboro and lit up. Nicotine, the only substance to calm raging nerves.

Her eyes automatically scanned the parking lot, assessing everyone coming and going from the parole office. Off to the left, across the sea of cars, sat a clean ten-year-old 1963 Ford pickup painted fire-engine red with bright chrome bumpers. It was parked skewed under a shade tree. The old cowboy from inside the parole office sat behind the wheel, smoking.

Was he watching her? No way would the mob subcontract with a broken-down wannabe cowboy. Right?

Imogene started up and drove fast, already late for a meeting she had never intended to make. But now that she had been released, a wolf amongst the lambs (as parole agent Humphries viewed her), life had to carry on.

She drove deeper into the heart of San Bernardino to the business center and pulled into the asphalt parking lot to a large Victorian house converted to an office in a residential area. She got out, put on her bonnet, tugged on the long white gloves, and walked to the front door. She turned one last time to check her back trail. Her breath caught. On the street, the fire-engine red Ford truck drove by slowly, the old cowboy driver giving her the evil eye. If he *was* gunning for her, only a fool would allow himself to be seen.

Unless he wanted to scare the sweet bejesus out of her.

Mission accomplished.

The question about him following her was answered.

E, what in the world are you smoking? Cain't you tell a man on the prod from one out ta get your sorry ass? That ol' cowboy liked what he saw back there in the parole office and jus' wants ta get him some of that sweeeet cherry pa-eye. You know what I'm sayin' girl? Look at you all gussied up, with the yellow sundress accented by that beeautieful white sunhat. And the white gloves...ooh-ooh girl you got it goin' on.

Inside the receptionist behind the desk, a well-put-together, heavyset woman with kind eyes said, "Mrs. Bea Taylor? The meeting has already started. This way, please."

Calling her "Bea Taylor," of all things. Her nickname from C-block. They had the receptionist say it that way on purpose, just to goad her. Leaving little doubt this was the enemy camp.

She had never been in a deposition and only read about them. The top-shelf attorneys for John Catskill pushed the lawsuit forward at lightning speed. Catskill wanted her to capitulate and sign the publishing contract post haste before some other publisher got a whiff of the deal and got the price jacked up.

She couldn't sign with anyone.

Not without hanging Lem out to dry. Lem, the Secret Service agent who had just kept her out of prison on a parole violation.

The receptionist's heels clacked in unison with hers on the polished hardwood floor. She stopped, hand on a doorknob, fake smile pasted on her round pie-pan face. "Before you go in, can I get you a water, some tea, or coffee? A Danish, maybe?" She looked Imogene up and down and added, "Two or three Danish maybe."

The catty wrench. Knee her in the gut, E. Go on, show her what you're made of.

Under duress, Ange, her old cellie from C-Block, spoke more often.

"Yeah, you sure can, babe. Get me a sixer of Schlitz malt liquor, the tall boys. That would be very kind, thank you."

The woman's eyes grew large, her mouth formed a little "O." She opened the door and stepped inside.

Imogene didn't want a beer. She only said it to take back a little ground lost after being forced to appear in enemy territory for the deposition. She needed to get herself prepped—pumped up for what awaited behind door number one.

She entered a room too small for the size of the table that filled it. One made of thick, expensive hardwood, mahogany maybe, polished to a bright sheen. Three men and a woman sat at the far end: John Catskill, senior editor of Delacorte publishing, visiting from New York; two attorneys from the law firm representing him; and the stenographer. Imogene knew how depositions worked from reading all of Erle Stanley Gardner while in the joint. She loved Perry Mason and intended to emulate him now. Shoulders back, chin up, she wouldn't take one iota of guff from these jaybirds.

If Humphries had sent her back to prison on a violation, she'd have finished out the rest of the original term, 25 to life, and never again seen the light of day. The deposition had not been a pressing problem on her radar until she'd walked out of the parole office.

What did it matter that John Catskill wanted to sue her pants off. Take everything she owed, including the house (paid for), the little red Gremlin (paid for), and the little dab of savings, $20,144.56. Most ex-cons didn't have that kind of nest egg or financial foundation. Not once the penal system regurgitated them back out into the world that hated them to begin with.

Imogene had continued to receive her social security while sitting in C-Block, money that accumulated with every lost day, week, month, and year. Most cons didn't receive social security. Weren't old enough. Most cons weren't sixty-three years old when they started their first stint in the joint.

The crux of the deposition was that Suz Davis, the neighbor to the east, had acted as a literary agent on an impromptu phone call with John Catskill. Together those two established a verbal agreement for Imogene to sell the rights to her novel, *Peekaboo POTUS*, for three hundred thousand dollars. A nice little bundle even by 1973 standards. Then, out of the blue, Catskill showed up at Imogene's door uninvited to secure a signature on said contract. That day just happened to be when Giancana and his thug-ugly came to get even for the funny money Imogene planted on him when he visited Dentco to commit his extortion, in his strong-armed protection racket. This was a much longer and involved story that exhausted Imogene, even thinking about it.

Imogene came in and took a seat across from the three, leaving a wide expanse of wood between them. She took off her bonnet, sunglasses, and white gloves. Making a show with the gloves, one finger at a time.

Catskill grunted and said, "Nice that you could you could finally join us. Twenty-five minutes late." He still sported a white bandage that started at his balding crown and ran down his forehead. He didn't have the right to sue for breach of contract. Not with only a verbal phone agreement and no unbiased witnesses. Instead, the deposition turned into a squeeze play. He sued for pain and suffering over getting pistol-whipped by Giancana, moments before Imogene shot Giancana dead.

Truth be told, Imogene did feel sorry for the poor sot. The doc used 157 scalp sutures to close the wound, one that would be visible for the rest of his life. But in his literary world, it would carry a huge cache along with bragging rights. He had been present when the great Giancana got "shuffled off this mortal coil." That scar, by her reckoning, almost made them square as far as the debt was concerned.

The older of the two attorneys, one with gray-white hair perfectly coifed, long slender fingers with a single ring, a wedding band, introduced everyone. None of their names stuck. He continued. "Ms. Taylor, where is your attorney?" He tried hard for debonair, speaking through his nose in a semi-haughty tone.

Get over it, dude, this is San Bernardino. Not Boston. Come on E, let's blow this pop stand. This guy is giving me the galloping gorples.

"I'm going at this pro per if you don't mind."

The man cleared his throat, "Ahem."

A tell he tossed out when he disagreed with something. Something she could without a doubt use in her favor.

"Very well. For the record, please state your name and date of birth."

The first question right out the gate, one that if answered would be perjury. A new charge, not to mention a parole violation. She'd stepped into a mine field and didn't know where to put her foot down next.

Imogene Taylor wasn't her real name; it was Alice Putnam. A name she had long ago discarded when she took up with her husband Wayne. They fled Arkansas after Wayne's armed robbery and car theft. She'd known nothing about either at the time. Fifty-six odd years ago. More than five decades. A long time for a lie to lie dormant and unmolested. No one would remember Alice Putnam.

"You already know my name. So let's dispense with the formalities, shall we? Let's just get right down to brass tacks." She met Catskill's gaze. "I'm sorry, John, for what happened to you. Really, I am. But I'm not the one who clunked you over the head with the gun. You should be suing him, the Cigar."

Gray Hair said, "Please, don't address my client and only answer the questions."

This guy must be sitting on a twelve-inch two-by-four. He's too stuck-up and mealy-mouthed to be anything else. Say something salacious and lurid that'll put him back on his heels. Go on, E. Do it. I gotta see this. Ask him if he can lick his own eyebrows with that tongue? Go on, git after it, girl.

"No, I won't know when we're on the record."

"Excuse me?" Gray Hair said.

"Look, Catskill wants my book. I'm happy to give it to him—"

Catskill interrupted her. "Wait. You are?"

Gray Hair held up his hand to silence his client. "Please, John, we've discussed this. Let your attorneys handle it."

"Don't you dare shush me. I'm paying your exorbitant rate. If Imogene wants to give me what I want, then let's talk turkey."

Imogene said, "Off the record."

"Ahem, I don't recommend this line of action. If it's not on the record, it didn't happen."

Catskill glared at him. "Stop the steno from recording or you're fired. How's that?"

"Ahem." He waved his hand at the woman on the steno machine. She stopped and stared straight ahead as if a robot that could turn off all audio and memory.

"Look, I'd be happy to give you the book. But after we had our little discussion on the phone, I realized there are things I wrote that can't see the light of day. Not without hurting people."

While in prison with anxiety, regret, and looking down that long tunnel of time, the thought of losing decades of life, Imogene had floundered about looking for an emotional crutch in order to survive. Ange, her cellie had been the one to suggest that Imogene start sending death threats to the president of the United States. Blame him for her incarceration. Go right to the top. She had to blame someone, right? Ange said it would give a needed distraction from the new life behind bars. The idea sounded bat-crap crazy, but there just wasn't anything else to quell her nerves. So she did it. During her tenure in prison, she threatened all three presidents as they rotated through the office. Sent poison missives that grew more creative with each passing month. Ange had been right, the solution of toothless threats did ease up on the prison stress. It also brought in several Secret Service agents to C-block to interview her to assess a threat level. One of which had been Special Agent Lem.

The tactic was meant to scare her straight, and instead only served as a momentary holiday from the mundane life in C-block. She continued the threats but then also wrote a novel called *Peekaboo POTUS*. A book about the assassination of a sitting president. She would never in all the world carry out such a threat. The book was merely a satire, a political allegory of the day's messed-up political, judicial, and correction systems.

After she got out with her tail, she popped up on the Secret Service radar as a possible threat. In the past two years, whenever the President of the United States made an appearance anywhere within two hundred and fifty miles of Imogene, Special Agent Lem took her to lunch and or dinner. If they had tried to detain her during the visit they would have violated her civil rights. During these five different outings with Lem—dates really—he opened up divulging secrets about the protection protocols used to keep the POTUS safe. Once out on parole, Imogene went back through *Peekaboo POTUS* adding in this new information and much more that gave the story huge credibility. And apparently huge salability.

On a whim, she sent several manuscripts out to publishers and thought the act no different than buying a lotto ticket. She never thought anyone would be interested in buying a story, especially from a broken-down old woman, an ex-con for crying out loud. She thought no more about it. When the phone call came from Catskill, in all the excitement, she forgot about the classified information Lem gave her and she used in the book. If she went through with the sale, Lem would be arrested and prosecuted for giving away government secrets.

And now Lem, out of the kindness of his heart, had applied pressure on the parole system to keep her out of prison. This when everyone else wanted her back behind bars: state parole, the Secret Service, the mob (because it would be much easier to take her out, once on the inside), and most of all her old cellie, Ange. What kinda world was it that thought an old woman needed to be incarcerated?

Catskill leaned forward, anxious now, his goal in sight. "Don't worry about all of that. I'll help you edit out anything you want. We can fix it, I promise you."

"I'm afraid the editing will strike too deeply at the heart of the book. That's why I chose to cancel the contract offer."

Gray Hair raised an accusing finger. "So, you admit there was a verbal contract?"

Imogene and Catskill both at the same time shushed him.

"You don't know me," Catskill said to Imogene. "Editing is my stock in trade. I'm very good at it, you'll see. Let's give it a try, shall we?"

A long, protracted legal battle was the last thing she needed. In a blink, all the words in the book whirled past as she calculated the cuts needed and how they would leave as an end product a whole lot of nothing.

Catskill held up his hand, his eyes closed. "Okay. Okay. Here's my final offer, four hundred thousand and…and it's a two-book deal. The second book will be nonfiction on your life up to and including—" He stopped, opened his eyes, fear suddenly present. His throat worked up and down as if the words grew too large to emerge out into the light of day. "Up to, and including the motivation leading to…the ah…the ah…what happened in your living room." His face blanched white.

Ah, the poor bastard. What's he got to complain about? He was knocked cold when you gunned those two A-holes. But it was sweeeet, E, I mean, your best friend

Ange here, loooved, loooved the way you stood there like Wyatt Earp and let 'em have it, cool as a friggin' cucumber. Now take a look at this little spineless dweeb, he's about to earp all over this gorgeous table. Hey, when you take the deal make 'em throw in this table would ya, E? For me, E?

Catskill held up four fingers gulping hard to keep his gorge from gracing them, spilling all over the gorgeous table. Ready to unload predigested coffee with cream cheese and apple Danish.

Imogene didn't look at Catskill. Instead, she shot Gray Hair a scathing glare. "Let me get this straight. I sign a contract for two books for four hundred thousand. One for *Peekaboo POTUS* and the other, as yet untitled, a nonfiction book on my life. If I do, you'll drop this spurious lawsuit over what happened to you in my house? Drop it with prejudice never to be resurrected again?"

"Ahem, now wait just a minute. I have to talk with my client before we make any kind of agreement."

Color suddenly returned to Catskill's face. "Yes. Yes. That's exactly right."

Gray Hair raised his hand with his long, elegant fingers. "Mr. Catskill, please, let us have a private conversation before you agree to anything. She's taking undue advantage here. You are holding all the cards. Not her."

Imogene, still looking at Gray Hair, "And in that contract, it will be written I have final say-so on the finished product of *Peekaboo POTUS*."

"No." Gray Hair slapped the table with a loud crack.

Catskill jumped six inches in his chair. He had a bad case of post-bloody-murder jitters.

He took in a deep breath as the excitement in his eyes winked out, shifting back to fear and then to ruthless negotiator. He raised a finger and pointed it at her. "No, that's a bridge too far, Imogene. Up to this point, I've been more than fair and…and…" His eyes suddenly defused as his mind scampered off to another place, a violent place where a man pointed a gun and unprovoked, used it as a club on his noggin. His hand gently probed his bandaged scalp as he mulled over an unvoiced problem.

He came out of his momentary fog. "I'm not a gun thug and I haven't killed anyone—"

Imogene opened her mouth to protest his disparaging remark aimed her way. He referred to how Imogene's husband, Wayne, had been killed, shot in the forehead in Imogene's bedroom. And twelve years ago, no less.

He held up his hand. "Wait. Just let me talk for one minute. You are a willful woman, Imogene Taylor, and now I am going to have my say. I won't use guns to get my way. I'm a wordsmith, and a word, one word, has just as much power as a gun. So take heed and listen to me closely. As I said, I've tried and tried to be a nice guy through all of this, and you have continually refused to meet me halfway."

Ha, this little weasel thinks he just grew himself a pair of balls. Don't he realize who he's talking to? "Words more powerful than guns?" Just ask my old man and his girlfriend which one gets the job done. Cut him off at the knees, E. Don't let him jibber-jabber anymore, git after it.

"I won't sit here and listen to—"

Catskill jumped to his feet. The chair flew back and hit the wall. He again raised an accusing finger and pointed it like a gun, his face bloated with rage. "No more negotiations. Negotiations are closed. You will sign a contract for two books for four hundred thousand, and there will not be a stipulation of any kind that gives you final edit. No ma'am. That's not going to happen. I wanted this project to be amiable, but you have forced me to be someone I'm not." He slid a prepared contract across the table at her. "Sign it. Alice."

Imogene sucked in a huge lungful of air. He knew. If he knew her real name, then he knew it all. Sweet baby bald-headed Jesus. He knew it all.

Gray Hair looked confused and started to ask about the name error.

Catskill said, "Sorry. Sorry, I meant sign it, Imogene." He pulled his chair back to the table and sat.

Imogene stared at him, her mind running at high speed for a solution to exit the box he just dropped her in. There wasn't one. Not if Catskill knew her real name. Life after prison always returned to the same issue, the tail—parole. If the state found out about her past, that she'd been masquerading under an assumed name all that time…well, that would be it. Ispofacto, slam dunk, right back to the joint.

Did every man she came into contact with have to exercise their male dominance? Sweet baby Jesus, this wasn't fair. When would women ever be equals?

Her hand, all on its own, reached across and slid the contract over. She signed it without reading. Signed it, "Imogene Taylor." Allowed the invisible cage to drop upon her, locking her into a car barreling down the highway, a car without any brakes. Destined to pile up one last time, in spectacular technicolor of blood and bone.

She stood, swept her white gloves off the beautiful table, and walked from the room without saying a word.

Chapter Three

Imogene got in her little red Gremlin and toured aimlessly around San Bernardino's downtown, her mind somewhere else, her hands and feet taking up the slack and doing all the driving.

Imogene should've gone straight over to Dentco and sat on the tall stool behind the counter, working the cash register, checking out the customers with their damaged food. A mindless job, something she needed in the worst way. The mundane distraction would help suss out a solution. Only there wasn't one. She would have to give up Lem. No two ways around it.

Two weeks had passed since the last time she worked. Who handled the job while she took the hiatus? Had Micheal Higginbotham found someone to replace her? For almost the entire two weeks, newsies camped out at Imogene's house and at Dentco looking for her. How could she work under those conditions?

Suz must've been hiding out at Micheal's.

The police had kept Imogene close at hand in a motel, the shabby Capri on Holt Boulevard that housed dope dealers, heroin addicts and hookers. This, while the cops continued to process the house as a major crime scene. The biggest in the town's history. Dour detectives came to the Capri three more times to re-interview her, trying to break what they perceived as a weak story. To find one that better matched what had happened based literally on where the bodies had fallen. They couldn't rectify in their pea-brains how Bernie came to be involved. Had Bernie not been there, they would've simply dusted off their hands to rid them of the sudden spate of violence and moved on. But Ol' Bernie was a civilian, a first-class citizen without one iota of justification for being in Imogene's living room at the time of the "Great Ma Barker shoot-out." That's what the newsies had taken to calling it. The cheesy fops. Assign a nickname, okay, fine. But at least use some creativity of their own and not a tired old cliché. And Bernie was the grade A citizen, liked, they thought. Imogene just couldn't tell the detectives about good ol' Bernie because it would implicate her further, pull her waist-deep into an already reeking cesspool.

For the first couple of days after the incident, she drove by her house trying to find Suz and talk to her. She had to be hurting emotionally, seeing those men meet their untimely demise in a most violent manner. She wasn't built for that kinda thing. Neither was Imogene, for that matter.

But Suz's car was never in the driveway. And her mom, Thelma, always sat in the same lawn chair in the same place in the front yard, dressed in a two-piece swimsuit. High-waisted with white and blue checks that should've had far more material to cover that body type. All those dern wrinkles. Imogene had nothing to talk about, but at least she didn't air her body out in public.

Each time with the sound of the Gremlin going by, Thelma would take down the cardboard covered with Reynolds Wrap aluminum foil used as a sun reflector held under her chin. She'd smile and wave like some kinda half-wit loon. As Imogene drove, dodging in and around the news trucks parked in the street, some espying her as the driver and giving chase on foot or in bulky news vans. The penny-ante fools.

Truth be told, the real reason Imogene drove by was because of the wooden crate under Mr. Majestic, the tall, graceful avocado tree in her backyard. The police had not yet found the box, or they would have Imogene back in custody, forthwith.

The neighbor on the west side, Bernard Lowery, the third unexplained dead man in the living room, just happened to be in Imogene's house, armed with a gun under his sweater vest. He arrived first that day before the Cigar and his thug-ugly could slip in through the back door. Bernie came over wanting information about the box he had stored in the garage over at Suz's house. He had the gun to shoot Imogene, if she didn't tell him. Of that there was no doubt.

But the gun-thug shot ol' Bernie dead after Bern's gun hung up on his sweater vest when he tried to draw. That short and immediate distraction, giving Bernie what he deserved, had given Imogene the opportunity to pull a gun and shoot dead the Cigar and the thug. A crisp snap of violence that happened in no more than a blink. Bam. Bam. Bam. Three dead men on the floor, just like that. Each time the scene played on the big screen in the back of Imogene's mind, she flinched. Her eyelids slammed closed and squinched down tight. Jaw clenched hard enough to crack dentures.

Bam. Bam. Bam. She jumped in her seat behind the wheel of the Gremlin as she toured the residential streets in San Bernardino, unsure of where to go next.

The police had just that morning cleared her to go back to her house. Booted her from the Capri no-tell motel.

But back at the house, the carpet was ruined with wide, jagged-edged blood spots where the three men had fallen. No way did she want to ever go back there. Too many terrifying memories.

Quit being such a big pussy. Man-up, girl, and git yo sorry ass home where you belong. You don't, some other heinous crap is sure to befall you. Bank on it.

See, right there. Ange would never use a word like *befall*. Imogene had used that word five times in *Peekaboo POTUS* and could name the pages and the line numbers.

Imogene turned the Gremlin around on a side street and headed home, her mind now all wrapped up in the most pressing issue in the bevy of problems plaguing her: the editing of *Peekaboo POTUS* and protecting Lem. Further down that list came the dead woman in the crate in her backyard. And lastly, the bloody mess in her living room.

In the rearview, a flash of red caught her eye. She looked with both eyes and didn't see anything. "You little bugger. I see you back there playing your silly kids' game of hide and seek." She stuck her foot in the accelerator. The little four-cylinder Gremlin didn't so much as surge.

You got no horses under the hood, E. You got nothing but a couple of tired, overworked squirrels.

How far she had fallen from the day fifty-odd years ago when she fled

Arkansas in a Studebaker truck that, according to Wayne, "ran like a striped-assed ape."

The Gremlin sped up slowly and took the next turn sharply, the tires squealing. She jerked the wheel and pulled into the closest driveway, one with a truck and camper, and laid down across the seat. She reached up and cranked down the rearview mirror to see.

Seconds later, that dern red Ford pick-up shot by like its tail was on fire.

Imogene waited for a count of ten, backed up, and drove in the opposite direction. The rest of the way home, the red pickup never reappeared in the mirror.

She made the final turn from Campus onto Hawthorne and spotted the truck parked in front of her house.

Dat-burn that cowboy's black-hearted soul.

She slowed, not quite coming to a stop, allowing time to think. She had never let anyone hoorah her and wasn't going to start now. She passed by the red truck and the old cowboy sitting behind the wheel as she pulled into the driveway. He got out and crossed the grass yard, cutting her off as she quickly made for the porch.

"What can I do for you? I got something of yours that I don't know about? Why are you on my property? Why in the world are you following me?"

The man's goofy smile didn't bode well for a high intellect. The man wouldn't be someone who worked crossword puzzles or participated in spelling bees.

"I prefer to talk inside rather than out here in front of God and all his minions."

"Get off my lawn. I don't hold with no bible-thumber tracking me down and telling me I'll be spending eternity in purgatory. This is my property, so git."

"It's not nothing like that at all. You're gonna wanna hear what I have to say. Trust me on this."

"No, I don't have ta trust you on anything." She opened her clutch, purse stuck in a hand that gripped the little .380 pistol. "I don't even know you. I'm not having the best day as it is, and you out here hoorahing me in my own front yard is making it worse. You get what I'm sayin' here?"

He reached around to his back pocket and came back with a sealed envelope. "I was asked to hand-deliver this to you."

She held out her hand. "Well, you delivered it. Now git." Court papers, no doubt, a subpoena or court order. Another problem to toss onto the heap.

He backed up when she tried to take it.

"This envelope comes with an explanation that only I can give. Can we please go inside and discuss this?"

The man's thin and wiry like a piece of jerked beef. I'm kinda interested to see what he's got on his mind. Hopin' it's somethin' like bronc ridin', if ya catch my meanin'. Wink. Wink. Neither of us has had ourselves a good ride in a month of Sundays. You know what I'm sayin' here, E? And hells bells, worst comes to worst you can take him, E. Jerk a couple of links in him 'fore you toss him out on his skinny ass. Go on, ask him in for a cool glass of sweet tea. Let's see if he can stay on this old bronc for the full ten seconds.

"All right then. You have two minutes to say your piece, then I'm tossing you out on your skinny ass."

He shot her that goofy smile again and followed along, up onto the porch. He waited while she unlocked the thick green door. Inside the hot air, still and musty, smelled of too many Marlboro cigarettes and…and a metallic reek. A scent of iron that made her gorge rise in her throat. She swallowed it down.

Dealing with the cowboy had deferred the thought of what awaited on the other side of the door, making it take a backseat to the problem at hand. Now the bloody remnants leapt up and slapped her in the face.

She entered on wobbly knees and tried not to look down at the three huge—once bright crimson now dark burgundy—patches in the gold high-low carpet.

And then marveled at how every smooth surface in the entire room was smeared with black graphite powder. Fingerprint powder. A person would never know the place had ever been clean.

The worst part, though, Joyce's, her daughter's portrait, lay broken out of the expensive frame and tossed willy-nilly on the floor. The outline of a boot print on the back from an inconsiderate cop. The inconsiderate bastards.

Imogene just wanted to back out of the house, light a match, and torch the whole shebang.

She moved right over to the divan and sat in the usual place, a perch that allowed a view of the entire house, such as it was. And through the big picture window, the outside that included the front of the now deceased Bernard Lowery's place to the west.

"Woo-we, I heard about what happened. But thunderation, its an entirely different thing to see it...ah up close...and—" He sniffed the air like a cur dog. "...and you know, smell it. "That whole mess the way it unfolded must've really been something ta behold. Scare the fluff right off a pillow, huh?"

The cowboy started to sit down in Wayne's old easy chair.

She gulped some air to keep from hurling. "Hold it right there, you jaybird. You're not staying long enough to get comfortable. Hand over that letter, say your piece, and get the hell out."

"So much for homestyle hospitality, huh?" He sat down anyway and took off his cowboy hat. His tanned skin stopped mid-forehead, the top part pale white in sharp contrast to the brown. Maybe he was a real cowboy and not one of those good-for-nothing drugstore kind. She kinda had a thing for real cowboys.

Didn't matter; it took every ounce of willpower to stay in the room and not bolt.

She lit a cigarette for the quick infusion of nicotine needed to grab the yayhoo by the scruff and toss him out on his ear. Then get back in her car, drive away, never to return.

She took in a huge lungful of smoke, held it, then blew it out. "You got one minute to spark my interest or—"

"Thunderation, you look pale as a ghost. You better just sit back and relax. Let me get you a glass of cool water."

"No."

He disappeared into the kitchen, his scuffed-up cowboy boots clunked on the green linoleum floor. The cupboard opened and closed. The sink water ran.

A glass of cool water was just what the doctor ordered, but that minor act of kindness would not ingratiate him in any way, not in her foul mood.

He came back into the living room and handed her the glass. She glommed onto it and drank half of it. The liquid cooled all the way down. Maybe the cowpoke wasn't the worst thing that could happen in a day already befouled beyond belief.

He stood in front of the coffee table. "You know this carpet is ruined. You'll never get this…ah stuff out. And leaving it like this is just a big, ugly reminder of an even uglier time." He bent over at the waist, pulled up his pant leg, and extracted a pearl-handled, Italian-made stiletto switchblade.

Run for it Eeeeee.

She sat back, glass in one hand, burning Marlboro in the other. "Ah, what the hell. I give. You got me."

He froze. "What's that you say?" He looked down at the knife in his hand. "Naw, don't be silly." He went down on one knee, pushed the button on the knife. The blade flipped out with a snick. He used it with too much familiarity, the little snick loud in the quiet room. He started cutting a big swatch out of the carpet. The crumpled burgundy spot left by neighbor Bernie Lowery. The sharp blade cut through the tired old carpet like it was nothing more than a sheet of paper. He tossed the first swatch over by the floor heater and got busy cutting out the one left by the Cigar's exsanguination. Half the white envelope stuck out of his pocket and stared at her. What could possibly be in that envelope that pertained to her?

"Wooo-weee girl, look at that man's beautiful ass. You could crack walnuts on one that firm and tight. I wanna get me some of that.

Ange wasn't lying, that was one nice piece of… "You wanna give me that letter so I can read it?"

He got up and smiled, only this time there wasn't any goofiness to it. None. He smiled with his eyes. He turned back to the job at hand. Instead of cutting the last swatch, the one left by the gun-thug, he picked up Joyce and put her back in the frame. Tapped it in snug with the butt of the knife and then hung her on the wall.

The bastard. He just ingratiated himself.

He got down on one knee and cut out the last swatch. He stacked them and picked them up like a big stack of cards. "Where's your outside trash cans?"

"Out back, down at the bottom of the stairs to the left."

He turned to go through the kitchen to the back door.

"Hey?"

He stopped and looked at her.

"I don't even know your name."

"It's Luke." The smile again.

"Luke, what?"

"Luke Short." He disappeared into the kitchen. The backdoor unlocked and opened.

"Ah, for crying out loud."

What now? The Marlboro man is damn near perfect, you ask me? Okay, scratch that, he's all the way live. He is as perfect as can be. Totally edible. I wanna bite that tight little ass.

Two minutes later, there came the clump of the cowboy boots on the kitchen floor, and the back door closed. The man was a sham, a con, and yet just having him around…having any living human present made life that much easier.

Joyce's portrait back up, the bloody carpet excised and gone, made a world of difference. She could breathe again. Even so he'd only get the original two minutes, then out on his ear. "Luke Short," for cripes sake.

He sat back down in Wayne's chair without any guile or expectation from his chivalrous act.

"Ah…thank you for doing that. You didn't have to. It was very nice."

He stared and said nothing.

"Now tell me what you want then get outta my house."

He lost the smile. "You are as hard as she said you'd—"

Movement out the front picture window caught her eye. She looked away from the cowboy. Outside, two black and white cop cars zoomed up to the curb in front of Bernie's house.

"Oh, my God." Imogene tried to stand and couldn't.

"What's the matter?"

"The police, they're back." She tried to stand again and still couldn't, not the way her heartbeat ran out of control and made her lightheaded.

The cowboy stood, went to the window, stood off to the side, and peeked out. "Didn't they tell you it was okay to come back to your house?"

"Yes. Yes. That's not it. Oh, God a-mighty. No. What a fool I've been."

He looked back at her as the cops got out of their cars and ran up to the front of Bernie's house.

"What is it then?"

"I guess the shooting kept me from thinking clearly that day." She wrung her hands. "But that's no excuse for not telling the cops about her sometime during the last two weeks."

"Telling them about who?" Now his voice sounded the tiniest bit stressed.

"Bernie," she pointed to the bare wood spot on the living room floor, the first place he cut out. "His wife is an invalid. A major stroke victim. She can't talk or even so much as move a single muscle."

"And?"

"Bernie's been dead for two weeks. Who's been taking care of poor ol' Dot?"

She looked from the window back to Luke Short.

Gone.

He disappeared without saying abracadabra. In the kitchen, the back door eased shut.

Luke Short didn't wanna talk to the cops. He must've taken off his boots before crossing the kitchen floor. In the law books, that was called a consciousness of guilt.

Imogene knew the feeling.

Chapter Four

Seconds later, two unmarked police cars rolled up and stopped behind the two black and whites. Men in suits exited. Homicide dicks.

Oh, dear lord. Poor Dot was dead.

Not from murder but from something far worse, starvation and dehydration. An absolutely awful way to go. She may have even died from just loneliness.

Imogene couldn't take much more stress before her body started jittering faster and faster until she turned supernova, then exploded. She walked out the front door and stood on the porch steps watching the happenings at the neighbor's, wringing her hands and puff, puff, puffing on the Marlboro.

She peeled her eyes away to look over at Suz's house to the east, hoping to spot Suz. Instead, Thelma had just walked out of the house carrying her lawn chair and a piece of cardboard covered in aluminum foil. She smiled and waved. The smile dropping off a cliff when her mind caught up to her eyes and peeped the cop cars one house over. Thelma dropped the chair and sun reflector and trundled over to the porch.

Perfect, that's the last thing Imogene needed.

"My land, what in the world is wrong with this neighborhood? Was it built on some kinda Indian burial ground? Morning, Imogene. Might as well set up a police substation at the corner. Am I right?"

Imogene puffed, not yet ready to engage in conversation with someone coco for Cocoa Puffs. "Have you seen Suz lately?"

"Hmm, no."

"Do you know where she's staying? I really need to talk with her."

"Good luck, I'm her mom, and she won't even talk to me. What's going over there?"

"I'm not a member of that organization, in fact, you might even say we are permanently at odds with each other. I don't expect them, any time soon, to come over here and brief me."

Thelma wore her hair up in a passé beehive dyed platinum and was dressed in the same high-waisted two-piece white-and-blue checked swimsuit. The outfit needed to be washed, she'd dripped mustard and catsup down the front in the most unfortunate places. All the sun worshipping tanned her skin nut-brown. White peeked out around the edges to her breasts. She looked healthy enough to live another seventy or eighty-five years.

"Well, you don't have to be so snippy about it. You're a rude dog."

"What else is new. Is Suz staying over at Micheal's? Is that it?"

"That's what I would think. She was over here last night to get some clothes. She wouldn't even let the poor man come in the house. He waited out on the street parked in his truck. She was never like this before. I think she gets this poor attitude from yo—"

"She was home last night? You just said you hadn't heard from her?"

"I said no such thing. Why would I say that when she came over just last night?"

"Oh, dear Lord. Can you please just tell me what—?"

Two men in cheap suits appeared over at the edge of Imogene's yard walking right toward them.

Thelma whispered, "Well, I guess they finally figured out who's causing all the problems around here. Good luck to ya. You want me to take care of your dog?"

"I don't have any dern dog."

"Your cat?"

"Go. Git."

She held her ground and smiled when the two detectives walked up.

"Good afternoon, ladies."

Imogene recognized both of them. The police department was too small for her not to know everyone, not after the last two weeks. Johnny Johnson—

a real original name, and James Albright, everyone called him JB. He was the easiest to get along with. They both carried clipboards with notes and drawings. Their guns in shoulder holsters bulged under the Sears and Roebuck suitcoats.

"How's Dot? Is she okay?"

JB looked at her queerly. "Who are you talking about?" He looked at his partner, John Johnson, to confirm that the question was in fact odd.

"Don't play your ignorant interrogation games with me. That's why you're here, for Dot. Bernard Lowery's wife, right? You two brain surgeons, in your misguided rush to justice, forgot all about Bernie's wife and left her to fend for herself. Didn't you? She's an invalid for cripes sake. You two will both be barking in hell over this one, that's for got-damn sure."

John Johnson smiled. "Taylor, you're the one off your nut. Dorothy Lowery died seven years ago. Her ashes are in an urn on the fireplace mantle."

Thelma took a step forward. "That house has a fireplace? These two houses over here don't."

Johnson looked at her in amazement, sizing her up for the free ride to the booby hatch.

"How do you know it's her?" Imogene asked. "In the urn, I mean?"

"It's the first thing we checked. We confirmed the death certificate. That's not why we're here. The mailman came by today and found a wooden box on Bernard Lowery's porch, a box with a dead woman in it. I don't suppose you know anything about that?"

Thelma took off at a quick walk, headed for Bernard's front porch to see for herself, muttering, "A dead woman in a box?"

John Johnson caught her by the arm. "Whoa there, lady. That's a crime scene."

They had found the box that was supposed to be under Mr. Majestic, the avocado tree in back of Imogene's house. Imogene's knees gave out. She eased down to the concrete step. How did it get from underneath the avocado tree, out to the front of Bernie's house?

Suz. Had to be her.

Suz came home last night, not to get fresh clothes but to move the box.

Two weeks ago, Imogene and Suz found the box in Suz's dad's garage at the bottom of a huge pile of hoarder junk. Inside, they discovered a dead woman. By mutual agreement, they chose to bury the box under the avocado tree in Imogene's backyard. They had originally thought the woman in the box was Thelma, Suz's mom. They didn't want to deal with the mess a dead Thelma would cause. The befouling of Suz's dad's reputation, the news hounds, and most importantly, the effect it would have on Imogene's parole. But Thelma, living in Alaska, read the obituary of Suz's dad and came down to pay her respects. Which threw a big monkey wrench into the whole mess.

Now they weren't sure who was in the box. But once Thelma arrived, Suz had insisted they turn the box over to the police because the victim's family would want to know what had happened to their daughter. Imogene had talked her out of it. Or so she thought. Then the little problem of killing three men in Imogene's living room sort of clouded the dead-woman-in-the-box issue.

Until now.

Imogene swallowed hard. "So, because I'm on parole for murder, you naturally think I would have something to do with any other dead person you find in the neighborhood?"

The words filtered down into her brain after she said them. Yikes.

John Johnson struggled to hold on to Thelma. "Well, it is a logical progression of things, don't you think? We'd be remiss if we didn't at least ask you about it, right?"

JB scoffed. "Don't listen to him, Mrs. Taylor. We came over here to see if you would come take a look to see if you can identify her. Would you mind?"

"The way you two have treated me the last two weeks, now you're asking a favor?"

"See, I told you it was a waste of time." John Johnson hesitated and shook Thelma by the arm. "Stop your resisting. You're not going over there."

"Oh, you want the murder queen here to take a look, but you won't let me?"

Imogene caught Thelma's eye. Thelma winked.

Two weeks prior, Thelma caught Suz and Imogene digging up the box the night before the shooting in an attempt to identify the occupant. For a total loon, at times, Thelma had flashes of intelligence that somehow leaked out around the crazy. More like a primordial ooze, though.

Suz moving the box to Bernard's porch really put the screws to Imogene. Not out of vehemence but out of Suz's misguided need to do the right thing. Bernard had already paid for killing the poor woman-in-the-box with a bullet to the chest. Sure, it was at the hand of a gun thug, but dead was dead. You can't pay that piper twice.

Imogene struggled to her feet. "Fine, let's get this over with."

JB, John Johnson, and Imogene walked next door. Thelma stayed back by the porch under the very real threat of arrest. She yelled at them, "Timothy Leary told me ten years ago this was going to happen. He can see the future. Too late now. Even if you did say you were sorry, I won't tell you who's in the box."

John Johnson muttered. "Everyone on his block needs to be rounded up and transported to Ward B."

Suz apparently had placed the wooden crate right on Bernie's porch with the lid halfway off. As they approached, a man in a suit and tie took photos, the flash attached with a cord to a clunky old camera. Expended blue flashbulbs, deformed and bubbled, littered the ground and crunched underfoot.

Just how many photos do they need? No wonder it took two weeks to clear the crime scene in the dern living room.

Imogene stared into the box and counted to ten. She didn't want to identify the woman too soon. When they dug up the box the night before the shooting, she figured out the identity of the woman. A good educated guess, anyway.

Maybe Suz was right; this was the proper thing to do.

She thought about feigning surprise and instead calmly said, "Oh, my goodness, that's Poppy Liu."

JB said, "Who? You mean you actually know her?"

She turned to him. "I don't know her. I know of her. She used to be one of the day nurses who cared for Bernard's invalid wife, who apparently now resides on the mantle inside. He must've killed her and put her in the box.

Years ago, by the looks of her."

John Johnson said, "She looks like a squashed horse turd and you can identify her just like that." He snapped his fingers.

JB asked, "Mrs. Taylor, how do you know it's her?"

"I don't for sure, but this woman here has long black hair just like Poppy Liu. Run her name CNI and NCIC, I'm sure you'll get a missing person hit. I believe it's spelled L-U-I."

"You see that, partner," John Johnson said. "She talks just like one of us. She's been in the system too long and needs to be back in prison where she belongs. I wouldn't be surprised at all if she was the one who actually killed this 'Poppy Liu.'" He made air quotes.

JB, disgusted, said, "Go run the name. Now."

John Johnson stared at him a long moment, turned heel and walked to the patrol car to call it in to dispatch.

"I'm sorry about him. He's just—"

"A turd cutter. You know it, and I know it. I'm going home. You need me for anything else, you know where to find me. I'd much prefer that you didn't, though. My house has been yours for the last two weeks. By the way, thanks for cleaning up after yourselves. That's sarcasm if you didn't pick up on it."

"Ah yeah, ah, sorry about the house. Thank you for helping us out, Mrs. Taylor. You saved us a lot of time. And we may have never identified her."

She started to walk away, stopped, and turned. "And for the record, I didn't kill her. But I am glad someone finally found her. Now her people will know what happened to her. Such as it is."

JB nodded and waved.

She shouldn't have said that last part. Dern her mouth. She stopped. Froze in her tracks. Sweet baby Jesus. Denying it like that, now they'll think she had something to do with the Poppy Liu killing. And there wasn't a dern thing she could do about it.

She trudged up the three concrete steps to the concrete porch and realized Thelma was conspicuous in her absence. She opened the door and entered, her eyes going down and to the left behind the chair just inside the door.

The cops had cut the twine she had tied to the screen door, the other end tied to a cluster of empty Schlitz Malt Liquor cans. An earlier warning system designed to alert when the Cigar came a calling. The grim reaper advocate.

Lotta good that did. The Cigar picked the lock and entered through the back door. She leaned down and picked up the beer cans that clattered together like the back of a car with a sign, "Just married."

She looked up and startled.

The cowboy suddenly reappeared, sitting in Wayne's chair. He drank a Schlitz pilfered from the refrigerator.

He held the beer up in a toast. "Didn't think you'd be walking back from that. Good for you. You must've one hell'va gift for gab. That's what I heard about you. That's why I'm here."

"What are you talking about?"

He took a sip and shrugged. "Usually, when a dead body drops, the closest parolee gets swept up first, guilty or not. You know that. It's jus' the way of the world. You just beat the odds. Good for you."

"Doesn't mean they're not gonna arrest me later on. But they'll have one big problem with me as a suspect."

"That right?"

"Yeah, I was in prison when she was killed."

Imogene didn't know that for sure, but it made a lot of sense. If she learned one thing about the justice system, it didn't have to make sense, not when it could throw an elderly woman in the can over an accident like the one that happened with her husband, Wayne. A system that let her do ten years before parole. Let her out with a dern tail ta boot. She wasn't no dern criminal. That tail irked her beyond belief.

Talking to Luke Short, she wished she could pull back the words, "in prison." Words that disparaged her character. A silly schoolgirl emotion that bubbled up over the old man sitting in the living room. A silly childhood crush syndrome that in no way fit comfortably in her lifestyle.

Oddly, Ange had gone quiet.

Probably also over the good-looking man present in the living room. He befuddled her. Or she was just lying back and soaking him all in. If he wasn't so debonair and handsome, Ange would've been spouting off salacious and lewd comments about what she wanted to do with the old cowboy. Imogene couldn't blame her; the man was easy to look at. She opened her mouth to tell him ta get the hell out and stopped. The need to be with someone, anyone, overpowered all else. A throwback to prison, where for ten years, Imogene was never without someone within ten feet of her. A person got used to that kind of social environment.

"Now, can you gimme my envelope?"

He sipped and stared. He had gray eyes. First time she noticed, and she should've right off. They made him look like a lobo wolf on the prod, gave him a latent, dangerous feel. One where he could, at any moment, snap at a hand that reached out to pet him.

"First, I wanna run something by you."

She owed him that much, after cutting out the carpet swatches and repairing Joyce, putting her back up on the wall. Joyce, looking down from up on the wall, gave what little solace was left in the world.

Imogene said nothing and waited.

He sipped. "What would you say ta workin' a couple of days in my pawn shop? It'd sure help me out. I'm kinda pinned between a bronc and the gate on this thing. You'd really be doing me a big favor. I'll pay ya good. You don't have ta worry about that."

"What I'd say to that is, gimme the letter and get outta my dern house. On the double."

"You are a scrappy one, aren't ya?"

"If I holler real loud, those cops next door will come runnin'. Sure, as God made little green apples, they will. And you don't strike me as someone who wants to grab the attention of those local gun-tottin' detectives."

"Huh? You don't take well to the male of species, do ya?"

She smiled at his attempt to sound educated. He was cute, no doubt about it.

She picked up the box of Marlboros, bumped one out, and lit up. He stared.

She finally said, "You follow me all over God's little half acre, even follow me into the parole office. All because you want me to work at your pawn shop for a couple a days? I'm not anyone's fool, and I don't appreciate you taking me for one. I have a lot of problems of my own and don't fancy stepping into any dog crap you're offering up."

"Did you hear the part about it being a big favor?"

"My ears aren't full of wax. I heard. But favors are reserved for friends and cute little dogs. You don't have floppy ears, and I don't know you from Adam."

"I was hoping you'd go along without me havin' ta do this." He eased up off one haunch, reached back, and pulled the envelope from his pocket."

He stood and took a step closer. He set the now crumpled envelope on the coffee table. "I'll need you there tomorrow at nine a.m. Holt Boulevard, north of Euclid Avenue, two or three blocks up on the right. West Valley Jewelry and Loan." He put his hat on and tipped it like a gentleman might.

"That's not gonna happen, Luke...*Mr. Short*."

He lost his smile.

"That's right, I read books. I know Luke Short is a popular writer of westerns. You lied to me about your name. First thing you did when we met was lie. Friends don't do that to friends. No way will I ever work for the likes of a liar. I'd say I'm sorry, but I'm not. I don't know you well enough to be sorry."

He walked to the door, turned, tipped his cowboy hat again. "It's been a pleasure meeting you, Imogene. See you, nine sharp. I'll have a big pot of fresh chuckwagon coffee waiting for ya."

"Not gonna happen, Kemosabe. I'd be crazy to take up with the likes of you. My parole officer's a real stickler, and fraternizing with an ex-con is number one on the no-no list. Hey, check next door, ask Thelma. She's more what you're looking for."

He left. Walked across the front yard, got into his red Ford pickup, and took off. Did it right in front of the cops he tried to avoid earlier when he took a powder out the back door.

The raw nerve of that man thinking he could order around an elderly woman. A defenseless elderly woman at that. She chuckled. Okay, well, not totally defenseless.

The letter on the table drew her attention. No way would she open it and play into his dumb-assed game. Not a chance. She puffed the Marlboro. Puff, puff, puffed. Gray-white smoke filled the air, not unlike gun smoke from two weeks prior. Those images would remain fresh in memory for many weeks to come. Maybe even years.

A heavy sigh rolled out. Who the hell was she kidding? She snatched up the letter, angry she had not fought the urge longer.

Chapter Five

Seven-thirty in the morning, July first, Imogene took a window booth at The Iron Skillet across the street from West Valley Jewelry and Loan. Set up a surveillance of sorts to watch the comings and goings. The red vinyl seat, the scents of coffee and vanilla, the donuts under glass on the counter, all combined gave off a nostalgic sense. She settled in for the long haul.

The pawn shop's front sat right on the sidewalk edge, which meant most of the parking was around back. Unfortunates fallen on hard times are ashamed of their penury, their inability to succeed in the game of Life. A parking lot where you enter off an alley works best.

A few spots out front were blocked off with city barricades. On Euclid, a wide boulevard of grass and ancient pepper trees separated north and south traffic. Grass enough to support the annual Fourth of July picnic, where every block had three or four U.S. states represented. Hundreds of picnic tables, red, white, and blue banners, and table cloths supplied by the city were in the process of being set up by city workers who wore jeans and orange shirts with the West Valley city emblem. According to The Daily Report, thirty thousand would be in attendance, up from twenty-five thousand the previous year. Not bad for a town of seventy-five thousand.

Imogene and Wayne attended the picnic and parade many times in the past; those memories are warm and endearing. Days firecracker-hot without any breeze for a hundred miles. Fresh hand-cranked ice cream, corn on the cob, short ribs, and homemade macaroni salad, Imogene brought and shared with everyone.

Loved the pageantry the parade afforded, even though it wasn't much as parades go. Some cheesy, rickety floats, convertibles cars with local celebs sitting high on the back waving like self-grandiose fools, high school bands, and lots of beautiful horses in formation with tall flag poles mounted in their stirrups. But most of all they loved the social interaction, the camaraderie.

Imogene and Wayne always sat at the California tables rather than the ones for Arkansas, doing everything in their power to bury their past, their old identities. Bury those old crimes that had faded away, the same as old Hollywood icons who once burned huge and bright. Then nothing. John Barrymore, who?

And yet, Catskill somehow figured out Imogene and Wayne's name game. In the deposition, he called her Alice. The son of a buck, she wanted to catch him in a dark alley some night and pummel him with a sock filled with sand. Pulp the little twit for causing such anguish using blackmail that left her no other option but to ruin a good friend, Secret Service agent Lem. Boxed her in a corner. She didn't like to be boxed in a corner.

She smoked Marlboros and sipped coffee with cream and lots of sugar. Nothing happened across the street at the pawn shop. The glass door remained locked.

An hour crept past. Then two. Still nothing. No one came through the door, even when the yellow pages said the store opened at 9:00 a.m. and closed at 7:00 p.m.

She ordered whole-wheat pancakes with eggs cooked runny and a tall orange juice.

Another hour passed. 10:30 a.m.

The high-class jewelry store next to the pawn shop started getting a dribble of customers, and so did the city's main post office on the other side. The shoe repair place next to the post office took in the most foot traffic. Patrons liked their old shoes and didn't want to give them up. Got 'em resoled to put another couple hundred miles on the bottoms.

To the north of the jewelry store, in a narrow shop, the front glass windows were covered in posters depicting a smiling mayor incumbent. Joseph Columbus. They called him Joe Co. He would be one of those smiling fools sitting on the back of a convertible. The man had a round face and was bald as a billiard. With those deep-set criminal eyes, he was lucky to get elected dog catcher. And yet he won three terms. No tellin' for taste. Or intelligence for that matter. By definition, fifty percent of the population has only a double-digit IQ.

Eleven a.m. a cop car slid to the curb outside the mayor's campaign office. First wove in between the temporary no parking signs to get it done. Above the law.

A tall, stalwart man in a tailored blue uniform with red hair walked in with a box under his arm. An elegant wooden box, the size of expensive cigars. Someone sucking up to good ol' Jo Co. The sun caught two gold bars on his collar and winked. A captain, probably vying to oust the current chief. Politics was cutthroat under the best of conditions.

Imogene opened her clutch purse and took out the letter Luke Short left the afternoon before. The one he set on the coffee table. Did it with the knowledge she wouldn't be able to resist looking inside. His smug attitude irked her the most. How he was so dern sure she would show up at 9:00 a.m., a slave now to his beck and call. That's what really chapped her butt fire engine red. That smugness.

She opened the letter and smoothed it out on the diner's table to read it for the umpteenth time.

While out on parole, she had sent letter after letter to Ange in C-block. All returned unopened, the envelope stamped in red, "Return to sender, address unknown." What did the post office mean by that notation? Address unknown, her achin' butt. Hellfire and crap matches, everyone who lived in the valley knew how to find the dern prison.

Imogene lived in the same cell with Ange for dern near ten years. Why wouldn't Ange open the letters Imogene sent?

She looked up from the letter and out the window. Her mind took a little vacation, harking back to something her ex-parole officer Nancy Do-right had said. An out-and-out lie, of course. She said there was never anyone named Ange or Angela who shared a cell with Imogene. That the warden for those ten years of incarceration had used Imogene to indoctrinate "new fish" to the prison system. He wanted her to teach them how "the cow ate the cabbage."

Said that Imogene was the "Grand Dame of CIW."

Absolute, unadulterated horse pucky. No way. Nancy Do-right only said it to mess with Imogene's mind. And as it turned out, she did a dern fine job of it. Those words continued to echo in her brain and make her crazy.

Until the cowboy dropped that letter on her coffee table that set her on a dizzying merry-go-round. Round and round and round.

At first, the letter confirmed Imogene's memories of having Ange as a cellie versus the fictional tale told by Do-right.

The letter on the table read:

My dearest Imogene

I miss you so. You cannot fathom the chunk you took from my soul the day you walked out of C-block. It hurt so bad I curled up for a week on my bunk and refused to eat. Refused to go out into the yard. Fat-assed warden Jeffers threatened to force-feed me if I didn't start eating.

I honestly didn't think you would make it on the outside. I thought you'd ricochet right back like everyone does. But not you. Not good ol' Imogene Taylor. If anyone could make it on the outside, you could. I should've known as much. We've heard rumors of how you're doing out there. All the stories are turning you into a legend. Good for you. I can at least say, "I knew her when."

I'm terribly sorry for turning your letters back unopened. I just couldn't stomach seeing your words, seeing that...well this is my cross to bear not yours.

Nothing's changed in here. They keep trying to give me a new cellie, but I raise so much hell they move the new fish out. I'm holding this spot for you, my friend. You'll get tired one day of that rat race and want to come home to mama where's its safe.

Anyway, I'm writing this as more an introduction. The man giving you this letter has asked me for a favor. I owe him big, Imogene. Big. I truly hate to pass this favor on to you and I wouldn't if I didn't absolutely

have to. Based on our friendship I hope and pray you will take up the
mantle in my stead and help him with his...little project.

> *Your long-lost*
>> *Devoted friend*
>> *Ange*

The night before, the first time she read it, her heart fell through the floor. She wept for hours, her mind shielding her from the obvious truth. A truth that later made her hate the world.

Separation from her friend wasn't fair.

And no wonder old people turned into grumpy old curmudgeons. She always said she never would fall into that ugly rut. But look at her now, hating the world. No, not the world, just the sadistic judicial system that would incarcerate a sixty-three-year-old woman for ten years. And when they did finally deign to let her out, they gave her a tail. A tail, dire and unforgivable. An evil that perpetually sat on her shoulder, a constant reminder of one big mistake that was nothing more than an accident. Twenty-five to life for an accident.

Now, sitting at the diner's table, Imogene once again tried her best to cherish the words in the letter and wished with all her heart they were true. She carefully folded the letter and slipped it back into the envelope. She crumpled it into a little ball and left it on the plate with the half-eaten wheat pancakes. She rose, straightened her dress, put on the sun bonnet, the mid-length white gloves, opened her purse, and set down the price of breakfast, plus a five-dollar bill for the tip. The memory of waitressing at Ozzie Eats back in the day, slinging hash and dodging randy truck drivers' roaming hands, kept her tips hovering at forty or fifty percent.

Out in the bright sunlight, she lit up another Marlboro, the fifteenth of the day, put on sunglasses, and walked to the corner to cross the street. The sun already bore down with an unyielding stifling heat that tried hard to pile-drive a person right into the ground.

No way did she want to give Luke Short what he wanted but the desire to uncover his real game gnawed at her like a redneck eating a chicken leg.

Two and a half hours late made a big enough statement in and of itself. She came to the pawnshop door and tugged. Locked. She took off the sunglasses, moved close to the glass, and cupped a hand for shade.

Inside, three glass counters in a horseshoe configuration contained jewelry, rings, watches, bracelets, and necklaces. Handguns, expensive cameras with long lenses. On the walls, lots of rifles and shotguns in racks. Some electric guitars and amps and other various sundry items that had little or no value. A large mirror hung on one wall opposite an old-time painting that looked valuable as far as paintings went. Though she wasn't an art snob.

How in the world would anyone choose Imogene Taylor for a job in a pawn shop? It just boggled the mind and didn't make one wit of sense.

Although for the last two years she did operate Dentco all on her own and made it profitable, when before the books bled with red. In the letter, Ange had said people were talking, telling stories, Imogene becoming a legend. Which now begged the question, had Imogene come out to the pawn shop for no other reason than to stoke her own ego? Find out if at least that part were true.

She took out her car key and tap, tap, tapped on the glass door. Tapped until Luke Short came from the back room. He sauntered over to the front door, arrogant and calm as you please. He unlocked it, opened it a crack. "You're late, Imogene. Go on home. We got someone else ta cover it."

"Fine by me." She turned heel and took three steps before Luke stuck his torso out. "Imogene, wait one dat bern minute, would you please? I swear ta gawd you are the most difficult woman to deal with." He looked up and down the street, a nervous jitter vibrating through his entire body. A man half-scared outta his wits.

But why?

The red-headed captain two doors down chose that moment to step out onto the sidewalk, headed for his cop car. He stopped and looked at them. They both looked back, neither wanted any kind of confrontation. The captain finally nodded. Chin in the air, he continued on, got in the black and white, and squeaked the tires leaving the curb. The cop car bumper brushed one of the no-parking barricades and knocked it over. The car didn't slow, just kept going.

"You gonna let me in or you gonna let me stand out here all day and melt in this hellish sun?" Sweat ran in her eyes and stung.

"All right, already." He stepped back and let her enter

He locked the door behind her. "Come on, we'll talk in the back."

Imogene walked behind him. "Hey?"

He stopped and turned.

"That painting up there, is that real?"

The picture depicted a sexy Rubenesque woman with fiery blond wavy hair lying on a fainting couch, partially draped in red velvet, but with plenty left to spark the imagination of the sexually oppressed. She wore a sated smile, her eyelids hooded—bedroom eyes. Her cheeks had just the right amount of red rouge. The painting looked a hundred years old or better and probably came from a bar along the Barbary Coast up Frisco way. A hand-painted original. An antique.

The cowboy took a step closer, leaning over the counter to see the white tag that hung from the gold-guild pictureframe. "Yes, it's real and very, very expensive."

Imogene yanked the .380 automatic from her clutch purse and shot the poor woman right in the breast. She'd aimed for the nose.

Luke Short jumped in the air and raised his hands to fend off the next bullet sure to be coming his way. "What in blue blazes is the matter with you, woman?"

She pointed the gun at *him*. This time aimed at his crotch. "Tell me what your game is. Tell me right now, or it's going to be Hi, Ho, good-bye Silver. And if you know anything at all about me, you know I have priors and will have no compunction whatsoever in shooting off your little Lone Ranger."

"Okay, wait. Wait. What are you talking about? I don't know what your—"

She extended her arm, getting that much closer to his little Lone Ranger.

"Okay. Okay, what do you wanna know. I'll tell ya. Sure, I will. I promise."

"If anything other than the truth comes out of that mealy mouth of yours—" She swung the gun around and shot the hanging mirror the size of a small car on the opposite wall. Shards clattered down in a racket that echoed and banged around inside the pawn shop.

His back stiffened. His jaw locked as if he accepted his own fate. "I have to replace everything you damage here, you evil gray-headed witch." He pointed his finger at her. "And you better keep in mind we have neighbors who'll report those shots."

She aimed at his foot and started to squeeze the trigger.

He held up his hands. "Okay. I lied. *I lied.* Is that what you wanna hear?"

"I wanna hear the truth and nothing but the truth or else. Now tell me the rest of it or lose a big toe."

"I wrote the letter. Okay, are you happy now?"

"I already knew that. My friend Ange can't read a word let alone write. Tell me the rest. What's going on here? Why did you want me to help you? And with what?"

He hesitated. "I'm…ah, no longer sure you're exactly right for what we have in mind. I mean for your…ah, position here at the pawn shop. I'm awaiting new instructions."

"Where did you get the information about Ange, my old cellmate?"

Luke looked as if he needed to think over that part before divulging it. "Okay, I was cellmates with Ange's brother up in the Q. He told me. I heard all about you all the way up there. You sounded perfect for what they have in mind here in the pawn shop and told them so."

Tapping at the front door drew both their attention. A blue uniform cop held his hands up to the window, peering in.

"Dumbass," Imogene muttered and casually dropped the .380 into her dress pocket. "Patrol tactics 101, you don't stick your face into a location where shots have been reported. Get the door and let him in."

She turned around and found Luke Short makin' tracks to the back. She yelled after him. "You're a dumbass, too. You think this guy's alone. He'll have someone covering the back, you idgit." She shook her head, walking to the pawn shop door.

The keys hung from the lock. She jingled the keys, getting the door open. "Oh, hey Hank. What's going on?" She knew Hank. He had picked her up at the Capri no-tell-motel one morning in a black and white cop car and shuttled her to the station for her second…or was it the third interview with the two brain trusts JB and his flunky John Johnson. Gave her the third degree over the three men who ended up dead in her living room. The same questions over and over, flailing that dead horse. She didn't budge one iota on the story. But on the way to the station, she had a nice talk with Hank.

Hank had sandy blond hair with a cute Tab Hunter smile. He looked and acted too innocent to be carrying a gun and answering dangerous calls for service. Trying to help people who couldn't handle their own problems, calling for someone who could.

"Oh, say hey, Imogene. What are *you* doing here?"

"I work here now. You wanna come in? I'm still trying to get things ready in here to open the doors. As you can see, we're running a little behind schedule today. You wouldn't believe all the crapola that goes on getting this place ready." She stepped aside. He came in a couple of tentative steps. Cautious, hand on his gun still in the holster.

"Would ya look at that mirror?" she said. "Broken in a thousand and one pieces. And it was taken in on a loan, ta boot. If the owner comes back to take it outta hock, it's gonna be my butt for sure. You wait and see if I don't get blamed for it." She winged it the best she could, the lies flowing like red wine from a gallon jug.

"What happened?"

"Oh…ah…atmospheric conditions."

"Huh?"

"Yeah, when there's a significant heat shift from cold to hot, glass will—" She pointed up to the shattered mirror. Luckily the shards had fallen obscuring the bullet hole. "—shatter just like that. And the heat out there today, you can pan-fry an egg on the sidewalk. Am I right?" Before he could answer, she continued. "So, the mirror, being glass, contracted. Over time, the wood frame dries out, pulling the mirror tighter and tighter. You add in that little bit of atmospheric shift and, voila, presto change-o. You have mirror soup. And it had to happen on my watch. Can ya believe it? I know I can't. The way it broke sounded like a gunshot in there. I kid you not."

"Huh. Never heard of such a thing. The heat contractions due to atmospheric conditions."

"Yeah, true story. Hey, whatta say ta some donuts?"

"Sure." He smiled hugely.

She put her hand gently on his chest and eased him out the door. "I'll take a maple bar and a cake with chocolate frosting and sprinkles. Thanks, Hank. Hurry back, I'm hungry enough ta eat an entire horse and spit out the hoofs."

"Ah, yeah, okay. Yeah, sure, Imogene."

She closed, locked the door, and waved to him through the glass. She turned and trundled back to the pass-through to go behind the counter. She didn't look back to see if he had bought the line of bull pucky she fed him and played out the ruse of being a busy new store manager.

Chapter Six

Luke Short waited for her in the back. "See, I knew you were perfect for this gig." He used his hands when he spoke. "You talked your way outta that shots-fired call slicker 'n snot. That was really something. You were cool as a dern cucumber."

They stood in the back room, one filled with double-sided shelves—stained dark brown. Cubbyholes packed with things people had offered up on loan.

What a logistical nightmare.

No way was any of this mess in order. Not well enough to work smoothly. If someone came in and wanted to pay off a loan to get their stuff outta hock, how in the world did you find it?

The place smelled of musty old gym socks. Poor lighting cast shadows everywhere, giving off an eerie sense of a B horror movie. As if a mummy might jump out at any moment. She never understood how a mummy could hurt someone. Just kick him to the ground and step on him. He's a mummy for crying out loud. A desiccated body of skin and bone wrapped in an Ace bandage.

"Do I need to pull my gun to get you to talk? Ta pick up where we left off."

"No. No. Come on back here. We can sit in comfort and jaw a little." He started moving before she could object. The storage area handed off to the furthest room in the back, a make-shift apartment with an old slat bed in the corner, a refrigerator that had seen better days and quietly rattled, a small table with a faded green Formica top, two matching chairs, the chrome speckled with rust, a coffee table, a broken-down couch and a comfy rocker. The whole place was dingy and yellowish from nicotine, and smelled of burnt coffee from the Bun carafe burning on the hotplate.

Luke sat on the sway-back couch and pointed to the rocker. "You take the nice chair. Go on, you'll love it."

"I'll stand, thank you. I'm not staying long. Start talking. Go on, wind up that propaganda machine you call a mouth and spew some falsehoods masquerading as truths."

He hesitated as if putting the words together in his head, taking them out for a walk first before airing them to the world. "Okay, it's like this. Old women are invisible, and—"

"Hold it. Who's an old woman?"

"Okay, take it easy. That was rude, I admit. A lady such as yourself. A lady with experience enough to talk an alley cat out of a tree. I had hoped the letter would work. But it appears they misjudged you."

"Who's they?"

"Just gimme a minute to explain before you start shootin' up everything back in this room, too."

Another pause, waiting for a reaction, not forthcoming. "Now keep in mind that cop coming outta the mayor's campaign office and the one that came a knockin'. Both saw your lovely countenance and can now identify you."

"Son, you're walkin' me into a corner I don't like." She reached into her dress pocket and pulled out the .380, mentally counting how many bullets remained: four. Plenty to make the little weasel hurt without killing him.

Contrary to popular opinion, she wasn't a killer, least not by her reckoning. "Spill it now, or you'll be walking with a cane the rest of your sorry life. I'm tired of this game you're playing."

He paused as if testing her resolve.

"You're not talking fast enough. I guess I need to get your attention. I'll just shoot that dumbass cowboy hat off the top of your head." She took aim.

"Wait." He held up his hands. "It's not me doing this. These people are dead serious. I was ordered to recruit you. They didn't tell me how. Just to do it. Don't shoot. I'm reaching into my pocket to get something. Okay? It should explain everything. Just take it easy. Just take it real easy."

She said nothing and gave him the stink-eye.

He slowly reached up and unsnapped his shirt pocket. He pulled out a Polaroid photo, set it on the coffee table, and slid it across. "Just so you know, this isn't me. This is part of their backup plan. They somehow knew my idea with the letter wouldn't work."

Before taking a look, she motioned with the gun, "Sit on your hands."

"Pardon?"

"I said, sit on your dern hands."

"Okay." He eased off his haunches and stuck his hands under him.

She picked up the photo and stared. "You sorry, sick sons of bucks."

"No, don't shoot me. That's my little niece Ida, my sister's kid."

The eight-year-old little Ida in a yellow dress sat tied to a chair with a dirty rag around her mouth, tears streaking her face. Eyes wide with fright.

"I don't know this little gir—wait. This little girl lives on Hawthorne, my street. I bought lemonade from her at her stand right out in front of my house. She was also selling avocados picked from the tree in my backyard. Picked from Mr. Majestic."

"That's right, that's her." He said. "Wait, *Mr. Majestic*?

"So, you're sayin' someone's holding her until you do something for them?"

"Yes. These people, they orchestrate jobs, make other people do their dirty work, and in doing so keep their hands clean."

Except for kidnapping. That's a federal damn offense. Come on, E, let's blow this hotdog stand, we got no interest in this fool's caper. Let him turn and burn. Not us, baby. Not us.

Imogene smiled, glad to have Ange back. "Where've you been?"

But she knew. Imogene's mind had kept Ange at arm's length until Imogene discovered the letter's true provenance. That's what generated so much pent-up rage. That someone would try and play her using Ange as a lever. The reason why she shot the mirror and that poor chubby lady on the wall out in the front room. Now she felt bad about popping off those two rounds. That wasn't like her, really, it wasn't.

"Pardon? I haven't moved. I'm sitting right here."

"Never mind what I said, keep talking."

"These guys, they do their research and purposely choose our kinda people. They're very meticulous and choose carefully. They have backup plans on everything. Backup plans for the backup plans are almost like playing a big game of chess. Like it's a game to them."

"Wait. Whatta mean people like us. You mean people with tails? People on parole?"

Sweet baby bald-headed Jesus, E. This is one hell'va an idea. Wish we thought of it, huh? They got a hammer on all the poor slobs that are involved before they even get started. They make it so it's twice as hard to go to the man over their kidnapped loved ones. To go to the pooolice. What a sweet, sweet deal.

"That's right. You pick up on things fast."

After pondering it a moment, she said. "No one's ever done anything like this, not that I've seen in all the caselaw books or the novels I read in the joint."

"Maybe you didn't read about it because these sons of bitches are good and always get away with it."

"Maybe so, but I don't have any kin they can grab and hold over my head." Even as she said it, the words tasted like a bitter poison in her mouth. How could she say something so callous and uncaring? Ida did nothing to deserve any of this.

Imogene didn't know her well, just saw her around the neighborhood riding her bike. The one time she did talk with Ida was a day Imogene and Suz cleaned out Suz's dad's garage and had put all the junk in the front yard with "Free" on a sign. The locust junkers descended and stayed waiting for more junk to be brought up the long, steep driveway. Ida saw the opportunity and set up a lemonade stand to feed the loco locust.

The conversation stood out in memory, clean and crisp. It wasn't often Imogene got to talk to a sweet little girl.

To be absolutely honest, though, Ida reminded Imogene of Joyce when she was the same age. Now the Polaroid photo of Ida tied to a chair caused a little ache in Imogene's heart. An ache that turned to anger. She wanted to shoot something or somebody. Silly how guns gave you that false sense of power. That need. That easy vent used for redemption.

The day Imogene asked Ida her name, the girl didn't respond in a normal fashion. She said, "My name's Ida. I'm adopted, and my new dad is Chinese."

At the time, Imogene wrote it off as a cheeky remark, as some idiotic pop culture saying or colloquialism, and didn't inquire further. But the odd conversation helped mark the memory for later review.

Luke Short again reached into his shirt pocket for another Polaroid. He tossed it on the coffee table. "I'm sorry about this, really I am. Before you look at that one, remember I was told to do this. Ordered to do it. They told me what to say and how to say it even."

She didn't want to pick it up. The puppet masters knew their job too well. The person in that photo would be emotional bad juju. No two ways about it.

But just like the letter left on her coffee table, the evil sister who shared part of Imogene's brain wouldn't let it go. That evil sister reached down and picked it up without Imogene's brain giving her permission.

Imogene's hand flew to her mouth to stifle a guffaw that slipped out anyway. She bent at the waist and laughed, to suck air into her nicotine scared lungs.

Luke said, "Are you kidding me? Laughing at something so serious?"

She tossed the photo back onto the table, reached down, and snuffed out the Marlboro on the shiny finish as anger replaced mirth. No one manipulated her and got away with it. No one. "That's a picture of my neighbor's mother, Thelma. Why on God's green earth would I give two craps about her? I don't." Without Luke Short noticing, she palmed both photos and slipped them into her dress pocket. He kept his eyes locked on the .380.

"Yeah, they said you'd say something like that. They were going to grab your neighbor, Suzanne, to put the twist on you, but they also need her for this caper. They're pulling her into it, too. They want Suz to appropriate a Dentco truck for this job. They want *you* to tell Suz about her mom and about the truck. Bring Suz with you to work tomorrow here at the pawn shop so they can keep a better eye on her. But I strongly suggest tomorrow you be here on time."

"My Suz? Are you kidding me?"

"Whoa, don't shoot the messenger."

Imogene paced back and forth, juggling the Marlboro box in shaking hands. Lighting up another one without putting the gun down. "Okay, what's the bottom line here? These A-holes have to be after something, what is it?"

In any battle of wits, the one with the most information wins. An edict from a book read while in the joint, written by a slimy politician. What politician wasn't slimy? Hence, *Peekaboo POTUS.*

Imogene needed more information. The who and the what. In this instance, the where and the why weren't nearly as important and would come later.

He shrugged. "Can I bum one of those coffin nails?"

She tossed him the red box.

He took one out. She tossed him the Zippo.

He lit up. "I don't know these guys, their goal. I can guess. They want us to steal something big. Has to be big to warrant this kind of planning and involvement. I was told we each have a job, and we're only told what we need to know to make our part work. We're not to talk about it either. We're all cogs in a much bigger machine."

Sometimes he spoke like a rube and sometimes like an educated foe who forgot he was supposed to be a rube. *He* could be the puppet master. Or at least one of them.

"Who did you speak to? Who told you all this?"

"Another con just like us, in the same kinda bind as us. The mouthpiece for this job. He has his own blackmail to deal with. Though based on what he said, I think he's only the information conduit and isn't directly involved in the job like we are. Just the conductor."

E, the more I hear about this thing the more I can't believe someone else hasn't thought of it before now. You all get caught doing whatever it is you're supposed to do, the puppet kings jus' walk away. No crap at all sticking ta them. Slides right off 'em like they're made a Teflon. A sweet, sweet deal.

"Come on. Show me what I'm supposed ta do. You say they want me to run this pawn shop. I don't have the first clue how ta do that." She headed out the way she came, throwing words over her shoulder. "I know nothing about no dern pawn shop."

They walked through the dark storage area and back out into the public part. Two people stood out in front wanting to come in, the bright noonday sun on them like a spotlight. One woman held a large brass tuba that glinted and winked. The man propped up a kid's two-wheeler bike that still had the tassels hanging from the handlebars. Tassels never last long on a kid's bike. The father took the bike from his own kid or neighbor kid to sell to satisfy a jones. One probably for heroin, the signs obvious in his demeanor. In the joint everyone called heroin "Hair-on." The poor child would have no idea why they'd been deprived.

Imogene walked right up to the front window and looked out, ignoring the waiting customers. Luke Short came over and stood beside her.

"Look at that over there," she said, "Directly across this wide grassy boulevard, in between those hundred-year-old pepper trees, see it? A big fat bank. Bank of The West."

"Yeah, but you just said it. It's across that wide boulevard. What's it got to do with the pawn shop? We're over here, and the bank's over there? We ain't gonna dig no tunnel that far."

She turned to look at him. "You're a con, so you know exactly what's at stake with your parole. What'd you do time for?"

He took the cigarette from his lips and flicked ash on the floor. "I think it's better we know as little about each other as poss—"

She gave him the evil eye.

E, don't put up with his crapola, reach down and grab a handful of man-grapes. Grab ahold of those danglers and give 'em a good yank. He'll change his tune, you wait and see if he don't.

"I am a kindly old woman who wants nothing more than to sit on my divan, smoke my Marlboros, and watch the world go by. Maybe on Friday nights, watch some Bonanza on the TV and sip on a beer. But men...men like you keep pulling me back into their world. Their slop. You don't start cooperating, you're gonna force me to do things I don't wanna do. You hear what I'm sayin'? Something not too ladylike."

The woman outside got tired holding up the tuba, set it down, and tapped on the window. Insistent, wanting out of the sweltering July heat. The one good thing about the pawn shop, the air conditioner worked like a champ.

"Robbery. Armed robbery. You happy now?"

She shook her head. "You dimwit, was it bank robbery?"

"Ya, dern you ta hell. It was a dern bank. But that bank right there," he pointed out the front window, "is too far away. According to what we know of the plan so far, we're supposed to be over here in the pawn shop. Robbing that dern bank as part of this here deal makes no sense at tall, unless we dig a long tunnel. And besides, that's not what they want me ta do."

She puffed the Marlboro and stared out the window. "It might make more sense if this thing that's gonna happen, happens a few days from now."

"Why's that?"

"Seriously?"

"Tell me."

"The All States Fourth of July parade. Tens of thousands of people will be out there in the middle of Euclid, having a picnic, having a parade. It's the perfect cover. What do they want you to do?"

He took off his cowboy hat and ruffled his gray locks. "Yeah, that does make a little sense, I guess. All those people can cause enough chaos to slip away with the loot. And I was told not to tell anyone involved anything other than what *they're* supposed to know."

She opened her mouth to severely castigate him when a small man in a black suit, a white on white dress shirt, wearing a yarmulke, came to the door with keys. Purple and red marked parts of his face, eyes, nose, and mouth with swelling and small cuts. Someone took a dislike to him. Worked him over but good.

Imogene hated any kind of tyranny, no matter what form. Unless, of course, the person had it comin'. This guy in no way had it comin'. He had victim written all over him.

He tried the lock, but the keys still in the lock on the inside thwarted his attempt. He tapped on the window. Tried to peer in. The bright white sunlight reflecting off the sidewalk washed out any view of the inside.

Imogene opened the door and let them all in.

"Thank you," he said. "I assume you're the woman who I am now required to train in *my* own business?" He turned before she could answer and spoke to the customers. "You folks, please go over to that counter and I'll be right with you."

"*Friend*," Imogene said, "you know as much about all this as I do. I got a hammer hanging over my head just like you."

He only grunted as if he didn't care that a vulnerable elderly woman was now at risk.

She followed the throng over to the counter, listened, and watched the man in the black suit during the two loan transactions.

Pretty straightforward. You filled out the receipt book that had three carbon copies, then you filled out a tag with a number and entered the tag in a thick ledger. The tags were attached to the tuba and in turn the bike. The part Imogene would have a problem with was the estimated value and in deciding how much to loan. He took a Polaroid photo of each item, taped those in a larger album on a page with the day's date. He then ducked down under the counter, spun a dial in a huge floor safe, pulled out a cash box, and paid for the tuba and the girl's bike. Thirty cents on the dollar. Criminal. Paying so little. Taking undue advantage of folks amidst a hardship. People adrift in a rocky sea of life.

She no longer felt sorry for his current plight.

The little old man watched them leave. Once the door closed, tears rolled down his cheeks, emotions he'd been holding back. The pure professional businessperson while in front of customers. He held up his arm, pointing. "My mirror." He turned. "My beautiful painting of Lillie Langtry. They're ruined. That's seven thousand dollars. More if I took it to auction at Sotheby's. Much more. But not now. It's not worth a dime, now."

Hyperbole. If it came down to it, Imogene wouldn't give a hundred bucks for ol' Lillie. Even if she did have a place large enough in her house for something so gaudy and ostentatious.

She opened her little clutch purse, took out a checkbook, and started writing a check. The other two paid her no mind and talked amongst themselves. Spoke of inane things of no great importance. Not with blackmail in the offing. Maybe the cowboy was right, old women were invisible.

The little man again turned agitated and pointed to the shattered mirror, "And that…that right there…is seven years bad luck." He looked up, his lips muttering a silent prayer to protect him against an invisible evil that stood amongst them, protect him against some hooky make-believe curse.

Phooey on all that noise.

Luke Short took off his cowboy hat and held it in front of him. "I'm real sorry, Mister, about your damaged property. I'll repay you somehow. I'll get you the money."

E, this ol' boy ain't no ex-con bank robber. Not with that kinda empathy. Unless he's jus' puttin' on a show for his favorite gal. I seen how he looks at you. He want's hisself some of that Imogene moooonpie. Go on, tell me you ain't jus' a little moist over this cowpoke. You tell me you're not, I'll call ya a liar and kiss your butt at high noon in the town square. We're friends and all, but E, kick out the little Jew, take that cowboy out back and show him exactly what Imogene Taylor's got under the hood—a super-charged V-8. Ride that bronc 'til you hear the buzzer. Girl, win yourself another one of them big shiny rodeo belt buckles and—

Empathy. Ange never used words like that.

Hearing the cowboy's entreaty to make good the damage, Imogene looked up from the check. "Ah, for crying out loud. All three of us have larger problems ta deal with than the lost value of a couple items in the store. I'm standing next to a crap-pile of guns, a violation of my parole." She pointed toward her bosom with the pen, "That's life for me if I catch a parole violation. I say we lock up, go in the back, and discuss every aspect of this conundrum. Pool our information and resources. Figure a way outta this mess. Put it hard to anyone and everyone who tossed us into the briar patch."

The little man shook his head. "I was told they'll be watching. They told me to tell you not to lock the door until closing. They said to act normal and under no circumstances are we to discuss about what's going between ourselves or anybody. Or else—" His hand shot up to his mouth. "I've already said too much." His hand gently probed the injuries to his face, remembering the past lesson.

The bell above the door jangled. They turned. A uniformed cop walked in. The little man in the black suit and yarmulke muttered, "Perfect. Just perfect."

Chapter Seven

Hank, the West Valley police department cop, stepped into the pawn shop and held a white bag with growing grease spots in one hand. "Here's the donuts you wanted, Imogene. Not as fresh as right out of the fryer, but not day-old either."

She smiled and took the bag. "Just in time. My stomach was worried someone had cut my throat."

Hank laughed too hard at a joke without legs. He suddenly turned serious. "Hey, I was back at the office and JB…you know good ol' JB. He wanted me to tell you—for the department, I mean. How sorry he was the way the department treated you. That it wasn't right." His eyes defused as if his mind suddenly diverted too much of his brain power to work another problem. "Hey, Imogene, aren't you on parole?" He pointed to the rifles in the racks on the wall and the pistols under glass in the counter showcases. "Aren't you—"

Imogene broadened her smile, waved her hand in the air in front of him as a distraction, took him by the arm, and stepped with him back toward the door. "Hank, you mind if I ask you a question? I know how conscientious you are and how aware you are of everything going on in your town, so I know you'll have the answer."

His expression turned worried. "Sure Imogene, shoot."

"I guess I'm working this year in this pawn shop and will miss the Fourth of July shindig out front."

They stopped at the door and faced each other.

"Okay?" he said.

"You see, I'll need to make a big fat money drop at the bank. You know, the daily receipts and all. Do you know if the bank across the street is open on the Fourth? I don't wanna have all that money left lying around."

"Oh, sure. They're open but with modified hours because of the holiday. Instead of closing at five they're closing at one."

She said, "That's when the parade starts, right? One?"

"Hey, that's right. I guess that's why they close at one o'clock, huh?"

If the entire police department was as amenable as Hank, someone could back up a tow truck, hook it to the bank, and just tow away the whole kit and caboodle.

She again eased him out the door, but couldn't lock him out. Not without raising suspicion. Hank stood outside. This time with his foot in the door. "Imogene, wait?"

She smiled. "I know, and I'm sorry for the bum's rush. I know what's bothering you."

"You do?"

"Of course, I'm a mother too, you know. You're worried about me. You don't have to be, it's perfectly safe working here. And I know you'll come by all the time to check in on me. Keep me safe."

Not at all convinced, he stuck his hand in the doorway. "No, wait—"

She smiled and gave him a gentle little shove. "As a mother, I also saw how you eyed that nice little chrome revolver in the display case. A Colt Detective Special, wasn't it? Come back later, I'll give you a deal that'll knock your socks off."

"What? I mean, you'd do that for me?"

"Of course, I will. We're friends, aren't we?"

"Yes, I guess we are. Thank you, Imogene. I'm working overtime on the Fourth during the parade. I'm standing watch down at the mayor's political office. Right here, just a couple doors down on the other side of the jewelry shop. I'll be there to make sure the mayor's office doesn't get vandalized. That'd be a real blackeye for the department. I guess everyone has enemies, right? I should make enough extra money to buy that gun you saw me eyeing. That is if you can see your way clear to give me a good enough deal."

"You name your price, it's yours. Now run along. I've got a lot of work to do." She gently pushed on him some more while trying to move his foot from the door with hers.

"Name my own price? Are you serious? Why that gun's gotta be worth—"

"Yes, Hun, whatever you want. I'll help you out with the price. Now get on, I've got a lot to do."

He nodded, his eyes no longer seeing her as his mind tried hard to rectify what had just happened. Poor Barney Fife.

She said, "Hank?"

"Yes, ma'am? Oh, sorry." He backed the rest of the way out of the pawn shop. She closed the door. He stood for a moment, staring in. With the angle of the sun, he could only see his own reflection in the glass. That big goofy look on his face made him out a fool. She did feel bad about gaslighting the poor soul. He was so young and eager, someone ignorant in the ways of the real world. He had better smarten up fast or someone on the street would hand him his butt, make a hat outta of it. Or worse.

Imogene turned. The two men at the counter stared as if she were some kind of magician, one who could make a cop disappear by snapping two fingers.

Imogene walked back to the counter, finished writing a check for eight thousand dollars, and handed it to the little man in the black suit.

He took it from her. Both men looked at it. Their mouths dropped open in awe.

Luke spoke first, "You have that kinda cash in the bank that you can whip out a check jus' like that?" He snapped his fingers. "Is it good? It isn't gonna bounce all the way down the street, is it?"

She gave him the evil eye, yet again. As far as men went, he needed more training than most.

"Okay. Okay. Then with that kinda cashola what the heck are you doin' wrapped up in all this mess?"

"That's what I wanna know. Can you please tell me?"

Tears filled the little man's eyes. He moved in, hugged Imogene. His small head nestled too comfortably between her ample breasts and stayed there, a puppy that found a home.

"E, this little guy's so small he could have a place on your dresser. Jus' set him up there next to the perfume bottles. You know what I'm sayin'? But don't you dare get funky with him. Not when you got Cowboy-Joe waiting in the wings for his wild bronc ride.

She let him have his fill and pulled him away. "Watch out for that check. I didn't put a name on. You lose it, and anyone can cash it."

He nodded, swiped at his face—at the tears. He filled in his name. "I am Alan Goldblatt, that's with two t's. Very nice to meet you, madam. I can't thank you enough. I cannot believe your generosity. Even when you had nothing to do with the damage. You are truly a woman of substance. And I might add, unlike any other woman in this town." He picked up her hand and kissed it.

E, watch him. Watch him! He's makin' his move. He wants some a that mooonpie. And let me say this, you are one dumbass dolt for giving up that kinda cashola when you didn't have to. He had no clue who crapped all over his stuff. Ruined it with errant gunfire.

"It was the right thing to do." She said to Ange.

Goldblatt smiled and shook his head in amazement. "Yes, it is the right thing to do. But not by you. You had nothing to do with this. You're a lady, a quiet, gentle lady. You're as much a victim as the rest of us. It's the evil men who perpetrated this…this immoral endeavor. I hope you don't mind me asking…" He looked down at the check for her name, "…Ms. Taylor. I would very much like to show my abundant appreciation. Tonight, could I please take you to a nice dinner at the Stuft Shirt in Upland."

Tolt ya, E. What'd I tell ya? Huh? Shove the little pipsqueak in the face, turn heel, and run for the hills. He wants to get into those big panties of yours.

Information would be the only way outta this fix. And good ol' Mr. Goldblatt with two t's had some to mine like a valuable ore. She wanted what he knew—had to have it.

"Yes, that would be very kind of you. Tonight, then, say eight-ish. I'll meet you there."

He bowed and kissed her hand one more time. "Madam, you are a breath of fresh air in a world filled with smog. I will see you tonight, then."

He hurried from his own store. Leaving two parolees to fly his pawn shop right into the ground. The odd thing, the fool was absolutely ecstatic about it.

She didn't want to feel anything about Goldblatt, no emotions. But that wasn't always left up to her.

Her acceptance of the dinner date was nothing more than an important calculation in a much larger game and had nothing to do with a love interest. But as always, that little cupid jaybird, the one with a reckless arrow flinging affliction, did as he pleased. The touch of Goldblatt's lips on her hand lingered. She shivered the sensation away.

"Oh, for goodness sake. Quit with the school-girl routine."

He looked to be what, E? Sixty-five, sixty-eight? He might be the one to mount and ride off into the sunset, if you get my meanin'?

Luke said, "What did you just say? Do you always talk to yourself like that?"

"Why don't you mind your own business."

He pointed in the direction of the front window. "That man's no bigger than a tick on a blue hound's ear. Hell's bells, I could pick him up and put him in my pocket. Yeah, that's right, he'd be a great pocket rocket."

Oh, sweet baby Jesus, E. The cowpoke's jealous as a calf on a strange mama's teat. Ain't it the way with men? It's feast or famine. Am I right? Tell me I'm right.

"I'm tired. I'm goin' home."

"No, you can't. They said we have to stay open 'til closing time, five p.m. Not a second sooner. They want you to learn how this place works. Feel comfortable here. They'll check up on us. You wait and see if they don't."

"I already know how it works. And if they do happen to ask, tell 'em I'm having dinner, tell 'em I'm out with the owner trying to glean additional information about the pawn game. And if they squawk about that, then tell 'em they can just kiss my rosy red—" She caught herself. For the last two years, while out on parole, she tried hard to shed that potty mouth she picked up in the joint. Tried to get back to the Imogene of old.

Now she sounded like some kinda King Arthur tale...the Black Knight of old.

"Yeah, about that dinner date," Cowboy-Luke said. "I'm thinkin' it might be better for you…I mean safer, if I go along."

"I can take care of myself, Tex Ritter. I want you to think real careful about your inability to tell me who's pulling your strings. The name. Because tomorrow I'm not gonna take no for an answer." She poked him in the chest with her finger. "You hear what I'm sayin'?"

He nodded.

Ange was right about the cowboy, he did have piercing gray eyes, with lips that begged to be kissed…silly talk for an old woman who just wanted to sit on the divan and smoke Marlboros, watch the day creep by on all fours.

"I'll see you tomorrow." She turned and walked out.

*　*　*

She drove home with her eyes constantly checking the rear view. Thuggish friends of the Cigar, the gangster who died of lead poisoning on her living room gold high-low carpet two weeks earlier, would eventually pop up. No two ways around it. It was going to happen. Just a matter of when. That reminded her to buy more ammunition for the .380.

How had her homespun life devolved to a point where additional ammunition was needed as a precursor to an upcoming second violent confrontation? Mind boggling to say the least.

She tried hard to put it out of her mind and couldn't.

The seatbelt across her shoulder and lap caused a twinge of claustrophobia. In her youth, she never suffered those kinds of maladies. Flaws in the human psyche. For some unknown reason, any feeling of restraint caused an abnormal level of anxiety.

And why didn't the law make all folks wear seatbelts? She had read that fifty thousand people died each year in car accidents. A crazy number. Especially when fifty-five thousand soldiers died in all of the Vietnam War. A war that just ended six months earlier. Fifty thousand folks a year killed in fatal car accidents. Unbelievable. Such a senseless loss of life. Half of which could be avoided if the law would just step in and make it a crime to drive without being buckled up. But people wouldn't tolerate having their freedom impinged upon. The fools. A small bit of freedom compared to risking life and limb.

She stopped at a stop sign. A new mother with a stroller, the expensive model with big wheels, rolled a newborn from street corner to street corner. Vulnerable while in the street. Imogene drove on and tried to stay focused on the issues at hand. Two of them when there shouldn't be any.

The blackmail situation at the West Valley Jewelry and Loan should be the worst problem. But it wasn't. Not when compared to the very real threat of a couple of mouth-breathers with broken noses coming to pay her a visit.

Everything she read in the joint, and in conversations with other cons, indicated that mob torpedoes no longer looked like the typical cliché. Now they could be anyone who wanted a piece of the contract put out on the street for the killing of a "made man." Of all things, a contract on a kind, gentle old woman who wanted nothing more than to be left alone.

The very idea got her blood up. She gripped the steering wheel as she came to a red stop signal. She tried to envision someone standing in front of the little red AMC Gremlin, pointing a gun at her through the windshield. Could she hit the gas and just run his butt over? The answer wasn't a resounding YES like it should've been.

Two weeks earlier, when she pulled the trigger and dropped the two thugs in her living room, the situation had been dire. Had she not acted, all would've been lost.

The armed man standing in front of her car scenario wasn't the same thing. She could simply duck across the seat and then drive around him. Thereby, circumventing the taking of yet another human life.

Each and every time she remembered the two episodes where she pulled the trigger, those memories came with a teeth-cutting edge. Jaw muscles knitted. Dentures ground together. They were not built for that kinda pressure. White flashes of violence disrupted calm emotional waves and pulsated through her entire body. She would never, ever shoot somebody again. The emotional price tag was too much to handle.

But she knew that wasn't true. There might again come a time where it would be her or them. And she would not just roll over and play dead. Not for the likes of them. Not for anyone.

The light changed, she drove on. The little car's air conditioner reminded her of the little train that could, as it fought a losing battle against Southern California July heat. Grueling and unrelenting, radiating in through the car glass. Heating the car metal like a rock next to a campfire. Making Imogene inside an ant under a young kid's magnifying glass.

Down the road, not more than a hundred yards, she again checked the rearview and froze.

Nobody was following, no one even looked suspicious or furtive.

No. The reason for the alarm was the particular sunlight that somehow caused a deep-set emotional response.

Homing pigeons are said to have compass-like navigational systems. She talked to a pigeon guy once who said the birds used the curvature of the earth and familiar light spectrums to guide them in their return flight home. Sometimes traveling hundreds of miles.

The afternoon sun in the rearview had hit a certain spectrum and sparked a horrid memory of Joyce, Imogene's only child. Imogene's lovely daughter.

In her mind's eye, the portrait of Joyce that hung over the TV flashed in memory. Joyce was a beautiful girl. In the painting, she wore a green dress with a white collar. She had her glistening brown hair in the fifties style pulled back off her face and curled. The painter gave her red lipstick and had ignored the tiny acne scars under both cheekbones. It had been so long since Imogene had seen Joyce, she'd forgotten what those little scars looked like. Would've forgotten her face entirely had the portrait not stared down at her day in and day out for the last twenty-five-odd years. Joyce never aging while Imogene continued to shrink and shrivel the same as a plump grape turning into a raisin. Over time, her mind and memory grew cloudy as Imogene continued to swirl down the drain of time. Drawing closer to the other side of eternity with each passing minute.

Joyce had been smart, the most intelligent kid in her sophomore high school class. Imogene might not have believed her daughter about that, not entirely anyway. But during parents' night at the high school, all her teachers said the same thing: "Whip smart." "She's really going places." "The way she does math, heck, she could even be the first woman astronaut."

Imogene listened to those same teachers talk to other parents about their kids to see if they blew smoke up their dresses.

They didn't.

Joyce was a true wonder. She had it all, beauty, brains, and tall like Wayne. Imogene would forever bask in that knowledge.

Totally lost in the memory, Imogene came to and no longer sat in the little red Gremlin driving down the street. Instead, she now sat on the concrete porch in front of her house, sipping on a Schlitz Malt Liquor beer and smoking a Marlboro.

The sun, low on the horizon, shot rays of fading orange, yellow, and red. She had no idea at all how she arrived there. It should've scared the bejesus outta her, but it didn't. Why worry about the small stuff when life, all on its own, kept trying to steamroll right over her. Mash her into the asphalt like that dumbass coyote who chased after the road runner.

The blip in lost memory was the first time that ever happened.

Huh?

Or was it?

Time just kinda skipped.

She emotionally blacked out and misplaced a small chunk of memory.

She whispered so no one else could hear, "Ange, you there?"

Senseless, really; there wasn't anyone around. Ange more than anyone would know what just happened.

Ange said nothing. Of course, she didn't speak when Imogene needed her the most. That would be too easy.

Imogene had read about how flashing lights could trigger grand mal seizures. Was that what just happened? Was it that peculiar light spectrum?

She sat back and tried to remember.

It had been the first part of July way back when. The afternoon the ominous knock came at the door. That same knock that sometimes echoed in her nightmares and soaked her nightshirt in sweat.

That meant the July light, the way the sun in its similar orbit for that time of year, the way it lit up the sky with its white-hot light, had somehow triggered her. Made her black out mentally for a time. Sure, that was it. At least now she started to understand the why.

The memory of that day long ago again tried to force its way into her mind. Just like the homing pigeon when it came home to roost. So did that horrid little nightmare.

She sat back and let it take her. Why fight it. Get it over with so she could move on with the bigger problems.

* * *

During summer school, two weeks after the teacher told Imogene Joyce was an exceptional student and going places—that's when the knock came at the thick green painted door at 744 East Hawthorne.

Imogene had been in the kitchen skinning a chicken carcass, putting the meat in the pressure cooker for the chicken broth to cook the Bisquick dumplings. Wayne's favorite.

She wore a nice day-dress with an old flower print apron over it. She wiped her hands on the apron just before opening the front door.

On the porch stood a frumpy-looking man and a police officer bearing horrid news no mother should ever endure. The words like acid etching into her brain. There on the porch. But at the same time not there.

Chapter Eight

Way back when, on that indelible July second, Imogene opened the thick green front door at 744 Hawthorne Street to an insistent knock and found that frumpy little man in a wrinkled brown suit and black-framed, round glasses under sparse, straw-like hair. He stood on the porch with a blue-uniformed policeman behind him. The warm breeze outside blew past the men and into the house, bringing along a sour-old-man kinda smell. One she would never forget.

Imogene whispered, "Oh, my dear Lord. It's Wayne, isn't it? Something's happened to Wayne. It was that dern disker wasn't it?"

Wayne kissed her goodbye that morning and told her he planned to disk Ruth Gordon's twenty-acre pink grapefruit grove up in LaVerne. Wayne and Imogene lost their own groves to blight, Santa Ana winds, heat and just poor luck. Maybe even some poor choices thrown in the mix. Wayne had taken to spot work, half-day jobs here and there to make ends meet. No way should he be out in those dern groves, not four hours at a time disking. Shouldn't be out there for one dern second. Especially not with his banged-up knees. He wore metal leg braces for crying out loud.

And driving a tractor?

He hugged her, kissed her lightly on the cheek as he always did. Said, "Imogene, don't answer the door today. I'm riding that deadly disk off into the sunset."

The disk, a lethal contraption pulled behind a tractor between the rows of citrus to turn over all the weeds and to make the dirt more arable. Old stories persisted of men who hit large rocks while disking. They got jostled off the tractor seat onto the ground. They went under the disk as the tractor continued on, no one at the wheel. The tractor didn't have a dead-man's switch. An odd name for something invented to save a man's life. One that had not yet made it to a John Deere.

Wayne joshed her each and every time with similar words, said it anytime he took a disk job. Thought it funny as all get out. Well, it wasn't. She wanted to slap the smug right off his face. But he had hugged and kissed her first. The scent of Old Spice mixed with the reek of burnt cherry pipe tobacco hung about him in an aura and always got her engine running. Though he had not ventured over to her side of the bed in quite a while now. If not for the pain in his legs he surely would've. Sure, he would've.

How could a man be a man when his knees ached forever and a day? So much so he let out little groans while he slept. Muttered to a dream doctor, "Just cut 'em off, Doc. Cut 'em off, dern you." His entreaties broke Imogene's heart. She would give anything to take his pain, all of it. If it were possible to hand it from one human to another. Take his pain so he would no longer have to endure such anguish and torture. He was too good a man.

When she pushed him about his legs he'd simply say, "Imogene, don't you worry that pretty little head of yours. Doesn't a matter one wit. In another ten years, they'll be giving out stainless steel knees like Halloween candy. You wait and see if they're not."

Pshaw. That would never happen. Stainless steel knees of all things. He was having on with her. Reading too much Jules Verne.

When awake, he never said word one about his own legs or the braces. Acted as if nothing at all bothered him. Wayne in his day could've been a twin to Gary Cooper. Gallant and brave the same as Cooper in *Sergeant York*.

That afternoon, when she opened the front door to the frumpy little man and the cop, that's how she knew it had to be Wayne. The Grim Reaper came to make his grief-filled notification about a gawd-dern disking accident.

Imogene's legs gave out. She eased down to the gold, high-low carpet. All the air vacated the world making it difficult to breathe. The West Valley cop opened the screen door, hurried in, and helped her sit in the chair across from Wayne's rocker/easy chair. That's what her eyes locked onto. That chair. And then the small brown pipe rack on the credenza next to his chair, the one that held Wayne's pipes. That was his place in her world. A place he always sat. He was always there. Even when he wasn't.

That same world that slowed its turn, now sped up again. Next she knew, the frumpy little man—a deputy coroner—took a knee in front of the chair holding her hand. His simple words the same as a pointed dirk penetrating skin, slicing through muscle, going deep, sliding off breastbone, piercing the heart and… "Your daughter Joyce succumbed to her injuries. She was DOA at San Antonio Community Hospital in Upland. You can claim her remains there."

"What? No. No. No. You mean Wayne. You're here for Wayne. Don't you dare play that evil joke on me. Not about my beautiful daughter. Not about my Joyce."

The frumpy little man looked up at the cop, then back at Imogene. "Did you hear everything I said? Is there someone here who can stay with you through this difficult time? Where is your husband, Wayne?"

A lump as hard as a cherry stone rose into her throat. "Joyce. Dear Lord, no! Not my Joyce! Please tell me you're lying. Tell me it's an ugly, ugly lie and I'll forgive you. Just tell me true."

She moved to the edge of the chair as if about to lunge at this interloper who dared to ruin her life. She loved Wayne with all her heart. But Joyce. Joyce *was* Imogene's life.

As an emotional defense, the frumpy little man dropped back into his droning monologue of what had happened, a repeat of how the "accidental death" occurred.

The air turned thick as clear Jell-O and warbled. Funny how Jell-O was made from ground-up cow's hooves and bones. Most people didn't know that little tidbit.

"…Joyce Taylor was riding on the back of a young man's 350 cc Husqvarna motorcycle."

Imogene stared at Wayne's pipes in the pipe rack and shook her head. "No. No. I don't believe you. I'm not going to believe you. So, you can just quit talking. Pack up your gypsy tent and move on, fella. I'm not falling for your snake oil show."

"…They weren't driving crazy," the cop said. "They just caught a green light and took the left turn too fast. Leaned over just a little too far. The foot peg caught asphalt, and…and the bike tumbled end over end. With the two riders in the mix."

End over end.

That's what the bastard cop said as he stood in their home. Said it just like that; "end over end."

Imogene couldn't get rid of the images freeze-framed in her mind, ones created through pure imagination. Her poor little girl caught up in a metal crunching somersault. Slapping asphalt, tumbling, shattering bone and skull. Tearing, rending skin and muscle. The body forever separated from the soul. And worst of all, Imogene hadn't been there to help her. Imogene had failed as a mother, as a protector. Her number one job.

Joyce was gone for good.

A long, low grunt slipped past her lips. The world spun round and round.

Time skipped for the first time.

Way back when.

* * *

She came to in a strange place. All the same color, beige or almost pink. Puce, that is, if her eyes didn't lie. Nothing else was in the room. She lay on her side, looking down the gentle slope in the floor that led to a drain. A ten-by-ten-foot room with a drain, a room that smelled of burnt rubber mixed in thick with despair. Did they come in and just hose down the whole place? Is that the reason for the dern drain? The next thing she noticed, her arms wouldn't move. Someone had placed her inside some kind of canvas contraption with too-long sleeves. Her arms in those sleeves pinned against her chest. Pulled up tight.

The single naked light bulb in the ceiling behind a metal grate blinded when she looked up.

"Hello? Anyone there?" Her voice croaked as if she'd been at a high school football game screaming for those Hedgehogs.

"Hello? Anyone?" Said it louder this time, almost screaming.

A loud clang made her cringe. She pulled her knees up to her chest. This had to be a nightmare. Nothing else explained it.

Nothing.

A rather rotund black woman wearing matching blue pants and top—hospital garb—with a white coat over it, trundled in. "Imogene, are you feeling better now?"

"Better? How the heck can I feel any worse? You got me trussed up like some kinda Christmas goose about to be shoved headlong inta the oven. Get your butt over here and turn me loose. Do it right now or else. I'll tell ya right now, I'm not one to trifle with."

The woman smiled with broad white teeth. "You're a pistol, aren't you? Least now you're coherent. You came in raving like a banshee. Do you remember any of that?" The woman produced a clipboard and a pen out of nowhere and took notes.

"This is all a bad dream, and I'm gonna wake up in about two shakes. Right? This is nothing but a bad dream."

The woman lost her smile and shook her head. She came further into the puce colored room and worked at getting Imogene up into a sitting position that made it more difficult to breathe. The canvas shirt, too tight against her chest, all but smothered her.

"Can you get this dern thing off me?"

"We need to talk first. Just a little. No sense taking it off if you're going to start climbing the walls again."

"Climb the walls. What the heck are you talking about? "Do I know you? Where's Wayne, my husband? Where am I? What is this place?"

The woman placed a hand on Imogene's leg. "Take it easy. I'll answer all your questions in turn. Your husband, Wayne, is fine. I just talked with him yesterday and—"

"You talked to him? He knows I'm in here? Then how come he doesn't come get me out of this seven kinds of hell?"

"Imogene, you're starting to get agitated again. Calm down, or I can't take off the restraining jacket."

"*You* put me in this gawd dern thing. Take it off. Take it off right now or I'll—"

The woman walked toward the solid steel door. "I guess you're not ready to be a lady and have a civilized conversation."

The thought of being alone in the room all trussed up, her breathing impaired, scared the bejesus outta her. "Wait. Wait, it's okay. I'll be good, come back. Please come back. I'll do whatever I gotta do to get outta this mule's harness."

The woman stuck her head out the door and said something to someone, then came back in. She sat down on the vacant floor next to Imogene as if they were two schoolgirls out by the smoking tree between North and South hall in high school, just talking.

Imogene said, "Can I please have a cigarette? It'll calm these dern jangled nerves of mine, at least take the edge off."

"No smoking is allowed while you're visiting here."

"Visiting? This ain't no garden spot that I'd call a visit."

Imogene clinched her jaw in anger and bit back an abundance of vehement words. Then said, "Go on, tell me what I gotta do ta get you to take this dern thing offa me?"

"We need to have a calm, civilized conversation. That's all. It's very simple. But I have to warn you, even though it's simple, it's going to be a very painful conversation. But one we have to have."

"Okay, shoot. I can take it. Give it to me, straight. I need to get home to my husband, Wayne, and my daughter, Joyce. They'll be worried sick about me."

A man came into the little room wearing all white pants, shirt, and shoes. Quiet as a mouse, not so much as a whisper of a sound. He looked like Mr. Clean from the TV commercials. He held a small paper cup and another larger cup with water.

The woman said. "Imogene, I don't want you to fight me on this. I want you to take this pill."

Imogene opened her mouth. The man emptied the little cup, dropping a blue pill on her tongue. He let her drink some water, then backed out and disappeared.

"What's next? You want me to stand up and jump through some hoops like some kinda pink circus poodle? I'll do it. Please, just get me the heck outta this harness. I'm having a hard time breathing, and I'm getting claustrophobic."

The woman took some notes, then looked up. Her tone came out softer, more caring. "Imogene, can you please tell me the last thing you remember before you woke up here?"

Imogene started to speak and froze as she harkened back. "I...ah...I was in the kitchen skinning a chicken, making some chicken broth for dumplings. Wayne loves his dumplings...and—"

All on their own and for no reason, tears ran down Imogene's cheeks. Burning hot little trails of fire. Suddenly, a smooth, warm blanket settled over her and relaxed every muscle in her body. She could breathe easy again. The muscles in her face relaxed, her mouth drooped open.

She turned to the woman sitting next to her in the ten-by-ten puce room that smelled of burnt rubber.

Imogene began to sob. "It's Wayne, he...he fell off a tractor in Ruth Gordon's pink grapefruit grove and went under the disker. Wayne's gone."

The woman moved around in front of her on her knees, looked Imogene in the eye. "Imogene, Wayne is safe at home. He's worried about you. He wants you better, so you can come home. I told you a few minutes ago that I talked to Wayne yesterday. Do you remember that?"

Imogene shook her head no.

"Has my daughter been asking about me? Has Joyce been here to see me? Does she know her daddy is gone? That he went under the disks?"

The woman didn't answer and put her warm hand on Imogene's cheek. "We'll get you outta that jacket and into a nice comfortable bed. We have quite a bit more talking to do and I hope you and I will become fast friends."

The man in white came back as if on cue and helped the woman get Imogene to her feet. The man worked at Imogene's back, unlacing the jacket.

That's when Imogene spotted the woman's name tag pinned to her white coat. "Doctor Angela, 'Ange,' Ledger."

Chapter Nine

Imogene woke to darkness and sat still, hardly taking a breath. Where the heck was she? What happened? Her memory scanned back, looking for what was real and what wasn't. She sat up in a corner, carpet under her bottom, legs, and hands.

The last real memory was sitting on the porch in front of her home at 744 Hawthorne, smoking and drinking a Schlitz Malt Liquor beer. She remembered that much. And while out on the porch, out to the left on the horizon, the sunlight had hit exactly right, hit that certain light spectrum. She wasn't at all sure how she got to the porch. The memory before that was driving the little red Gremlin home from West Valley Jewelry and Loan. She read somewhere how stress can cause memory to skip. At least she thought she read it somewhere.

And lately life had for some reason kicked her in the teeth, given her enough stress to can it in mason jars, put up it the same as summer fruit.

Now time had skipped yet again. And she was…she was sitting in the dark. Was this purgatory? Had a gun thug snuck up on her while she sat immobile on the porch, her mind defused and focused on an ugly past. Snuck up, stuck a gun to her gray and black mop of hair, pulled the trigger, and now she sat in purgatory. Heaven's waiting room. Unable to ever advance due to violations of the Ten Commandments. The big one, thou shalt not kill. Times three.

She had killed three men.

Wayne and two thugs. There wasn't any parole in purgatory. You did the full sentence.

Eternity.

A wayward yelp slipped past her lips, one she couldn't take back.

Moments later, there came a rattle from a newspaper and: "Imogene?"

A kind voice from a darkness that turned into a soupy dimness as her eyes adjusted. The blackout blinds did their job to a point.

"Imogene, don't be afraid, it's me, Suz."

"Dern it, girl, you scared the water outta me. Thought I was about to have a conversation with ol' Beelzebub himself. Thought he'd tell me I had a permanent room in his resident hotel. Come on, give an old woman a hand up." As she said it, the memories of what happened that same day flooded back. Imogene had a Polaroid picture in her dress pocket of a hostage held by dark forces. A hostage named Thelma. Suz's mother. And worse. Much worse. A small girl named Ida.

Suz offered her hand. Imogene took it and struggled to her feet, knees whining in pain. That's when she realized she stood in her own bedroom and that she had been sitting in the opposite corner from where Wayne had been when she mistook him for an intruder, twelve years back.

Mistook him for an armed robber who terrorized their neighborhood. From across the dern room, she had pulled the trigger and shot poor ol' Wayne in the head. The love of her life. The last vestige of anything that resembled an anchor in her life cut loose and set her adrift.

Any other time, under those circumstances, she would've missed the shot. She wasn't a gun moll by anyone's estimation. But that night when she shot Wayne, Lady Luck tossed her snake-eyes. An accident, pure and simple. Yet a jury of her peers saw it differently. The judge gave her twenty-five to life. None of those who sat in judgement, the jury or his honor, took into account the emotional trauma incurred during the incident. Had she not been a strong woman, she might've turned into a babbling idiot in need of shock treatments.

She got out after ten years on good behavior but with a tail. A tail that now threatened to tug her back into the joint to finish out her term. Fifteen years still remained, a guillotine poised overhead. Fifteen years, the same as a death sentence to a seventy-five-year-old. All because of what? That she had somehow been chosen to run a pawn shop loaded with firearms while a couple of gunsels attempted to rob a bank during a Fourth of July Parade? Her book, *Peekaboo POTUS*, was an outrageous satire she thought would never sell. But this robbery premise flat-out took the cake. No author could write this story because no reader with any common sense would believe it.

But there she stood on shaky knees, smack dab in the middle of someone else's conspiracy to commit.

The room suddenly closed in on her. "Come on, lend an old woman a hand and let's get outta here." She had not slept in the room one night since she shot Wayne. Suz came over and stood close, lending a shoulder for Imogene to lean heavily on. They went out to the living room where Suz deposited her on the divan in the regular spot. She set the folded Daily Report on the coffee table. The patchwork floor looked like hell, where the bloody sections were cut out by Luke Short, exposing the hardwood floor in missing, uneven swatches. She'd call first thing in the morning and order new carpet.

Imogene lit up a Marlboro and spoke through the smoke that came out of her mouth, mixing with the words. "How'd I get in there?" Before Suz could answer, Imogene looked out the big picture window, startled. She muttered, "Sweet baby Jesus. What day is it? What time is it?"

The sunlight position on the grass, the brightness meant she'd slept through the entire night and into midmorning.

"It's Tuesday, silly. Yesterday was Monday. This Thursday is the Fourth and the All States picnic and parade. We got a table off of B Street, you and me. I'm excited. Anyway, you ended up in your bedroom because me and Mike found you last night out there on your porch babbling. We helped you into your bed, but you fought and struggled like a sack full of alley cats. Said you never slept in that deathbed and wouldn't start. We finally let you go. You crawled over to the corner of the room where you sat and talked to someone named Ange. Talked to her long into the night. I got tired and slept on your couch. I heard you when you woke up. I came in to check on you. There, now you're up to date. I really hope you'll let me drive you to the doctor to get checked out. The way you were…last night…well, it scared me. I'm worried about you, E."

Imogene puffed and puffed the Marlboro. Suz's words hurt and scared her. "I don't mean to be an ingrate. I just wanted to know what happened, is all. And thank you for looking out for me." She mulled over a lie that might work to explain the previous night's aberrant behavior and hesitated, floating it over to her friend.

"You're welcome. Now will you let me take you to the doctor to get checked out?"

Imogene waved a hand and smiled. "Pshaw. It's nothing and—"

"E, you didn't see yourself last night. You were—"

"Outta my head with delirium?"

"Yes, you could call it that. Yes, that is a likely description."

She tried hard to get all the guile from her expression and hoped for contrite embarrassment. "You see…I have a sickness—"

"What are you talking about? We're best friends, and this is the first I've heard about any illness?"

"Take it easy. It's something silly, really. I…ah…I have malaria."

Suz's expression shifted to confusion. "Malaria? Have you been out of the country, to Africa, Southeast Asia, or South America? I didn't know you used to travel."

And as always, what happens when one practices to deceive, one lie begets another. "Yes, when I was a teen, my father—we owned a chain of hardware stores before Sears and Roebuck mail order catalog crushed us. I told you that part before. When we were still flush with cash, my father sent us on a world cruise. Daddy worked so hard he never had time enough to spit and stayed home. He sent me and mother on one glorious vacation. One for the books, to be sure."

"Really. Oh, how interesting, E. Please, please tell me all about it."

Imogene puff, puff, puffed on the Marlboro and stared her down. "You just said we're friends, is that right?"

By Imogene's tone, Suz turned scared. "Yes, of course we are, E. Why would you even say such a thing?"

"Friends don't bushwhack friends."

"What are you…Oh. I am sorry about that. I couldn't live with myself with that girl in the box…Poppy Liu. Her family had to know what happened to her."

"You put me in a crack with the police. I was questioned."

"What? You were? Why? I put the box over there on Bernard's porch, so they would think he did it. He did do it."

Suz was so young and naïve it made Imogene smile. "I'm on parole for murder, for crying out loud."

"Yes, but that was an accident when you shot—" Her hand whipped up to cover her mouth. "Oh. That's right, they don't know you like I know you. They'll automatically think that—I'm so sorry, E. I didn't mean to—"

Imogene waved it away. "It's over and done with. Don't worry about it."

How could she be mad at Suz when Suz stepped up and took the blame for capping the two thugs in the very living room they now sat in. Took the weight that surely would've seen Imogene back in C-Block.

But it wasn't over and done with. Those two detectives would be all over her until they figured out she was in CIW when the murder occurred. Until the coroner rendered a TOD, a time of death. They'd be all over her at a time when she was enmeshed in the dern pawn shop caper. A caper not of her doing. A caper she wanted no part of.

And just like that, part of the answer to the *who* bubbled up to the top of her brain. The answer was so easy she should've seen it long before. Everyone involved in the heist was on parole. Handpicked. That meant they had to be chosen from a slew of parolees. That meant there had to be a parole connection feeding the puppet masters information. A catalog of parolees to choose from just like the catalogue from Sears and Roebuck.

E, Now you're cookin' with gas. I figured that one out a long time ago but thought it better if you happened on to the answer your ownself. I'm not always gonna be here to pull your chitlins outta the fire. Time you stood on your own two feet.

Imogene reached down, stuck her hand in her dress pocket, and fingered the Polaroid photos of Ida and Thelma, Suz's mother, being held against their will. At the same time, Imogene's eyes fell to the paper on the coffee table. The headline read "Mayor Joseph Columbus signs historic contract to build a fifty-million-dollar speedway race track in West Valley." But that wasn't what had caught her eye.

She grabbed up the newspaper, pulled it closer to read the item below the fold, almost down at the bottom edge, "Man dies in fatal car accident."

"What is it, E?" Suz rose from the chair and came closer.

Imogene read on:

Last night at approximately 8:31 in the evening a trash truck stolen from Upland city yards broadsided a Mercedes coupe pulling out of The Stuft Shirt restaurant on Euclid just north of Foothill Boulevard. The driver of the Mercedes was killed instantly. The two vehicles caught fire and burned to the ground before Upland Fire Department could arrive on scene.

The driver of the Mercedes has been tentatively identified as Alan Goldblat, the owner/ operator of the West Valley Jewelry and Loan located on Euclid Avenue in West Valley. The driver of the stolen trash truck evaded arrest and is still at large.

Anyone with information on this incident please contact Upland police department, traffic division.

Oh, my gawd. Goldblatt was at the restaurant to have dinner with *her.* If she had made it to the dinner date would she too be part of that car-be-que? What a horrible way to die.

E, look, the newspaper spelled his name wrong. It's supposed to be Goldblatt with two t's. Shame ain't it. Couldn't even get his name right in the last thing ever written about him.

"What is it, E? Did you know the gentleman who died in that wreck?" She stood close now, looking over her shoulder.

"Yes...I mean no. Not at all. The car accident just reminded me of something. It called up a long past memory, that's all."

Out the front window, two men in suits came across the front yard at a fast clip. Determined. One came up onto the porch, the other hurried down the driveway headed around back.

The men came on too fast. There wasn't time to react. To flee.

They were cornered.

Suz saw it too. She got down on one knee and took hold of Imogene's hand.

Imogene's other hand reached into her dress pocket for the .380, her hand turning frantic when it wasn't there.

Suz whispered, "Oh my God, I'm so sorry, Imogene. Mike took the gun."

Imogene looked up at her. "You just killed us both."

Sorry for the words she said the second they came out, slicing through her best friend. Suz didn't know any better.

"The way you were acting last night we didn't—"

The screen door opened. In stepped a man with a gun in his hand. He stood just a little shorter than Wayne's six-foot-one with a square forehead and a doughy face. Ugly as sin.

E, if I had a dog that ugly, I'd shave its butt and make him walk backward.

A crash came from the kitchen. The second man kicked in the door to make entry. He came through into the living room. He, too, held a gun. They meant business and weren't about to be deterred.

The one that came in through the back wore a dark blue three-piece suit with a thin pinstripe, the more expensive worn by the two men, which wasn't saying much. He had dark hair and a pencil-thin mustache.

"Erv, lookie what we have here. Both hens in one place. Doin' us a big favor." He waved his gun. "Come on, youse two get in the bathroom."

Erv the dough-face said, "Hold it, boss, someone just rolled up out front."

"Watch her hands, she's an evil witch." The boss moved over and peeked out the front picture window.

John Catskill from Delacorte Press hopped out of his rental car with a huge smile on his dumb mug. The white bandage on his forehead there from when he was pistol-whipped the last time he came to Imogene's home. Bright sunlight reflected off the bandage, gave it a white glow. In his hand he held a white envelope also catching the light. Probably the check for *Peekaboo POTUS*. She signed the contract at the deposition. He wanted to remain in Imogene's good graces, have a good working relationship. Nothing made for great relationships like a big fat check with lots of zeros. Everyone became your friend. This, according to Ange.

"We gonna do all three, boss?"

The boss said to Imogene, "Who's the dude? You don't get rid of him, he takes the plunge with the two of youse."

Imogene shook her head in wonderment. "You're a couple of dumbasses. Just step over ta the door and let him get a look at you. That's all it'll take."

Catskill hopped up the two concrete steps headed for the door. Erv stepped over in front of the screen door. Catskill froze, hand up to knock. Erv wasn't the man who pistol-whipped him across the head, but he *was* cut from the same bolt of cloth.

Don't sit there, fat dumb and happy. Now's your chance, bum rush the shorter dude. Do it right now while they're distracted. You got no other option. Get your fat butt up off that divan and rush him. You got nothin' ta lose. Bitch-slap him into next Tuesday.

The window of opportunity to make that move slammed shut. Catskill took one look at Erv and backed up. He missed the two steps and fell off the porch flat on his back. He scrambled, got up, dropped the envelope, and ran for his car.

"Huh," The boss said. "You're right, that little weasel's got water for blood. Now, back to the business at hand. Get both your asses up and into the bathroom. I won't tell you again."

"Hey, Boss? Take a look at the floor, the carpet's been cut out."

"So?" He paused as his expression turned blank while his mind played across the reasons why the carpet would be cut up. His expression suddenly shifted to anger. He pointed with the gun. "That where the Cigar met his untimely demise?"

Unable to flee anywhere, Suz put her face into Imogene's shoulder, hiding from the ominous threat, an ostrich with her head in the sand.

Don't sit there useless as tits on a boar hog. Negotiate. Use your words. The ones I taught ya when we were in C-Block. Leverage. Use your leverage, for crying out loud.

"Negotiate with what? What leverage?"

"Lady, you got nothin' ta negotiate. In your case, the fat lady has done already sung her song. Now, I'm not gonna tell ya again. Move your ass."

Every bone and muscle in Imogene's body shook with fear. She had to appear cool, calm, and collected or all would be lost. She picked up the red box of Marlboro's. "I'm gonna have a cigarette first. You're not afraid of a girl and an old woman, are ya?"

Erv looked at the boss.

"Yeah, why not. Go ahead. Don't let it be said I don't have no feelings."

She lit up a cigarette. Suz took her face out of Imogene's shoulder not understanding what just happened. She looked at the two thugs. She whispered, "This is the absolute worst kind of deja vu. History repeats itself, but not usually this soon. Right? This whole thing just happened two weeks ago. But this time I don't see a way out."

The nicotine did the job, sanded the edges off Imogene's jangled nerves, and allowed one sort of common sense to squeeze among all the stress with a possible answer. "This is your territory, your turf, right?"

Erv opened his mouth to answer.

"No," The Boss said, waggling his gun in the air. "We're not gonna do that. We're not talkin' here. This ain't like in the movies where we cop out to every little thing just before youse two get rescued. Ain't gonna happen."

Imogene shrugged. "Okay, your loss." She didn't push it and let the bait lie fat and cozy between them. Let it entice the big fish. You can't move too fast or you'll spook 'em.

The Marlboro burnt down too quickly. She tried to take small puffs.

Didn't matter, the two thugs would get antsy soon enough and move whether the cigarette was finished or not.

That's right, you can squeeze a lotta living into the time it takes ta burn one cancer stick. E, quit doin' the dick-around and get on with it. Lay it out for 'em or it's gonna be too late. Trust me on this, girlfriend.

Imogene squinted the way she believed a gun moll might and pointed her burnt-down Marlboro at the men. The long ash about to cascade to the carpet at her feet. "So, if this is your turf, that means you know all about the big bank robbery that's gonna happen, right?"

The Boss chuckled. "That's enough of this crap, get your asses into the bathroom. Dead men walking will say anything to get out of what's about to happen. In youse two's case, dead women walking. Heh, heh."

Imogene struggled to her feet. Suz glommed on to her arm and silently started to sob. "Come on, kid." She put her arm around Suz to hold her up.

"Boss, what if she's tellin' the truth? What'll Big Mike say if something happens out here and we don't know about it? Something big happens and we don't do a thing about it?"

"Naw, she's blowin' smoke up our asses. She'll say anything ta save her own skin. You know that. We see it every time. We're not gonna fall for it. We're not a couple of chumps."

Erv shrugged. "What's it gonna hurt to hear her out?"

Chapter Ten

In Imogene's living room, The Boss hesitated while he mulled it over. "Okay, fifteen seconds and that's it. Spill it. Or I'll drop you right where you dropped The Cigar. Poetic justice and all that kinda crap."

Imogene stared at him, trying for unafraid. "There's a syndicate that's planning to rob The Bank of The West on the Fourth of July."

"Boss, ain't that our bank. The bank where we keep—"

"Shut your face. Don't say another word. Not one more word."

He rushed over to Imogene, stuck the gun under her chin, his breath hot on her face. Humid. "What kinda game you playin' at, Girlie? Huh? I can draw this out, make it last. You'll be one sorry ol' crone."

Imogene grabbed onto the gun and pushed it away. "You wanna act like a gun thug, go ahead and shoot. Go on, get it over with. Shoot. Make yourself into a big man killin' an old woman."

Suz backed up until she hit the wall. Her eyes wide, absolutely sure another murder in the same living room was about to occur.

The boss stuck the gun into Imogene's throat, his face contorted in rage, skin mottled red.

Suz yelled. "She doesn't care if you pull the trigger. Can't you see that you idgit. She did ten years in prison for murder! She's not afraid a you."

The boss took a step back. The heavy pause hung fat between them.

"That true? You do a dime for a killin'?"

Imogene said nothing.

"Where? Tell me. Where'd you do your time?"

Imogene said nothing.

Suz squeaked out the words, "Tell 'em, E. Please just tell 'em the truth."

Imogene had made her peace with the world and braced for the bullet about to enter her body in search of vital organs. After all, she deserved to be shot. She killed Wayne.

She killed Wayne.

Tears burned her eyes. She didn't want Suz to see her weakness. Her shame.

Suz didn't want to die, especially not out of Imogene's selfishness, some misplaced sense of pride. Imogene looked over at Suz, who nodded. Imogene looked back at The Boss, "C-Block, CIW."

"Bull pucky. I don't believe you. They don't have old crones like you in lockup. Doesn't happen."

"Believe what you want."

"Okay. Then what'd they serve for lunch on Saturdays?"

"Seriously, that's the only test you can come up with?

"Do ya know, or don't ya?"

"A stale bologna sandwich and a mealy apple."

"Well, I'll be a son of a…What's this caper about at the bank?"

"I'm on parole, and I'm being blackmailed into helping. If I don't they'll turn me in to my parole agent. These people are gonna rob The Bank of The West on the Fourth of July during the All States Picnic and Parade."

Erv said, "That's good, Boss. Real good. And it makes a lotta sense too. We mighta done the same thing if it wasn't our own bank and—"

He spun on Erv. "One more word and you'll top the dogpile of dead broads. You hear me this time. I won't tell you again. *Shut your trap.*" He took several deep breaths, getting back in control. He looked at Imogene. "How do I know you're not makin' up all this crap just to get out of having your tickets punched?"

"If I tell ya that, how will I know you won't just—"

"Don't play games with me, doll. I'm not here to play games. Tell me, or deal with the consequences. You give me the straight skinny, I might be inclined to give youse both a stay of execution." He smiled, smug at his use of big words.

"I'm being made to work at the West Valley Jewelry and Loan by these people. This pawn shop is right across the street from the bank. There are two others that I know of who are also similarly involved. None of us have been told all of the pieces in how it's going down. They're going to use the parade as a diversion when they rob the bank. The bank's only open till one o'clock and the parade starts at one."

"Nothing but empty words. Gimme some proof."

"The proof's right there on the coffee table. Right under that fat bazoo of yours."

He looked down but held the gun stuck in her gut. "Where? I don't see nothin'"

"The newspaper, right there."

"Pick it up, show me."

She again put her hand on the gun and shoved it way. She bent, picked up the paper, and held it out for him. "Right there, that news story about the car accident."

He snatched the paper away and took two big steps back, almost tripping on the patchwork carpet. His eyes going to the article. "How does a car accident prove a thing?"

"For Pete's sake, it's there at the bottom of the news item."

He looked up, gritting his teeth. "I've had it with you, Grandma. No more games."

"Imogene, whatever it is, just tell him. Quit messing with him. Please just tell him."

Imogene looked at her friend, then back at The Boss. She stepped over close, scanned the article, and pointed to the important part. She read it out loud.

"The driver of the Mercedes has been tentatively identified as Alan Goldblat, the owner/ operator of the West Valley Jewelry and Loan located on Euclid Avenue in West Valley. The driver of the stolen trash truck evaded arrest and is still at large."

The Boss looked at her cockeyed, the obvious evading his pea brain.

She said, "Goldblatt is the owner...was the owner of the pawn shop. He was a loose end. They killed him because of it. Because of what he knew."

"Huh. Who's running this gig?"

She shrugged. "I told ya. Everyone is a cutout. No one has all the pieces. I won't know until it gets closer to the day…to the Fourth. Today's the second."

He started to shake his head, a non-believer.

She said, "Everyone involved is a parolee. That's part of the motivation they're holding over our heads. The other part is—" She reached into her dress pocket, the one with the photos. How had Mike and Suz not found them the night before?

The .380 had been in the pocket on the other side.

Erv pointed his gun at Imogene, "Watch it, Boss."

"Take it easy," Imogene said. "You think if I had a gun I wouldn't have already shot your dumb asses? I can't believe I got had by a couple of Woolworths five-and-dime thugs. Shameful is what it is." She showed The Boss the two Polaroid photos, one of Suz's mom, the other of Ida.

The little girl who lived down the lane, E. The only true victim in this whole kerfuffle.

That last word caught Imogene looking. Ange never used words like kerfuffle. It shook Imogene. Two weeks ago, her previous parole agent had told Imogene that Imogene had never shared a cell with anyone named Ange. When words like kerfuffle bubbled up they scared the water outta her. Reminded her that the world might not be as it seemed and that the ground she stood on wobbled and moved beneath her feet.

The Boss took the photos from her. Ida's sorrowful image, her cheeks wet with tears, tied up and gagged, that's what convinced him. He nodded and started to back away even more, "What kinda animal throws a kid inta the mix? I'll take care of 'em myself, I find out who it is."

She snatched the photos from him.

"Who are they?" he asked

"The child is from around the corner on the next street over, the niece of a man named Luke Short, somebody else who's caught up in all this mess. He's also on parole for bank robbery. He only knows a tad more than I do."

"And the other?"

Imogene looked to the side at Suz. Suz's mouth dropped open. She leapt forward and grabbed the photos from Imogene's hand. She looked at the one, stunned. "Mom? This is Thelma, my mom. What the heck's happening here, E? First Poppy Liu in the crate in our garage, then the extortion and the…the killing and now this. How can the world be so screwed up? What do they want with my mom?"

"I'm so sorry, Suz. They want you to steal a Dentco truck to use in the heist. They want you working in the pawn shop until the robbery. They wanna keep a close eye on you till it goes down. I was about to tell you when these two sorry excuses for men showed up."

"Why, E? Why?"

Imogene shrugged.

Erv said, "We've done jobs just like this. Well sorta. We sit with the bank manager's family while he goes and opens the bank's vault. When you shot The Cigar…killed him, our enemies saw it as an opportunity ta rub our noses in it. Using the two of youse ta kill two birds with one stone. So ta speak. They're hittin' our bank. That's why this is all happening. It's not really about you. It's just your bad luck ta be stuck in the middle of it."

The Boss turned to face Erv. His body shaking with rage, his face bloated red. He took two steps closer to Erv and spoke. The words came out in a forced croak. "What…did…I…tell ya? I don't care who you're related to. I don't care if Big Mike is your uncle. You just crossed a line."

"Come on, they deserved to know what's going on and—"

The Boss shot Erv in the upper leg. Imogene and Suz both jumped and yelped.

Erv fell to the floor, gripping his leg, groaning loud enough ta wake the dead. And probably alert the neighbors.

"You," The Boss said to Suz. "Get him some towels. You. You have any duct tape?"

"It's in the kitchen in the junk drawer."

"Get it. And you better not come back with anything else in your hands. You understand what I'm sayin'?"

"Yeah, I understand. Dumbass. And let me tell ya, the way you're handling this, well, you won't be winning spelling bees anytime soon."

"Was that a crack? What'd you mean by that?"

"Exactly." She kept going into the kitchen.

Suz came out of the only bathroom with some towels, one hand-monogramed with "Imogene" and "Wayne." Imogene did the needlework with tender loving care.

"Now, put the towel around his leg and bind it tight with the tape." He moved over close to supervise the two women. Imogene and Suz both got their hands bloodied administering first aid, trying their best to stem the flow and save his life. Erv turned pale as a sheet.

Imogene used the duct tape, wrapped it tight. The blood eased to an ooze.

The Boss shook his gun as a carpenter might with a common hammer. "Erv, we need to come to an understanding about what happened here. You dropped your gun, and it went off. Just like that. You see what I'm sayin'?"

Imogene nodded. "I think he does. Leave him alone. Can't you see he's in all kinds of pain? You shot him for crying out loud."

"Shut your trap. I won't tell ya again."

"E, cool it. Seriously. You're acting crazy, just like last night."

"You better do what the pretty broad tells ya. I'm at the end of my rope here."

Imogene opened her mouth to rebut the ignoramus. Suz skip-hoped over to Imogene and a little too brusquely put a hand over her mouth. Suz's skin tasted of iron from Erv's blood that covered her hand.

The Boss hooked his hand under Erv's arm and helped him to his feet. "We good, Erv? Or I gotta drop everyone in this room to make it right?"

Erv nodded, his face a rictus of pain as he hopped on one leg to the front door. The Boss turned and spoke over his shoulder. "I'm not through here. I'll be over ta visit that pawn shop. When I do you treat me like any other customer. You understand? You better have more information on this bank job or else."

Suz said, "Yes, sir, we understand."

Imogene tried to pull off Suz's hand, but Suz kept walking Imogene back, forcing her hand in place.

The front door finally closed.

They were gone.

The house let go with a huge sigh of relief, at least that's the way it seemed.

Suz stood at the big picture window and watched Erv hobble across the front yard with The Boss helping. Watched until they got in the car and drove away. She staggered over to Wayne's chair and plopped down. She leaned over and put her face in her hands, not caring at all about the blood. "What are we gonna do?"

"If you hadn't taken my gun last night, this would all be academic. We'd have two more bodies cooling on the living room floor." Imogene didn't know where those words came from. She didn't like this new callousness. She'd tried hard to put away the ten years she spent in stir, but it just kept pulling her back. Kerfuffle didn't help, set her on edge.

Suz looked up, angry, her face now streaked with blood. "Killing two more men. Really? That's your answer to get outta this mess? And what about the other more pressing problem, the one with my mother? What are we gonna do about that? I can't believe this. I really can't."

Imogene sat back on the divan and, puff, puff, puffed a Marlboro. "Nothin' else we can do but play out the hand dealt to us. Unless I'm missing something, and you have a better idea."

"E, there are times when you are the kindest, most gentle person I've ever met. Then other times it's like what just happened and…and you're someone else entirely. E, you're…you're Doctor Jekyll and Mr. Hyde. But lately, more Doctor Jekyll. Can you please, please bring back the nice Imogene, so we can talk. I really need to talk to the nice Imogene."

"Oh, pshaw, I'm the same person. I just adjust to the world as it changes around me. It's the law of the jungle. You adapt or get run over. And I won't get run over. Especially by the likes of those two twits."

Suz stared at her. Imogene didn't like what she saw in Suz's eyes. "I'm sorry. Yes, please, let's talk this thing through. I don't want you angry with me. We're too good friends to be angry with each other. You're my only friend, Suz."

Suz held her gaze a moment more with that same expression of disappointment. She rose, went into the kitchen, and came back out with a thick-bladed butcher's knife, the one Imogene used to slice the pork roast Wayne loved so much. Served it with homemade, chunky apple sauce. That life two lightyears ago buried under ten years of C-block memories.

For a fleeting second, Imogene thought Suz might've slipped over that tenuous razor edge of common sense and fell headlong into insanity. Sometimes it happened that way. The mind isn't made of steel. The brain's nothing more than a vulnerable, soft, and spongy organ, susceptible to internal and external pressures.

Suz held the knife by her leg while looking down at Imogene.

Imogene looked up at her, all the while puff, puff, puffing on a Marlboro. The spell broke.

Suz walked with a slight sway in her gait over to the area next to the television. She got down on one knee and started cutting out the gold high-low carpet where Erv fell and bled profusely. Silently worked at it.

Anger again rose up in Imogene, Suz was too nice to be cutting bloody sections of carpet from her neighbors living room floor.

Suz suddenly stopped halfway to her goal, three sides to the rectangle cut. Her head dropped lower as if she just realized something and the thought froze her hands. She looked up and smiled.

Imogene asked. "What?"

"This keeps up, you're not going to have much carpet left."

Imogene smiled back. Suz started to laugh. Imogene laughed right along with her.

Relief. Pure unadulterated relief. Not moments before, they had been on their way to the bathroom with a bullet to the back of the head, their destiny.

Stress over life and death incidents could do that to a person, make 'em laugh. Black gallows humor that bubbled up right after the grim reaper, with his dark cape and sickle, sauntered by without stopping even long enough to tip his hat. Leaving behind a cold chill up a person's spine.

Chapter Eleven

In Imogene's living room, their laughter died an untimely death. With a sputter and a cough. Suz got up from the floor, walked to the back door in the kitchen, the one standing open with the frame shattered when The Boss kicked it in. She tossed out the square of carpet that fluttered down past the ten concrete steps to the backyard. Then she tossed the thick-bladed butcher knife into the sink with a clatter.

Imogene couldn't see any of this but sussed it out based on sounds alone. Suz stopped at the fridge, opened it, and pulled two Schlitz Malt Liquor beers from the six-pack. Leaving one left. She came back, handed a beer to Imogene, then sat in Wayne's easy chair. Imogene glanced at the clock on the credenza and held up the beer. "I usually don't imbibe unless it's Friday night after five. It's ten o'clock in the morning for cripe's sake."

She still couldn't get over how time had skipped and left her wanting. She lost an entire early evening, a long night, and part of an early morning. Gone.

"You don't want it, leave it for me. I rarely, if ever, drink, but lately it seems like the right thing to do."

"No. No. I'm good." She pulled the ring tab. The beer hissed out a wonderful hoppy scent, one that masked the iron reek of warm blood that still hung in the air. The reek of flop sweat left by the gunshot Erv.

Up on the wall above the TV, the portrait of Joyce looked down, judging Imogene. Always judging. Joyce witnessed everything that had happened in the living room in the last two weeks. Two separate days of gunplay. Blood and mayhem.

Was gunfire some kind of contagion? Did Imogene's first shot, the one where she shot Wayne by mistake in her bedroom twelve years earlier, had that been patient zero? When the virus was introduced into the environment? And then this same virus in some way attracted other patients of violence similarly infected? Called them to a meeting of the minds in Imogene's living room? Imogene sipped the bitter beer and contemplated the idea. This, a kernel of another book that just raised its lovely head and said, "Look over here, look at me." Imogene loved writing now, the way it transported her away from this world that no longer viewed her in a favorable light, no longer allowed her to toss sevens. Just snake eyes.

Imogene came out of her funk to find Suz sipping her beer and staring at her. She asked, "What were you just thinking about?"

"Nothing."

"Tell me, E. I have a right to know. My mother's been kidnapped and held against her will until I steal a truck. That gives me a right to know."

"Truth?"

"Of course, I want the truth."

"I was thinking about writing another book." Suz had read *Peekaboo POTUS* and claimed she loved it. One of only two people who read it; Suz and John Catskill. The same John Catskill who, not fifteen minutes ago, fled, falling backward off the porch. Imogene looked up and out through the picture window. The envelope still sat where Catskill dropped it in the lawn. The white glowing bright in the sun.

"Writing another book? With all that's going on? You're kidding, right? We need to think of a way outta this mess. We need to get my mother back."

Imogene took the photo of Ida from her pocket and tossed it the short distance to Suz.

Suz picked it up. "What's this?"

Earlier, when The Boss held the pictures, Suz hadn't seen the photo of Ida, only the one of her mother. And maybe in all the stress of the moment, including the part about being taken into the bathroom, made to stand in the tub and shot in the head—maybe that had clouded poor Suz's hearing. Blocked words from getting to her brain.

"Oh, no. E, this is Ida from around the corner on Bonnie Brae. That's who you were talking about? I'm a big horse's ass for just thinking about mom." Suz had never known her mom, not until two weeks earlier when she appeared out of nowhere.

Imogene looked at her, sipped the Schlitz Malt Liquor, and puff, puff, puffed on a Marlboro. She'd already lost track of what number cigarette she was on for the day. She picked up the pack and counted. She tried to limit her smoke intake to two packs. Twenty in each. Forty cigarettes total. The brutal warning on the side of the cigarette boxes started to get under her skin. So only two packs a day. That was a favorable limit.

Imogene's mind flitted again like a bee from one flower to the next. Thelma was a full-blown whackadoo, and although being kidnapped was a heinous crime to happen to a person, Thelma might not even know she'd been grabbed. In fact, the kidnappers would rue the day they grabbed that fruit loop.

Two weeks earlier in Imogene's living room, Thelma admitted to having sex with Bernard Lowery, the neighbor. Bernard, as it turned out, had been the killer of Poppy Liu. The girl in the wooden box hidden in Suz's garage for years and years. The same Bernard Lowery who died in Imogene's living room, shot by a gun thug, and not Imogene. Bernard owned one of the bloody carpet swatches Luke Short cut out with his authentic Italian Stiletto knife.

The night Imogene met Thelma for the first time, Suz brought her over to the house. They both sat in the living room. At that time, the working theory was the dead woman in the wooden crate found in Suz's garage, and as yet unidentified, was Suz's mother. Suz had just randomly showed up that night with this strange woman and asked the woman to tell Imogene a story.

The woman's hair was dyed platinum blond and stacked on her head in a beehive, a throwback to the sixties. She wore low-cut jeans that exposed most of her hips and flat stomach. She also had on three long, multicolored strands of hippie beads that swung from around her neck.

This unidentified woman at Suz's coaxing told a wild tale, one still vivid and alive in Imogene's memory. The entire scene from two weeks ago replayed the same as a movie on the big screen in Imogene's head.

* * *

The woman with the platinum colored beehive who sat in Wayne's chair said, "It all started when—Well, my mother was dying, you see, and I took a trip to go see her one last time, clear across the continent of these great United States. In New England. Boston. I'd never been on a plane. This was oh, twenty-odd years ago. Jets were still brand new. 1953. Yes, it was in '53."

Imogene looked from Thelma to Suz. Suz put her index finger to her lips to shush Imogene's questions, then pointed to her ear, wanting Imogene just to listen. Suz now looked angry. Maybe even beyond angry. Incensed.

What the hell was going on?

Thelma continued unfazed. She picked up her beads and twirled them as she spoke. "I got on the plane nervous as a cat." Rattle. Rattle. "At the time, I had never so much as taken a train or a bus, and I now found myself on this…*in* this big, long aluminum tube with wings. A beast too large to fly. At least not so high in the air like that. To fly at all, really. It was like something out of a cheap sci-fi magazine. How could something that had to weigh forty tons get up in the air and carry all those people hundreds of miles? It just wasn't right. It went against nature. The plane didn't have any feathers. Truth be told, I was scared outta my wits. I only tell you this part to be fair, to show you I wasn't myself. I shook like a leaf in a high wind, and I sweated right through my blouse."

Imogene took a long slug of Schlitz Malt Liquor and wished she had some pruno, a prison alcohol concoction Ange used to make in a plastic bag hidden in the cell toilet, strong with a lotta wang to it.

You think I'm a few tools short of a toolbox, this woman here is a total whack-job, Imogene. Tell her to get the hell outta your house 'fore some of it rubs off on ya.

Truly, Imogene had enough problems without Suz draggin' in some fruit loop off the street. She trusted Suz and decided to let the crazy street person carry on. Maybe just a little more. There had to be a reason why she brought her into the house.

"I climbed all those stairs up into the belly of this huge silver beast and then just walked right in, dumb as you please. In a kinda daze, I found my seat. Then they wanted me to strap in just like they do to the loonies in the loony bin. You know, just before they shoot you all up with Haldol that makes you babble and drool." Thelma waved her one hand, with the other she swung her beads. "Sure, I knew all about flying, that it was supposed to be safe and all, but this was just how I felt. I had a hard time wrapping my mind around it."

Exactly what mind is she talking about? This gal is cuckoo for cocoa puffs.

The irony of hearing Ange tag the woman as crazy made a lump rise in Imogene's throat and again question what Nancy had said about Ange. That she had never really been there in C-block. Which meant she was never there at all. Past or present.

Then who was talking in Imogene's head?

"All this new stuff, the plane, the seat belts—the other passengers who got on and acted like this wasn't a big deal—made me want to yell, 'You dumbshits, how is this gonna work? You think we're all just going to rise up into the air and fly like birds? Are you kidding me? Are you all outta your ever lovin' minds?'"

Thelma had risen up in her seat and now calmed, easing on back. "Anyway, all this mess made me have ta pee. I had to pee bad but was too afraid to unbuckle and get up. I stayed sitting strapped in like they insisted. Just like Dr. Frankenstein insisted when he strapped down the monster before he reanimated him with electricity. Right? Are you with me on this? Am I right? That's another thing. Why would Dr. Frankenstein strap down the monster? He didn't know he was going to be a monster once he put the juice to him. Right? So why strap him in? So, that just begged the other question: why were they strapping *us* into our seats? Right?"

"Thelma?"

"What? Oh, yeah. Sorry. I sometimes get off track. Anyway. I strapped in like everyone else. That day I was a lemming ready to go off the cliff with everyone else because in the end when it was all said and done, I really did need to see Mom.

At this point, I'm a real nervous Nellie. And I may or may not have smoked a doobie in the airport bathroom before I boarded. You know just to settle the nerves. I wanna put that out there, so you'd know where I was coming from. Anyway, this huge, ungodly beast rolls down the runway, and at first, it struggles into the air like it can't make it. Like it's not going to make it. I hold my breath the entire time and claw the armrests. Everyone around me just sits there, calm as you please, reading books or magazines, or eating Planters peanuts from those packages that had the peanut in a top hat and cane, dancing without a care in the world. That's irony if you ask me.

"Now here's where the story starts to get a little weird."

Just now it's getting a little weird? You look "weird" up in the dictionary and you'll find a picture of this looney bird, the one sittin' right here.

"This man, a guy sitting across the aisle, stared at me like I had a big zit on my nose or something. I mean every time I looked I caught him staring and then looking down at his watch as if he had a very important meeting coming up. A meeting up in the air at the top of the world? Yeah, right.

"I was sitting mid-plane in a window seat, trapped against the wall. After about an hour or it might've been a couple hours…I don't wear a watch. I don't want time as a friend or worse, an enemy. You ignore her, and she leaves you alone. You know what I mean?" She held up her arms as an example. "Look, I'm only fifty-five and I sure don't look a day over twenty-five. Am I right?"

Huh, thought she was sixty-eight or better. Whatta you think, E?

"Anyway, I couldn't take it anymore, I just had to pee or burst one of my bladders. I walked down the aisle, my legs making me out like some kinda drunken sailor. I make it to the bathroom door and look back. That same man followed me, walking right at me real fast with something big in his hands the size of a suitcase. But it was this cardboard box. His eyes were trying to tell me something. To watch out, that some unknown danger was creeping up on me from behind. Something like that." She shivered, shaking off the fear-filled memory.

"I didn't know what to do. I jumped into the bathroom and closed the door. Tried to close the door.

"The man stuck his arm in and blocked it. I fought with him to get it closed. He said in this frighteningly harsh voice, 'I'm trying to help you. Stop it. Listen to me, we don't have much time. Get down on your knees before it's too late.'

"'Let me alone, or I'll scream. I swear I'll scream.' Then he did something really strange. He shoved into that small bathroom that big box. All the cardboard pushed me away from the door. His arm snaked in, grabbed onto a red handle sticking out and jerked it. The box exploded into nothing but yellow, lots and lots of yellow that smelled of rubber and squeezed me hard against the wall. It filled every open space. I couldn't breathe. Couldn't get my lungs to work."

Thelma stopped and looked at Imogene for a reaction. Imogene sipped her beer, no longer interested. She just wanted the stupid story to end, get the two visitors the hell outta the house. She needed peace and quiet to think.

Suz said. "That's not the whole story, go on, tell her the rest. What was the yellow thing, and where was the man from?"

Thelma nodded. "The yellow thing was a life raft, okay? He'd shoved it in with me and inflated it as sort of a giant cushion. I couldn't move a muscle. He'd slammed the door before it inflated. I was stuck. No one could get in or out of that bathroom." She paused again and swallowed hard as if the retelling caused her great angst.

"Thelma?" Suz said.

"Okay. Okay." The words gushed out of her. "The man was from the future. He was sent back there to keep me alive. The plane crashed. I was the only one that survived. I found out later that I'm a princess from some forgotten planet, banished here to this one forever. My people are to this very day still out there looking for me. There, are ya happy now? I said it. You're sure not laughing this time, are you, honey?"

Imogene didn't think it was funny either. Not in the least. "Suz, thank you for this brief interlude from reality, but I'm tired. Could you please just—"

Suz held up her hand. "Wait, that was just the basis for what I really wanted you to hear. Thelma, tell her the other part."

"What other part? Oh, you mean that I'm your mother."

The beer slipped from Imogene's hand and fell to the floor. Foam roiled out the hole, an imitation of how her brain felt squishing out her ears.

* * *

Back in the living room, Imogene's hands still shook from the adrenaline that had surged over the threat of death. The nicotine probably didn't help. She took a long chug from the Schlitz and swallowed back a bubble that, if released, would rise and turn into an unbecoming belch. She was friends with Suz and all but had been trying like heck to rehabilitate a somewhat tarnished reputation.

"Well," Suz said, "Do you have a plan for how to get my mother back from these people? Start from the beginning. What's this about a bank robbery, and why am I supposed to steal a truck? Maybe you told me, but I'm a little sideways on all that just happened. It's coming back to me a little at a time."

"We should get going. We both have to work at the pawn shop today. We're already late."

Suz jumped to her feet, the beer in her hand foamed over. "Wait just one minute. Are you implying that if we're not there, they will hurt my mother?"

That was a distinct possibility based on all the hostage and extortion cases Imogene had read in the joint.

"No, of course not. But we should get going."

Suz nodded and eased back into the chair and took a chug from the beer, determined to finish it before they left the house.

Imogene, for the umpteenth time, looked out the picture window like she did every day while sitting in the same place on the divan. Keeping an eye on the world so it didn't sneak up on her and pull the wool over her eyes.

Something strange came into view.

She muttered. "What the hell?"

Chapter Twelve

Out front on the lawn, a woman bent over to pick up the envelope dropped by John Catskill in his headlong flight to escape. Imogene did a double-take. The woman was Thelma, Suz's mother. The kidnapped woman in the Polaroid photo.

Suz read Imogene's expression, jumped up from the chair, and looked out the picture window. "Oh, my God. It's mom." She dropped her beer. It soaked the bare wood in one of the open wounds in the carpet. She ran to the door. "Mom. Mom." Thelma, out in the yard, stood from being bent at the waist and turned. She smiled and held up the envelope. "Look what I found. It's got a check in it for Imogene. It's a lot of money. I found it right out here. Can you imagine, right here in the front yard. What's it doing out here? More money than I've ever seen in one place."

Suz ran and hugged her. A touching scene, even for the callous-minded Imogene.

What the heck, huh, E? You ever thought you'd see that woman again. I know I wrote that dingbat off. For good, too. Fish food is what I thought. They always say, God looks after the simple-minded. And that woman there is about as simple as they come. Right, E? You with me on this one, E? Gimme a high-five if you are?

Suz put her arm around her mother and escorted her up the steps of the porch and into the house. Imogene had watched the scene play out while drinking her beer and smoking her Marlboro.

Thelma came in and immediately marveled at the cutout swatches in carpet. She looked up, smiled, "Looks like you got a huge termite problem. Huh?"

Suz said, "Mom, come on, sit right here and tell us what happened to you."

Thelma sat. "What happened to me? Nothing happened to me, Baby Doll."

Suz kept her hand on Thelma's shoulder as if Thelma might again suddenly disappear.

She patted Suz's hand. "Dear, I like it when you call me mom. When you call me mother, not so much. Okay? Are we clear on that topic?"

"Oh my God, mom, what happened to your neck and look at your arms." Tears filled Suz's eyes, her words choked with emotions. Red marks and scratches covered Thelma's neck and arms. Her wrists had marks from the tape that bound her to the chair as depicted in the photo.

"What are you talking about? Oh, that? That's nothing. A man friend tried to get fresh. I showed him women aren't soft and cuddly, like he may have thought. You have to do that every now and again to remind 'em that the male species don't rule the world. Women do."

Gender. The dingbat means gender, right E? Not species. Hang around this one too long and the marbles in the brain break loose and rattle around. I'm tellin' ya E, it's contagious.

Suz swiped at her tears, smiled, and laughed a little at the inanity of the statement, also relieved her mother was okay. "Mom. Mom, it's okay. We know what happened to you. You don't have to pretend it didn't happen."

"Whatever are you talking about, dear?"

Suz picked up the Polaroid photo of Thelma duct-taped to a wooden chair and held it out to her. "They were holding you against your will."

"Oh, my land." She took hold of the photo to steady Suz's hand.

"Now you remember? It had to be just awful. I'm so sorry it happened to you."

Thelma looked up at Suz, who stood close by and blinked with big eyes. Bambi in a Disney flick. Doe-eyed and innocent. She put her hand up to the platinum colored beehive hairdo, patted it, and referenced the photo. "I've looked better, don't you know."

Suz got down on one knee, "Mom, you're holding it in. It's okay. You're safe now. You can let it out."

Thelma let a patronizing smile crawl slowly into her expression. She patted her daughter's cheek. "Honey, this kinda thing has been happening to me since they came for me in that airplane crash. I always manage to get away. See. I'm sitting right here, aren't I?"

Imogene had enough of the idiotic babble. "Do you know where they were holding you? There's a little girl still missing. We need to find her."

"Oh, dear me. You're kidding. They have never taken anyone else in the past. Only me. They just want me to relinquish my crown, and I refuse to do it. I didn't see anyone else, and I would've if a little girl was there."

Imogene picked up her cigarettes from the coffee table and stood. "We better get going to the pawn shop. We're late. We'll take two cars. I got something to do after I check in, after I spend a little time in the shop, to show them I'm there."

"But Mom's back now. We should go to the police."

"Seriously. Think about what your mom just said and plug that in with what you just said. There's a huge disconnect. The police will laugh us outta the station house."

Not to mention the part about Imogene being on parole. Any contact with law enforcement was an extremely bad idea.

Suz's expression shifted to conflicted. "But what about mom? They might come back for her." Tears rolled down her cheeks. Suz, the poor girl, too innocent and not callous enough to accept the real world for what it was. Some folks never accepted it. Went through life their heads in the sand, whispering, "That didn't really happen. That's not true. No. No, I don't believe it." All of those sheep ripe for the slaughter.

Imogene stumbled a little in one of empty squares sans carpet and looked down, so she didn't do it again. Suz glommed on to her and hugged her.

Thelma stood up from the chair and looked a little jealous. The hug continued. Imogene relented and finally put her arms around Suz. Let her guard down just a smidgeon and realized how much she enjoyed her best friend. The comradery. The desire to be needed. Imogene craved it, needed more of the physical intimacy a good friend afforded. She closed her eyes and hugged back. In that brief moment Imogene caught a glimpse of Suz's world, one where bad men didn't hoorah women, beat, kill or strangle them.

A fantasyland not anywhere close to reality. But one Imogene now never wanted to leave.

Suz tried to pull away. Imogene held on a moment more before relinquishing the hold.

"Thank you, E, I really needed that."

A lump rose in Imogene's throat, embarrassed at the emotions. She didn't know what to say in return. "My name doesn't start with an E. Why do you call me E?" They had the same conversation before. Imogene knew Suz's answer. But this was what good friends did when they wanted to change the subject, shift it to something more comfortable.

She shrugged. "I first envisioned your name as *Emogene*. Once I started calling you E, it just seemed so…so right. I hope you don't mind."

"We're friends. You can call me whatever you like."

Suz's eyes welled up and her chin quivered, getting ready to really let go with the waterworks.

"Come on, let's get going before you're crying too much to drive." She hurried past. Too late, tears had already filled Imogene's eyes.

Out front, Imogene waited in her little red AMC Gremlin for Suz and Thelma to make it down the porch steps and into the yard. Some people just didn't know how to move along and get things done.

Suz came over to the Gremlin. Imogene rolled down the window.

"I'll have Micheal come over and fix your back door, so you can secure your house. I just now tried to lock it. It's pretty messed up."

"Thank you. How's he working the schedule without you and me? Who's working at his two Dentcos? I'll be back in a week, once this is all over. Please tell him that. Once Fourth of July is over, I'll be back."

She patted Imogene's arm. "I'll make sure he holds the job for you. I know how important it is to your parole. Here's that check from your publisher Mom found in the yard."

Imogene tossed it on the passenger seat. "I'll see you at the pawn shop in a little while. You be careful and watch your rearview for anyone following you."

"Ah, E, now you went and got me scared all over again."

"Don't be scared, they still need you for part of their scheme. They won't do anything until it's over and done with. Two days from now, that's when to worry."

"And then what?"

Imogene shrugged. "If you can't be a witness against them, nothing. So, don't *see* anything you're not supposed to."

"How am I supposed to know what I'm not supposed to see?"

Imogene smiled, started up. The Gremlin engine drowned out Suz's words.

Imogene backed down the driveway while her mind munched on the problem of the bank job, not unlike the way she wrote her novel. She started from the beginning and asked herself what do the players involved want? She went down the list one at a time ticking off motivations. And actually, started to get somewhere. Developing some ideas. Two solid ones.

She came out of this mental funk and found her hands and feet all on their own had driven around the corner to Bonnie Brae, the street Ida lived on. A black and white and a detective's car sat in front of Ida's house. Imogene's subconscious must've figured if Thelma was no longer in the kidnapper's custody maybe Ida also escaped. That kind of information would definitely change the game. If Ida was loose.

Imogene drove on past without slowing. Her parole tail precluded her from doing the right thing, stopping and checking on the little girl's welfare.

Smart move, Girl. Walkin' up ta that door with those cops on scene, well, that'd put your tit in the wringer for shore.

"I'm not without a conscience. I wanna find out how Ida is doing. She could be home just like Thelma."

Now she was talking to someone who wasn't there. Had she been doing that all along and just realized it?

She made a U-turn on Berlyn Avenue, drove back, and parked on the opposite side of the street.

Don't do it. I'm tellin' right now. Don't do it.

"Dern you. I won't kowtow to no tiny voice in my head. They could've found her and she's been hurt."

With her purse on her arm, she walked across the street and onto the driveway. John Johnson, of all people, walked out of the house. It couldn't have been JB, the nice one. Ida's mom and her father, a Chinese man, looked out the front living room window, anxious as if Imogene might have news about their daughter.

That's right. Ida had said her adoptive father was from China.

"What the hell are you doin' here?"

"If you haven't noticed, I live right around the block. That's sarcasm by the way. I point it out to you so there's no misunderstanding."

"Who's your parole officer? I'm gonna give him a call and get your ass thrown back in the can. Now, I won't ask you again, what are you doin' here?"

JB, the nice detective, came out the front door, a notebook and tape recorder carried in the same hand. His charcoal gray Sears and Roebuck suit was pressed and neat. "John, go back in and sit with the family." John Johnson gave Imogene the evil eye before turning to leave. JB faced Imogene. "Can I help you with something?"

"Yes, thank you. I was concerned about the police cars out front. I have a friend who lives here."

JB took a step toward her. "Is that right? Who?"

"Ida, she comes around and picks avocados from the tree in my backyard, and a while back she even set up a lemonade stand out in front of my house. She was supposed to start mowing my yard on Sundays. I haven't seen her lately. I'm worried about her. Is she all right?"

"She's gone missing. When's the last time you saw her?" He pushed the button, activating the recorder.

Crapola.

"Ah…that would be…about two weeks ago. Yes, I'm pretty sure it was two weeks ago. She was supposed to start mowing my yard, but you kind gentlemen roped off my house as a crime scene. And then outta the goodness of your generous hearts, put me up at that lovely roach-infested establishment, called The Capri Motel." Imogene cocked her head to the side and smirked. Then smiled.

JB returned Imogene's smile. His brown hair combed to the side hung now off his forehead over light brown eyes. He hadn't shaved since the day before, giving him a rugged outdoors look. One that could definitely catch on and become a wildly popular fad if a movie icon tried it. He came closer, his eyes growing more intense. "You're scaring me here, Imogene."

"I am?" Imogene tried hard to cover the squirm that rolled through her body, tried to suppress it. Ange might've been right about stopping, about sticking a big fat bazoo into the lion's den.

That dern conscience, the little angel that sat on her shoulder. Instead, she should've listened to the all-red guy with the pitchfork and spiked tail on the other shoulder. Kept going right past the house.

JB stopped moving. He now stood too close, right up in Imogene's space. His breath smelled fresh from cinnamon Dentine gum. His eyes tried to drill right through hers.

She put her hand on his suit over his chest and instead of pushing—that would've been misinterpreted—she backed up. "You're supposed to be the nice one."

Imogene's face flashed hot as she suddenly remembered something terribly important. Her body shifted into full panic mode. The two Polaroid pictures in her dress pocket, the one that had Ida duct-taped to the wooden chair. That one would be the end of her. She couldn't let the cops detain her. Handcuff and search her. To do so meant a free bus ride back to the joint for another twenty-five ta life sentence. This time for a kidnapping she had nothing to do with.

All because she listened to her dern conscience. What the heck was it good for except ta get a decent person inta trouble.

"How exactly does a broken-down ol' crone like me scare a big strong cop like you?" She tried for flirty, self-effacing, but wasn't good at it. She needed more practice coordinating the promiscuous smile, the faint cock of the head, her eyes on his feigning interest. At least that's how Ange told her it worked.

He took a step forward, again entering and violating her personal space, a tactic he must favor to pressure a criminal. Probably one from the Jack-Booted Cop's Handbook under Interrogations 101: hot light, rubber hose, and obstreperous language.

"Imogene, when I said Ida was missing, you didn't react. You skipped over the reaction part and went right to the question I asked."

"And I thought you were not only the nice one, but the smart one as well. Have you forgotten my history? I get nervous anytime I'm around police. You, as a police detective, asked me a question that went directly against my penal interest. You said Ida was missing and then asked when the last time I'd seen her. According to *Miranda v. Arizona*, you're required to read me my rights before you ask any questions against my penal interest. Did you get all that on your tape recorder? Hmm?" She feigned interest in the recorder in his hand.

His expression shifted to angry. She'd pushed him too hard. But what she'd also done was set up a solid defense if this whole mess ever ended up in court.

She said, "I'm sorry, we got off on the wrong foot. I'm not the ogre you think I am. Really, I'm not. I just stopped by to check on Ida. That's all. I am truly concerned about her, especially since you now say she's gone missing. You've never been on parole, so you can't possibly know how I feel or think while around police. I'm scared. Parolees defend first, react second. I'm sorry, please, let's start over. Is there anything I can do to help find Ida?"

His eyes eased off, the smile that had turned into an edgy grin turned back to a smile. "Yeah, I see what you mean. Sorry about that. So you saw the cop cars and just stopped to see what was going on?"

"No. That's not what I said. I said I know a little girl who lives here and stopped to check on her welfare. Please, can we dispense with the word games. I'm innocent. You're looking for a donkey to hang your hat on. I'm not that donkey, honest, I'm not, Detective."

He took a step back, checking the tape recorder to make sure it continued to memorialize the contact.

Ah, crapola. He wasn't backing down.

"For the record," he said, "Please tell me where you've been for the last oh, let's just make it the entire last twenty-four hours?"

"I actually thought we were friends. At least that we had some kind of understanding. I'm not the evil person you apparently think I am. I don't know how I can convince you of that."

"Imogene, don't dodge the question, that's a play a hardcore con would make. It's what the guilty do. Let's get through this, shall we?"

"Fine. I have a new job. I work down at the pawn shop on Euclid just north of Holt Boulevard. I was there all day yesterday. There are witnesses to that effect. After that I came home and—"

"That's Alan Goldblatt's place, right? West Valley Jewelry and Loan?"

Imogene put her head back, looked to the sky, and closed her eyes. "Ah, crapola."

"What, Imogene? Is something wrong?" His tone turned heavy with sarcasm.

"Look, I saw the Daily Report today, saw that Alan Goldblatt died in a fiery car crash. And here I am sticking my big bazoo into your problem that has nothing to do with me or with Alan Goldblatt. I'm on parole. And I know you're not going to believe me."

"Keep going. This all might resolve itself very quickly with what you say next. Where were you last night after work? Do you have a strong alibi for those hours?"

She smiled and tried hard to show relief. "I have a perfect alibi for last night when Alan Goldblatt died in a car crash—*an accident,* I might add. I was at home with my neighbor, Suz, and her boyfriend, Micheal Higginbothom. She stayed with me all night because I wasn't feeling well. Now see, I'm not the big bad wolf you think I am."

"Suz, *the woman* who shot to death two men in your living room two weeks ago?"

"Saint Peter on a cracker." She held out her wrists for the handcuffs. "Here, go ahead and do it. Take me in. Because you're not believing anything I say."

"Take a step back from this situation and look at it from where I'm standing. I honestly don't want to believe you had anything to do with what happened in your living room two weeks ago. And by that, I mean *you,* being the one who actually shot those two men."

Sweat broke out on Imogene's forehead. This was the first time anyone said out loud what they really thought happened.

Why the heck had she stopped to check on Ida? She should've listened to Ange. From now on, she'd always take Ange's suggestions.

Dern straight you will. It's too late now. He's gonna throw your sorry ass in the can until he gets this whole thing straightened out. By that time, it'll be too late. You'll have already caught the chain down to CIW.

"What am I gonna do?"

"Excuse me?" JB asked. "Did you say something?"

She said, out of turn. "Sssh, please just one minute."

Bonehead. You forget everything I taught ya in C-block? Cops are sharks, you give 'em a juicier hunk of bloody bait, he'll trade you in a heartbeat for something better.

Imogene said, "Okay, let's horse trade." She pointed to the recorder and ran her finger across her neck.

He hesitated, then shut it off. "This better be good."

"You got nothing on me because I didn't do anything wrong. I swear to you I'm not involved in any of the things you're investigating. But as a sign of good faith, I'll give you something good. Something I just happened into."

"Tell me."

"We have a deal? Am I going to jail today?"

"Depends on what you have."

"You don't have a thing on me, and you won't find anything. I just don't want to go to jail and wait until you figure it all out for yourself. One of us will have to trust the other. One of us has to blink."

"You got the most to lose."

"And I thought you were a gentleman. You're just like all the others. I guess I have to trust you, don't I?"

"I guess you do. I don't have all day."

"Someone's gonna rob the Euclid branch of The Bank of the West at one o'clock during the parade on the Fourth of July."

Chapter Thirteen

Two hours later, Imogene entered the pawn shop to find Thelma and Suz behind the counter, along with Luke Short, dealing with a throng of folks taking loans out on personal property they brought in to pawn. The customers growing unruly over the delays. Boisterous. Complaining.

She stood just inside the door, trying to catch her breath, puff, puff, puffing on a Marlboro. The heavy-duty air conditioner cooling her body, drying the flop sweat in her armpits and down her back. Why she was so short of breath?

Stress. Had to be all the stress.

JB had really put the screws to her about the bank job. She regretted letting that big black cat out of the bag. Bad luck times ten. Telling cops about the bank job seemed like a great idea in the moment. A sleight of hand trick to keep the photos in her dress pocket from being discovered. To keep from going to jail.

JB took the bait all right. He saw the information as a stepping stone to promotion. She could see that part in his eyes while she explained it to him, the way they came alive with excitement. She didn't tell him all of it. Couldn't. Not without implicating herself. Told him that a good friend—an informant—knew about the bank job. The informant, someone she met in CIW while doing her ten-year bit. The informant beyond reliable. As solid as they come.

JB had insisted on the informant's name before he let Imogene walk. She had no choice and told him, "Angela Ledger."

On the drive from Bonnie Brae to the pawn shop on Euclid, Ange went ballistic, yelling and screaming about violating The Code, about ratting her out. Throwing her to the wolves. Wolves who would *tear the very flesh* from her bones.

What a drama queen.

Imogene couldn't get a word in edgewise to tell Ange that she already resided in C-Block at CIW, and that the cops couldn't lay a glove on her for the robbery. Ange would have none of it. In the end, Ange went silent, brooding like a small child who had her candy taken away and then was told to go stand in the corner.

When talking to JB, Imogene left out the extortionist putting the squeeze on her. Left out the mob. Left out what she knew about poor little Ida. Imogene had to leave all that out or risk having the FBI brought in. And talk about screwing things up. The FBI couldn't find their asses with both hands. While she researched her book, she read all about how they operated. Any investigation for them takes a minimum of two years. Usually longer.

No, Imogene had played that part well, giving JB just enough information to whet his appetite. Enough that he'd have to let her go on the pretense that she would dig up the names of those involved.

Only the end result of spilling about the robbery served to wedge her even tighter into the problem. The added stress built up almost to the point of smothering her.

Now, three players came to the table over the same bank job. The extortionists, who set the job up in the first place and proved their vile worth by killing poor Mr. Goldblatt. Then the mob with The Boss and Erv. The bank actually belonged to the mob, for crying out loud. A place they apparently laundered their ill-gotten gain…and now the cops.

Sweet baby Jesus.

She put a hand to her head and moaned, trying like heck to find a way out. No positive scenario came to mind. Not one. People were going to die. No two ways around it.

The worst part, when Imogene took a step back to go over in her mind how it all came together: *she'd* been the one to bring the other two factions into the game, the mob and the cops.

The mob and the cops.

Just thinking about those two being involved made her heart flutter.

One good thing, though, something Ange used to say. "Look at it this way, cain't get any worse." Imogene first heard it while working in the prison kitchen. Ange whistled through her front missing teeth as she stirred one of the mega round vats of chicken stew with a baseball bat-sized paddle. She paused, whistling her poor rendition of a show tune, reached into the soup vat, and with two fingers pulled a blue rubber glove from the afternoon's lunch. The kind used when cleaning sinks and toilets. She held up the glove on the paddle for all to see. "Well, lookee here. Guess it cain't get much worse than this."

Remembering Ange's guileless expression when she said it made Imogene smile.

Standing just inside the pawn shop door, Imogene put a hand to her chest, looked at the Marlboro, tossed it to the shop floor, and ground it out underfoot. One thing for sure, old Goldblatt kept a clean shop, the fastidious little gnome. God rest his soul.

If only Ange would cool down long enough to talk to Imogene like a sane person. Ange possessed the best criminal mind Imogene ever knew. Ange could figure a play out of this mess, Imogene was sure of it.

"Ange?" She whispered.

The folks at the counter were too wrapped in their pin-headed, small-brain problems to notice Imogene standing by the door cooling her heels, gathering her wits.

Imogene whispered, "Ta heck with ya, lady." She bumped out another Marlboro and lit up. She walked the thirty feet to the counter and lifted the pass-through. All the inane chatter added to her rising anxiety level.

She put two fingers in her mouth and let loose with a whistle that pierced the ears. Everyone froze.

Luke Short finally noticed her as if she just appeared outta the ether. "Imogene, am I glad to see ya. Can you help us out here with this whole process? We're a little confused in the steps. There's too many steps."

"No, we're closing the store for one hour. Everyone, please step out. We'll reopen once we get some administrative things worked out." A man with a bad rug on his head, holding a teddy bear and a beat-up portable TV, yelled, "I will not wait another hour. I'm on my lunch break, and it's almost over. Where's Mr. Goldblatt? Where's Alan? He never treated us this way."

The others chimed in, all talking at once, the noise grating on her last nerve. She whistled again.

Silence.

She looked at Luke. "Did you at least get the floor safe open?"

He nodded.

"Ah…" she said. "Let's see. Gimme…" She quickly counted eight customers. "Gimme four hundred dollars."

The talk of that kind of money kept the people on the other side of the counter quiet, waiting to see what happened next.

Luke didn't hesitate. He squatted, reached into the safe, and came out with four hundred dollars in fifties. She took the money. "Now, each of you will get fifty dollars as a show of good faith. Come back in one hour, and that fifty will work as an advance on what you're offering for the loan." Imogene didn't wait for the people to say a word, one way or another, and handed out the fifties.

In the shattered mirror across the store—the mirror she shot—she caught Suz, Luke, and Thelma's images, their mouths agape.

The patrons snatched the bills from her hand, afraid she might change her mind. They fled a little too quickly. The man with the bad rug dropped the crummy portable television. The crash to the floor made them all jump. The tube shattered, scattering glass and puffing out gray picture-tube powder across the waxed floor. Rug man took off without looking back. He kept the ratty teddy bear under his arm. Probably forgot it was there. The fifty-dollar bill was five or six times the money he would've received on a real loan.

The last customer exited. The bell above the door gave a final ding.

Silence.

Finally.

Luke spoke first, "You know that money's gone for good. Those idgits won't be back."

Imogene glared at him. "Thelma, please go lock the front door. You two follow me into the back. We gotta talk."

Suz said, "What about the four hundred dollars? That'll come out of our own pockets."

Imogene's mouth sagged open at the blatant ignorance. *"We're being made to rob a bank.* A little girl's life hangs in the balance, and you two are worried about four hundred dollars? Seriously?"

Suz nodded, "You're right, E. We weren't thinking straight."

They headed to the far back room, the studio apartment. From behind, Luke said, "And besides, you're eight thousand ahead."

"What?" Imogene asked, still walking.

"Didn't you read the papers? Goldblatt bit off the big one last night. No way did he have time to cash that check you gave him yesterday. Probably burnt up in—"

Imogene stopped. Luke bumped into her. They stopped in the darkened warehousing section. She rounded on him. "A man is dead. Is that all you can think about? A check he may or may not have on his person during that horrendously painful and violent death?"

"Oh, yeah, sorry. That does sound a little callous, the way you say it."

"Callous, it sounds like you're some kinda wet-brain sociopath lacking all empathy. You better work on that, or you'll find yourself without friends."

She put the Marlboro between her lips and puffed out a cloud of smoke. She poked him in the chest with an index finger. "Now. You're gonna tell me the rest of what you know. Describe to me who contacted you and told you to pull me into this. Then tell me your part, what you're supposed to do. Don't even think about giving me the ol' okeydokey. Not this time, Pal."

He visibly squirmed. "Imogene, I was told under penalty of death not to say one word."

Thelma had locked the front door and now caught up with them where they stood in the warehouse area amongst the towering shelves filled with pawned junk. From above, a colorfully painted yard gnome stared down at them. Judging. "What'd I miss? What's going on? Dang it, it's not fair I had to be the one to lock the door."

Imogene ignored her and continued to glare at Luke. "Your niece is being held by some ruthless people, and you're going to stonewall me on this?"

He turned smug. "Not for nothin', Imogene, but how exactly do you think telling you the information is gonna help our situation? What are you, Batman or something? Wonder Woman?" He gave Suz and Thelma a weak smile, soliciting help and not getting a drop.

Imogene poked him harder this time. "You just crossed a line, my friend. You have thirty seconds ta tell me or face the consequences."

He raised his hands and waggled them. "Ooh, I'm scared."

She spun and took off, headed back the way she came. The others followed and stopped where the hallway opened to the customer area. She moved behind the counter and looked around. She picked up a heavy brass lamp in the shape of a Maltese Falcon and slammed it down on the locked display counter, shattering the plate glass.

"Imogene?" Suz yelled.

She raked the glass clear with the falcon, reached in and grabbed a beat-up Colt Detective Special, a .38.

Luke muttered, "Ah, crap."

Thelma giggled, "This is about to get real. Wish I had a doobie ta burn."

"Imogene," Suz said. "Don't do this."

Imogene held the gun and looked back at the trio. "Luke, time's ticking. You gonna talk?"

Luke squirmed and said to Suz in a lowered tone. "You think she's crazy enough to do it?"

Thelma cut in, smiling at Luke. "Do polar bears eat yellow ice cubes?"

Suz said, "Unfortunately, after all that's happened. I'm guessing you better tell her what she wants to know."

"I can't." Then louder so Imogene could hear. "I can't tell you. I'm sorry."

She spun around and scanned the wall of boxed ammunition until she spotted .38s. She pulled the box at the bottom of the column, toppling all the boxes on top. They clumped to the floor. Spilt rounds clattered about like marbles in some kind of weird children's game gone awry.

She opened the box, pulled out the cardboard drawer, and grabbed six bullets. "Fifteen seconds, Luke. I consider you a friend, but I'm not goin' back to the joint. I am not gonna let Ida get hurt because of your ignorant loyalty to people you don't even know." She opened the carriage on the gun, thumbed in the cartridges as she walked toward him. "Suz, you and Thelma, step out of the way. My hand's shaking ta beat the band." She finished loading and jerked the carriage shut with the flick of her wrist, the way she saw Mannix do it on TV.

Thelma let out an evil cackle as she grabbed ahold of her daughter's arm and pulled her out of the line of fire. "You might wanna close your eyes, daughter, blood spatters ya know."

Luke's eyes grew large. "Don't do this, Imogene. Please don't do this."

"Ten seconds."

Luke looked around for an escape route.

"You run, I'll just put one in your back." Words that didn't belong to her. Words only used as a threat to get what she wanted.

"Imogene," Suz yelled. "This is insane. This isn't you. Bring back the good Imogene, please. Don't do something you'll regret."

Imogene moved to within two feet of Luke, who shook with fear, too scared to flee. "For a cowboy, you sure lack grit. You gonna tell me what I wanna know?" She stuck the gun barrel in his crotch. Suz was right. This was the CIW Imogene, the C-Block Imogene, and not the harmless old woman who sat on the divan smoking two packs of Marlboros a day while watching out the picture window as the world passed by.

Luke nodded and gulped. "The guy who started all of this, he's a big black guy. He has some gray in his hair. Not a lot, just some. Brown eyes. He has brown eyes. He wore jeans, Levi's I think and...and black shoes, the kind with crepe soles so you can sneak up on folks."

"What else?"

"Ah...ah oh, yeah. His jeans, they were ironed. I noticed because at the time I thought who the heck irons jeans."

Imogene let the gun drop to her side. "Ah, crap on a Ritz."

"What?" Suz asked. "Do you know this guy?"

"Yeah, I guess I do. Like Luke said, it's odd someone would iron his jeans. The fastidious black bastard."

"Who is he?"

"Don't you worry your pretty little head. I'll deal with him."

"What are you talking about? You're…you're a woman. You're seventy-five years old and wear cat-eye glasses, for cripes sake. These are hardened criminals who'll do anything to get their way. They've already kidnapped two people. We need to turn this whole mess over to the police and let them handle it."

"That's just it, kid. The man Luke just described, he is the police."

Suz's shoulders slumped. "Oh, dear lord."

Thelma smirked. "Quit with the crocodile tears. None of this mess can hold a candle ta bein' shoved inta a plane's bathroom at thirty-five thousand feet and having a man from another planet inflate a life raft seconds before the whole shebang plows inta the side of a mountain. I'm sorry, but it doesn't."

Luke looked at her queer. "Say, what?"

"Exactly," Thelma said. "I wouldn't be surprised at all if these weren't the same people behind that whole airplane mess. They're really just after me. All of you are just extra."

Imogene ignored the comment. It was getting easier to do. "What did this guy tell you about your part? What are you supposed to do during the bank job?"

"He…he asked me if…well, if I was really a yegg or if it was just a rumor that I was."

Suz asked, "A yegg?"

Imogene answered before Luke could. "A yegg is a safe cracker. And that's real bad for us."

Luke nodded.

"What else did he tell you?"

"He said that on the Fourth…you guessed that part, Imogene. I was impressed, really, I was. He said that on the Fourth, I would get a phone call here at the pawn shop telling me what to do and how to do it. You two are to help me with those orders. Whatever the guy on the phone says, you two are supposed to help me."

"What about me?" Thelma asked, "What am I, chopped liver? I can help you rob a bank."

Imogene ignored her again and asked Luke. "That's it?"

"Well…he also— He scared the hell outta me under the threat that if I told anyone at all he would cut off…cut off a certain…ah, appendage. That's the word he used, too. Call it an appendage, like it was some kinda afterthought. And now I went and done it, told all ya all. I'm gonna be speaking soprano. I just know it."

"You're supposed to be some kinda fearless cowboy. Buck up will ya, Nancy?" Imogene handed him the loaded Colt stock first.

He waved his hands and took a step back. "I don't want my prints all over that. I'm not goin' back ta the joint. No siree bob, I ain't."

"Oh, for heaven's sakes." She put the gun in her dress pocket. The weight pulled down on the waist and made the dress look funny. She needed a lighter gun like the one Suz and Micheal took from her.

"Thelma, you're up. Come in here and sit down." Imogene guided her into the studio apartment and set her on the couch. The other two followed along and took seats in the room.

Cool, calm. Collected. Thelma said, "I don't know what *I* can tell you."

"Please, just do this for me. Sit back, close your eyes, and try to remember. Just start talking. From the beginning, tell us what happened when the man grabbed you?"

She started to sit back and close her eyes, and abruptly sat forward. "He didn't grab me, I went with him."

Imogene looked over at Suz, who rolled her eyes.

"Okay, then start with that. Where did you first see this man, and what did he look like?"

"Oh, I was walking down the street…ah, it was on Campus Avenue. Not far from the house. Yeah, that's right, Campus. I was goin' ta get some pizza at Gino Brother's Pizzeria on Fourth Street. You know, over by Grove. There's not a thing ta eat in my daughter's house 'cept green leafies in the fridge. I'm not a rabbit, by the way. This guy in a panel van, he pulls over. Leans across the seat and rolls the window down. Says, 'wanna ride?' I say sure, you bet. My feet were sore as heck by this time from these shoes. Just look at 'em." She looked over at Suz as if the shoe issue was her fault. "Baby, I need some new shoes."

"Get back to the man in the panel van. What did he look like?"

"He was short. I'd describe him as just below medium, maybe even go as far as calling him smallish. He had a rat face with a big bazoo. That's why I got in the van with him in the first place. I thought that if anything happened I could easily yank on that big nose of his and kick his sorry butt outta the van. Take the van and drive it ta get the pizza." She looked at Imogene. "I don't just get into a car with any Tom, Dick, or Harry. I know you're thinking that, Imogene. Judging."

Imogene puff, puff, puffed the Marlboro and rolled her hand in front of Thelma. "Come on, stay with the story and forget about the dern pizza. Then what happened?"

"I don't know."

"Mom, what do you mean you don't know?"

She looked down at her hands in her lap. "I think…well, I think someone else was in the van. A hand came from behind with a white hankie. I don't know what happened after that. The van suddenly smelled like chemicals."

Luke whispered, but loud enough for all to hear. "Ether. The bastards used ether on a woman."

"Then what happened?"

She shrugged. "I woke up in a room taped to a chair and no one around."

Imogene came closer. "What did the room look like?"

"I don't know, like a cheapo motel room. I had a headache like someone was splittin' my skull with a sledgehammer ana wedge. I couldn't think straight enough ta pick my nose."

Luke asked. "How'd you get away?"

She turned to look at Luke. "I kinda stood. I mean I was taped to the chair and all. You could see what I mean in the photo. Can I have that photo?"

"Mom."

"Okay. Okay. I got up on my toes and backed up real fast right into the fireplace. This motel had a fireplace made of rock. I did it again and again until the chair broke. That's how I got the marks on my arms and hands and legs. All taped up and crashing inta that fireplace."

Imogene leaned over close and took Thelma's hand in hers. "When you got out, do you remember the name of the motel?"

She shook her head. Her chin quivered. She was about to cry. In the back room of the pawn shop, they had forced her to relive the awful encounter. The thought gave Imogene a little emotional heartache. The poor woman.

"It's okay." Imogene patted her hand. "One more question, okay?"

"I'm doin' the best I can. I'm tellin' ya, I had a bust-head hangover and I didn't even drink a drop. I swear. I openly admit that me and Mr. Smirnoff had a clandestine affair for a few years, but I'm over all that. The half-pint bastard."

"I believe you. But I want you to concentrate. In the room, what did the carpet look like?"

She looked up, her chin quit quivering. "The carpet? Yeah, that's right? I remember that because it was odd."

"Go on."

"It was old, and instead of putting in new stuff, it looked like someone used spray cans to make the color darker. From puke brown to a spray-can blue."

"Ha." Imogene stood and headed for the front door. The others followed.

"Imogene?" Suz yelled. "You know where mom's talking about?"

Imogene stopped at the shattered counter, took the Colt out of her dress pocket, dropped it in amongst the glass shards and other guns. She carefully took out a Walther PPK .380.

"It's the Capri Motel."

Chapter Fourteen

Imogene made four passes on Holt Boulevard and two in the back alley before setting up in the parking lot of the defunct *Joe Co's Stationery and Supply* across the street from the Capri Motel. Imogene had a two-week forced stay at the bedbug-infested fleabag. Got to know the environs, the perverted office clerk, and most of the folks who inhabited the fifty-room business that should've been red-tagged by the city.

Nothing looked out of the ordinary. Same rundown cars parked in front of the motel room doors. The same kind of rundown street people coming and going from the rooms. The down-on-their-luck, the mentally off, the addicted. All of them busy in their nefarious activities without acknowledging the world around them.

None of whom she recognized.

The front office run by Earl Biggers wasn't visible, blocked by the rock grotto that used to have water running over a small waterfall into a pool with bright-colored koi. Now the empty pool and the grotto behind the nonexistent waterfall contained trash: fast food wrappers, empty 40s, syringes, used plastic baggies, torn-up toy balloons, and a bent-up chrome car bumper from a parking-lot crash that occurred years before. The plate attached to the bumper was from Nevada, "The Mother Lode State."

Framed faded color photos on the wall inside the office depicted a beautiful Capri back in the glory days when movie stars on their way from Hollywood to gamble in the speakeasies at Big Bear Lake stopped in for a quick afternoon tryst.

John Johnson—or now it may have even been JB after the way he treated her in front of Ida's house—had told the twenty-four-hour-a-day clerk, Earl Biggers, to put her right next to the office. She assumed so Earl could keep an eye on her while she waited out the forensic people going through her house. Their theory being that the room close to the degenerate clerk would allow him to call if she tried to take it on the lam. More than once during her interrogations they gave her the ol' "Don't leave town or else," routine. Where exactly would she go?

For two dern weeks she lived in that interminable hell hole.

Her motel room door opened to that dern grotto that smelled foul, like a raccoon died right after a skunk hosed it down with stink. Ugh.

The others, Luke, Suz and Thelma all wanted to tag along but that woulda been like herding cats. The yammering alone during the surveillance would have been enough to eat lead from the Walther PPK. She smiled at the thought of those three trying to run the pawn shop. Pure chaos.

This way she sat alone, puff, puff, puffing Marlboros, already deep into the second pack. Today might be one of those three-pack-a-day aberrations she worked hard to avoid. But come on, she'd made one of her biggest mistakes since getting out on parole by stopping in at Ida's house. She almost caught the chain back to Chino over one simple mistake based entirely on empathy for a little girl.

Stress. Nothing but pure teeth-cutting stress.

"Come on Ange, say something. I'm goin' outta my head sittin' here twiddling my thumbs."

Nothing.

Ange was still angry about her name being offered up as a rat to JB.

Imogene tried to channel Bessie Gottschalk, the strong female lead in *Peekaboo POTUS*. What would Bessie do in a case like this? Surveil the target location or make something happen? Bessie, bold and brazen, wouldn't sit on her butt waiting for the bad guys to raise their ugly heads. She'd "kick it in gear and get after it." Bessie's favorite saying, one used a little too often in the book.

But in the real world, calm calculated logic said that once Imogene talked with anyone at the Capri, the cat would be outta the bag. The bad guys would know someone was onto them. This would put little Ida at risk.

In this instance, Bessie would say, "You can't put the toothpaste back in the tube once you've stomped on it."

Maybe Imogene used too many hometown bromides in the book. The next book would be less folksy and instead grittier. Life wasn't a bowl of cherries. More a defunct grotto used by ne'er do wells as a trash receptacle.

She puffed the Marlboro down to the filter, used the last of the cherry to light the next one and flicked the butt out into the empty parking lot with the other two.

"Ange, come on, quit being a butthole and talk to me."

A Yellow Cab pulled up in front of The Capri.

Something out of the ordinary. Exactly what Imogene had been waiting for.

The entire two weeks at the Capri no one ever pulled up in a taxi. The motel occupants could barely make rent, let alone afford that kind of luxury. Their favored mode of transportation was strictly shoe leather. Some didn't even have shoes. The skin on the soles of their feet thick as pizza crust.

She leaned forward over the steering wheel as if getting closer would make the cab occupant exit faster. Instead, the fare in the backseat continued to jaw with the miffed driver.

The driver threw up his hands. His angry, muffled words didn't make it across the busy Holt Boulevard.

The woman got out. The cabby exited too fast, teetered almost going to the ground, still waving his arms, yelling. Apparently, the fare didn't have the money.

The woman—

"Oh, dear Lord."

The woman was Thelma.

What in the blue heck was she doing at the Capri? But Imogene knew. Back at the pawn shop, Imogene made the mistake of blurting the name of the motel Thelma had described, where the puppet masters held her captive.

Dern her crazy soul. She would ruin everything. She already had. Just by pulling up out front in a taxi cab.

Imogene started the little red Gremlin, drove over to the driveway to wait for traffic to clear before she could cross. The new angle allowed a visual into the office window. The degenerate Earl Biggers talked on the phone. He was a pig who took advantage of down-on-their-luck women trading sex for a room. Exploiting them.

He waved his hands animatedly as he spoke. He knew all about Thelma, had recognized her from the moment she pulled up in the cab. He was warning the puppet masters of the abrupt status change. Earl wanted to know what to do. Wanted help.

Traffic cleared. Imogene gunned the Gremlin. The little four-cylinder engine roared like a domestic cat. The car jetted across four lanes on Holt Boulevard. The car's front end banged up into the motel driveway. The cabbie and Thelma swung around to see the commotion.

Imogene pulled up and stopped behind the cab. Thelma smiled and waved. That cued the cabby that Imogene was a friend. He rushed Imogene, yelling about the unpaid ten-dollar fare. Thelma fled to the office.

"Thelma, wait. You wait right there."

The cabby, emboldened and unafraid of the old woman before him, put his hands up toward her chest and stopped her.

While in stir, she read two books on judo and was still channeling Bessie Gottschalk from *Peekaboo POTUS*. Imogene took hold of the cabbie's hand, twisted it around, and put him in pain compliance wristlock. At seventy-five, she couldn't do hip tosses or mid-air flips, but she could do the simple wristlock. About the only judo move she *could* do.

The mustachioed man went to his knees, muttering and near to tears. For the briefest of moments, Imogene reveled in this newfound control over men. Then realized she was hurting someone. She let go. The man crabbed away. She opened her purse, took a folded twenty out of the coin purse, caught up, and handed it to him. He didn't thank her, his expression one of fear and at the same time fascination. He gained his feet, backed away, turned, mounted his cab, and fled.

She turned and looked through the office window.

"Sweet baby Jesus."

Thelma had the Colt Detective Special pointed at Earl the perv. The gun Imogene had loaded back at the pawn shop was tossed back in the display case.

Ange chuckled. *I couldn't stay mad at you, Baby Girl. And this here is too funny to keep mum about. A whackadoo with a gun about ta cap a lowlife perv. Nothing but fun can come outta that, huh? Am I right, E? Am I?*

"Glad to have you back. Not happy with you leaving when I needed you most. We're going to talk later. Bet on it."

Imogene put her purse up on her arm, straightened her dress, opened the glass door, and entered the small lobby that bled over into the office, separated by only a scarred customer counter. Thelma stood on the other side in the small office area. Earl, on his hands and knees, looked up into the barrel of the Colt.

Imogene had been there two weeks earlier after she looked down the barrel of The Cigar's gun as he stood in her living room. That barrel the size of a train tunnel. The train already on its way and at any second about to burst out.

Thelma had flipped the pass-through over when she entered. Imogene walked into the office and sat in the pig's easy chair. Earl begged. Pleaded with Thelma, asking her what he did wrong. He turned. "Please, Imogene, tell her I only run the office. That I got nothin' to do with what goes on here. Tell her, please. She's crazy. You can see it in her eyes. She wants to know where the man is. When I asked her what man, she said the man with the yellow lifeboat who smells like rubber. Are you kidding me here? Do you know her? Please tell her not to shoot me."

Thelma waved the gun around, her eyes wild, the platinum beehive hair on her head swaying from side to side. The whole can of Aqua Net the only thing keeping it atop ol' Smokey.

Tell her ta shoot him in the foot. I wanna hear him squeal like a pig. Please, E? Tell her. She'll do it if you ask her to. Ange's tone shifted to anger. *Do it, E. This pig has no right to live. Not after the things he's done to all those women. He's one of those...one of those...what do you call 'em...a my-o-gone-ist. A myogonist.*

Imogene casually reached into her purse for the Marlboro box, bumped one out, and lit it while both of them watched. She flicked the cigarette ash that really didn't need flicking and said, "Misogynist. The word you're looking for is misogynist."

Thelma's expression shifted to confusion. "I wasn't looking for any word."

Imogene flicked her cigarette again. "Earl, listen to me very carefully. I'm going to ask you some questions. If you don't answer them correctly, I'm going to direct my cohort here to shoot you in the foot. Then the leg. Then the hip. You understand? Before we start, please tell me you understand?"

Before he could reply, Thelma interrupted. "I'm your cohort? Really? I've never been a cohort before." She waved the gun some more, like a cook at IHOP with a spatula. "I kinda like this whole thing we got going here. It's kinda like being in a gang. I never had any friends, and now I'm in a gang."

E, tell her to shut her yap and jus' start shootin'. I can't take any more of her yammering. No wonder her planet banished her to Earth. Huh? Am I right, E? Am I right?

"Thelma, we're working here. Cut back on the yammering and let me talk, okay? Just point that thing at his foot, and when I tell ya to shoot, you shoot. Not before. You understand? Don't pull the trigger until I tell you to."

Earl yelped out, "Oh my God, Imogene, you're serious, aren't you? What'd I ever do to you, huh?"

"Of course, I'm serious. Have you ever known me to mess around or joke with you? Earl, we're not friends, never have been, never will be. Now, first question. I would recommend you take a second before you answer it. Because, like in court, I won't ask a question I don't already know the answer to."

Thelma again looked confused. "That doesn't make any sense. Then why would you ask—"

"Thelma, pay attention."

"Okay. Okay. I don't know if I like being in this gang."

"Earl, first question. It's a softball. An easy one. What is the room number where the men kept my friend Thelma locked up?"

His mouth dropped open and then slammed shut. He realized he'd been had and didn't have any way out.

"Okay," Imogene said, "I guess we have ta put a timer on the answer. Wished I had my egg timer from home."

"Now?" Thelma asked. "Shoot him now?"

"Not yet. Earl, ten seconds."

"Nineteen. Around in the back. Room nineteen."

"That's why Thelma didn't know the name of the motel. You had her out back where the doors open to the alley."

"Didn't have no one nowhere. I told ya, I'm not involved. You know that. I keep my nose outta everyone's business. It's the only way to survive around this place."

"Except when it's a woman who doesn't have any money and needs some place to stay. Moving on. This is going to be a tough one. Tell me true or take a bullet. Which room are those men keeping the little girl in?"

His eyes went wide. "What are you talking about? I don't—"

"Now?" Thelma asked. "Shoot him now?"

Imogene held a hand up to Thelma. "Earl, look at these two photos. One is of Thelma here, and the other is a little girl who we're still looking for."

He looked at the two Polaroids. "Oh, nooo. No. No. I had nothing to do with this. I swear ta Gawd. All I did was rent out one room to those people. That's it. Just one. They gave me a phone number to call if anything happened. I don't even have a name. The phone number was on a slip of paper."

"You rented the room to what people? Get ready, Thelma."

Thelma pulled the hammer back on the gun, the click loud enough to make Earl pee his pants. The urine reek filled the air. She lined the barrel up on his foot.

Earl pulled his foot back, trying to get it under his body. "Wait. I'll tell ya. You know him."

"I know him?"

"Sure. I rented the room to Dirty Pete. He had cash and asked for one room for a week. Cash up front."

"The same Dirty Pete that lives in room eleven?"

"Yeah, that's him. He's also the one who gave me the paper with the phone number. But he left. Took off. Said he came into enough cash to catch a bus back to Little Rock."

"Dern their sorry hides. They used a cutout."

"A what?" Thelma asked.

"Someone that's used to fill a link in between this turd and the bad men we're looking for. A cutout stops us from going any further."

"That's smart. These are smart guys, huh, Imogene?"

Earl shook his head. "See, I told ya I had nothing at all to do with this."

Imogene put the cigarette in her mouth, squinted from the smoke, and stood. She took the Colt from Thelma and eased her back out of the way. Imogene leaned down a little, a hand on one knee, to talk to The Capri's twenty-four-hour clerk with wet pants. "Listen here, Earl, you say anything to anyone about what happened here, and I get arrested. When I get to court, I'll tell 'em you knew all about the kidnappings. That you were in on it. You understand?"

"I won't say a word. I promise. I swear on my kid's eyes."

He's got kids, E? That's just not right. That's coyote wrong. You gotta do something' Anything. Don't let him off. Not without letting him know who you are. You're Imogene Taylor, for cripes sake.

"I think she's right, Earl."

"Think who's right? What are you talking about?"

"Okay, this is going to be the hard part."

"The hard part?"

"Unfortunately, it is for you. Not for me. We're talking about the carrot and the stick. Only in this case, you get the stick first."

"No. I don't like the sound of—"

Imogene shot him in the foot. The shot, an explosion that continued to reverberate against the walls in the small room.

Earl screamed and grabbed his foot, leaving behind a bloody swath.

Thelma said, "How come you got ta shoot him?"

Imogene raised her voice over Earl's yelling. "I did that as a warning. Don't you ever exploit another woman. I hear about it and I'll be back. If I come back, I won't be shooting you in the foot. I'll shoot you in the source of your problem. You understand? Tell me you understand, Earl?"

"Yeees. Yes. Yes."

"Come on, Thelma, let's go."

She followed along, going out the front door. "Can I get that gun back?"

"No."

"Where we goin' next?"

"To see another man?"

"You takin' me with you?"

Imogene stopped and waited for Ange to weigh in.

Ah, hell, E, might as well. This loon is good for a laugh.

Imogene said, "Sure." And handed the Colt back to her. "Keep in mind it only has five shots left."

Chapter Fifteen

Within fifteen minutes after parking across the street from the San Bernardino Parole office, Imogene took a small packet of Kleenex from her purse, made some makeshift plugs, and put them in her ears. Thelma continued to yammer nonstop. Her favorite topic: the kingdom of poor souls that had to soldier on without their Queen. Thelma, in her rant, postulated that this world that belonged to her was a small planet in the shadow of Pluto and rattled off coordinates that in no way could be real.

E, Pluto's too small to have a planet hiding behind it and—

Imogene puff, puff, puffed a Marlboro, burning it down twice as fast. The tobacco crackled and sparked from the abuse. She held her hand up to stop Ange. "You want me to argue with her over—" Imogene looked at Thelma who'd stopped mid-yammer.

"You talking to me? You never did tell me what we're doing here."

"We're watching for my parole officer to leave work. We're gonna follow him."

Thelma rose up in the passenger seat of the little red Gremlin and looked around. "In this car? It's red and stands out like a—"

"Would you like me to drop you off somewhere?"

"What? No. 'Course not. I'm just saying you need a nondescript car to tail someone. I learned that much from *In Cold Blood*. You see that movie? Freaky. I'm not kiddin'. It's in black and white and literally scared the water outta me. But I love me some Robert Blake. I'd go out with him in a hot second. I just know he's the kindest, most gentle man you could ever meet.

He'd never hurt a fly, not like in that movie."

Please, please drop her stinky butt off. Take her ta the Greyhound station, it's right down the street. Send her off ta Timbuktu, good riddance and see ya later. You don't, I won't be responsible for what happens. I won't, E, I'll do her dirty. I swear I—

"Why do we wanna follow your parole officer?"

Anything was better than listening to her yammer about the purple kingdom hidden behind Pluto.

"We're following him because I think he's the guy who wound up Luke Short like some kind of tin soldier and put this whole mess into play."

"Why do you think that?"

"For one thing, everyone involved is on parole, so there's a definite parole connection. And Luke Short said the man who threatened him was a black guy who wears ironed Levi's."

"Huh? Seriously? Your parole officer did that ta Luke? Don't know if I believe any of it. Sounds kinda like a wish and a prayer with a lot of coincidence thrown in with a cuppa Tide laundry soap."

Imogene shrugged. "Why don't we just sit here and think about this for a minute. Quietly?"

She nodded and sat quiet for the count of ten. "I like to talk with you, Imogene. I don't get to talk to a lot of people. Ta tell ya the truth you're the first person who believed my story about the airplane."

"I what?"

"Don't you believe me?"

Imogene didn't want to lie to her. She was woe to lie to a friend. "Of course, I believe you. Why wouldn't I?"

Thelma reached over and put her warm hand on Imogene's.

E. I can't take this anymore. I'll give you a clue you missed finding on the little girl if you dump her sorry ass off at the Greyhound station.

"I didn't miss a thing. You're just jealous."

Thelma sat back as if slapped. "You feeling okay, Imogene? Sometimes you spout off like...like maybe you're just a little bit nuts."

Ange cackled loud and hard at that one and said, *Kettle, meet Pot*

This one made Imogene smile.

But she lost the smile in half a second, suddenly turning all business. She reached down and started the Gremlin. Parole agent James Humphries just walked out of the parole office. "Here we go."

Thelma pulled the .38 from her purse and held it up. Imogene gently took it from her. "I don't think we'll be needing a gun for this."

Giving Thelma the gun in the first place ground on Imogene's nerves the moment she'd done it. What was she thinking? She wasn't. The kinda mistake that could and would spiral down into a black hole that equated to C block at CIW.

Humphries walked down the sidewalk to the parking area. He wore black shoes with crepe soles just like Luke described. He carried a worn soft leather business satchel with a long strap over his shoulder.

And wore the Levi's with razor pressed crease.

"You sure we don't wanna shoot him?"

"Positive, we shoot the suspect, how will we find out where he's hiding, Ida?"

"Good point."

Humphries got into a faded orange Opel Cadet. He drove out onto the street without looking each way before entering. His mind pondering something heavy. Like being a direct participant in a dual kidnapping and bank robbery. He too might only be a puppet doing what he was told.

Imogene pulled out into traffic and followed.

You know, having that gun links you directly to the shooting of that pig. You're on parole, E. Dump it. Dump right it now. Don't even give it another thought. Every passing minute the odds stink worse. You'll get pulled over for shore. That's jus' the way life works. Then what? Huh?

Imogene, out of instinct, looked up in the rearview as if Ange was in the backseat, a backseat driver in a life that hadn't been right since Imogene shot Wayne.

Imogene whipped over to the curb and stopped next to a storm drain. "Open your door."

"What?"

"I said open your door. Hurry, he's getting away." She flicked open the carriage, dumped out the five live rounds and one empty shell casing. Thelma opened her door. Imogene tossed the gun down the storm drain and hit the gas. Thelma's door came closed all on its own.

She wove in and out of cars trying to catch up to the Cadet. She came right up on Humphries' bumper before she realized it and had to back off using the brake. He had to have seen it. She brought her hand up to her face as cover, a fool's makeshift disguise. She watched Humphries' rearview for his eyes to lock with hers.

He didn't even look up.

The man's a fool, E. You kin roll right up on him and he'd never know it. Not till you capped him in the back of the head. Think about it. You'd get a new parole agent. A nicer one.

"I'm not a killer and you know it."

Thelma sat back in her seat. "Hmm."

They followed Humphries in and out of traffic on main thoroughfares until he turned down a tree-shaded, residential street in a middle-class neighborhood of Rialto.

Thelma had gone quiet after Imogene's last comment about not being a killer. Least she now knew how to shut her up. Imogene loved Ange to death, but Ange continued to believe that Imogene was just like Ange, a stone-cold killer. That wasn't so. Wayne's death was an accident. Those other two in her living room didn't count, they had called their own game.

Thelma said, "He lives here. He's not going to lead us to her, is he?"

"Nope."

Offer still stands. Drop the loon off and I'll give you a clue. It's a good one, E. You're gonna kick yourself in the butt for missing it.

Imogene was a lot of things, but a fool wasn't one of them. She understood the dynamic of how Ange talked to her. How that communication was a safety outlet for emotional distress. A release valve. That or go crazy. For ten years, Imogene shared a small cell with Ange. In ten years, you really got to know a person. One of Ange's favorite sayings echoed in Imogene's head, "We're butthole to elbow up in here." Ange had been around too long now to let her go.

Maybe that was why Imogene put up with Thelma. Well, sort of put up with her.

No way in God's little green acre could Ange give clues about something in the real world. It just wasn't possible.

She drove by the house Humphries pulled into and caught the address number. She would need it for later. At the next intersection, she whipped a U-turn and looked over at her passenger. "You hungry?"

"My mama always said to eat whenever ya get the chance, 'Cause ya never know when you'll get your next meal. It could be days down the road.' I remember her saying that like it was yesterday."

Probably was yesterday. The woman's a full-blown loon.

Imogene said to Thelma. "I'll take that as a yes."

Imogene eased back in the seat, let her elbow rest on the open windowsill, the warm wind blowing in on her face. She smoked and drove, going over everything that had happened step by step. If Ange knew something, it stood to reason Imogene would already know it as well and had just missed it.

"Imogene?"

She looked at Thelma.

"Are you…are you talking to…pretending to talk to people to make fun of me. To taunt me?"

"Of course not. Don't be ridiculous. I'd never do something like that."

Now she felt like a grade A heel.

Thelma nodded. "You seem like the sanest person I've ever met. So, you see my problem. How could someone like you—"

"Look, I'm not making fun of you. I was in prison a lot of years. Too many years. In that small cell the only way to stay sane was to talk to myself."

Thelma smiled, her whole face lit up. "That makes perfect sense. Of course, you would talk to yourself if you were alone for so long."

But she wasn't alone. Ange had been with her the entire time. Physically in the cell, talking non-stop. Wayne would've called a woman like Ange, "A gab-about." His pun on gad about. He always laughed at his own jokes. Imogene missed the hell outta him.

She pulled into an A&W hamburger joint painted brown and orange, stopped with her foot on the brake, and reached into her purse. She handed Thelma two twenties. "Why don't you order me a large root beer float and a double cheeseburger with fries. I'm gonna sit out here and smoke a bit, think about our next move."

She took the money as blatant disappointment filled her expression.

"Sure. A large root beer float. Forty dollars. That's a lot of money for—"

Imogene glared at her. She got out and trudged toward the restaurant. She stopped at the open door, looked back. They shared a knowing moment. Thelma turned and entered. Imogene put it in reverse, backed out.

And left.

Thelma was much better off without Imogene dragging her around committing felonies. A mile down the road, she again looked in the rearview. "Okay, you rude witch. I did what you asked even though it ripped my heart out. So, you better have something good. Go on, spill it. Tell me right now."

Ange said nothing.

Hot rage flushed Imogene's face. She pulled to the curb. "You talk ta me right now or...or—"

Keep your big panties on, girl. I'm right here.

"Tell me."

You still have the photo of the little girl?

"You know I do."

Take it out and look at it real close. The clue's been right there under your nose this whole time.

Imogene pulled out the photo and looked at it. Ida sat taped to a chair just like Thelma's photo. The background pitch-black, nothing in the room could be identified or even seen for that matter. Someone carefully framed the shot so as not to leave anything for the court ta hang 'em high.

"You're yanking on me, Ange. There's nothing here. I mean nothing at all but a scared little girl."

Are you so sure?

"What are you talking about?"

Are you so sure she's scared?

Imogene moved the photo closer to her nose, lifted her cat-eye glasses, and looked into Ida's eyes. "Well, I'll be a monkey's uncle. I think you're right. Her mouth is turned down in a grimace, but her eyes are telling a different story. She's faking it. Someone asked her to act sad and scared and this is her doing it."

What's that tell ya?

"That's she was probably told they were just playing a game. But it could still be the bad guys asking her to do it. This doesn't mean a thing."

Ange didn't respond.

Imogene looked at the photo. Stared into Ida's eyes. She tossed the picture on the passenger seat, took her foot off the brake, and hit the gas. "Dern your sorry hide."

Hmm.

Fifteen minutes later, Imogene pulled up and parked on Bonnie Brae all the way down at the end by Berlyn. The police cars no longer sat in front of Ida's house.

She didn't want to consider what it would mean if Ida's family were somehow involved in the bank robbery. The poor little thing would have foster care in her future.

The sun sat on a false horizon of rooftops. Half an orange glowing orb cast an eerie yellow light that made it difficult to watch the house. Her stomach growled. Had she eaten anything at all today?

Nope, nothing but cigarettes and coffee. Nicotine and caffeine, the breakfast of champions. Now she wished she'd stuck around for that root beer float, cheeseburger, and fries from A&W.

She could stand to lose a few lbs. That's the way Ange referred to them. Lbs, as if not saying the whole word kept them from sticking to her hips while eating the starchy diet at CIW.

That orange orb slowly sank behind the rooftops, leaving a bright shadow in her vision that almost made her miss the car backing out of Ida's driveway.

"That's Ida's driveway, right? Talk to me."

Crickets. Nothing but crickets.

"Ange?"

"Ah, dern your sorry hide." Imogene started up and drove behind the car that headed west toward Campus.

This time, the driver of the car kept checking his rearview. She reached behind the seat to get her surveillance bag. Bessie Gottschalk always kept one in her car. Imogene had no need of it while watching the Capri or the parole office. She put on a blue Dodgers ball cap and then sunglasses over her prescription cat-eye glasses.

But that idjit Thelma, she had it right after all. How could a person in their right mind follow someone while driving a red AMC Gremlin? Imogene knew all about surveillance from her research writing *Peekaboo POTUS*.

When she got out on parole, she treated herself to a brand-new car. She chose red, so it would be easier to spot when coming out of the grocery. Her memory not being what it used to be. Who'd have ever thought she'd need the car for surveillance, especially one where her life depended on it.

Now she tried to remain inconspicuous behind a Chinaman driving a yellow Toyota 240Z. How did he afford a car that cost a king's ransom, $3700.00, new off the showroom floor? As compared to $1800.00 plus tax and license for her little Gremlin. Twice as much. Had JB and John Johnson checked in Ida's stepfather's garage when they questioned him about Ida's disappearance? Talk about a missed clue.

That's not the right question to be asking.

"What am I missing?"

If he's in on it and he did put the grab on that sweet thang, why'd he call the police ta report her missing?

Imogene again looked up into the rearview mirror, expecting to see her old cellmate back there giving advice. "Som bitch, Ange. What the heck's going on?"

Ange wasn't there and said nothing.

"Naw, doesn't make any sense, why grab Ida?"

You already know. Talk it through. I have faith in ya, girl.

Imogene nodded and let her hands and right foot manipulate the car while she shifted all brain power to the problem at hand.

"Why kidnap your own kid? That's the question. Why? I got nothing,

Ange. You're gonna have ta give me a hint on this one."

Come on, E. You're doggin' it here. You're Imogene Taylor, for cripes sake. This is an easy one.

"Ange, I'm tellin' ya I can't—"

The yellow Japanese car turned into the Holiday Inn on G Street.

Go on by. Go on by. Don't act the fool and pull right in behind him. Go on by. That's it. Now, make a quick Union. Go. Go. Get back there before you miss what room he's going in.

Imogene turned into the drive and took a left in the parking lot just in time to see Ida's adoptive father climb out of the 240Z, stand in the open door, and look around. Checking for anything out of place. Checking for tails.

Rule number one in surveillance, act like you belong in the environment. More important, don't ever stare at any one thing.

Imogene pulled in and parked three cars down from the Z car. She took her time getting out. Her biggest asset: no one would expect a 75-year-old woman to be tailing them. With her purse on her arm, she moved down the walkway smoking a Marlboro a little too fast. When she came even with the Z car she nodded and mumbled, "Evening," to the Chinaman and hoped he didn't remember her standing in his front yard talking to JB.

Old women are innocuous. No one notices them. No different than fall leaves on the sidewalk. All of them the same. All delicate underfoot and too easy to ignore.

Imogene had forgotten about being in his front yard, about him looking out his kitchen window. How could he not recognize her? Sweat broke out on her brow.

Girl, you gotta go full nuclear option on this one. Play it hard, or he's gonna remember you.

Imogene muttered, "Easy for you to say."

She stopped. Froze for a moment. She turned around and backtracked to Ida's father, who still stood in the open door to the Z car as if at any moment about to flee.

"Ah, excuse me," she said. "I live on Hawthorne right off of Campus. I've seen this car in the neighborhood. You really can't miss it. It's a real beaut. Must've cost you a small fortune."

He stared, blinking.

"Huh," she said. "Just wanted to be neighborly. If this *is* the same car, I mean. There can't be too many of 'em around. Especially not this color."

He said nothing.

"Okay, well, good evening ta you." She started to turn.

In an aggravated tone, he said, "What are you doing here?"

"Excuse me?"

"What are you doing here? At this hotel."

"I don't know you, sir. I don't think it's—"

"Why are you here?"

"Harrumph. If you must know, my house is being fumigated. You know, tented for pests. I know it's a little shameful to admit having bugs, but that's what happened just the same. Termites in the foundation. Had I not acted 'aggressively,' this according to the Terminix man, the buggers could've taken down my entire house. They have to tent the whole shebang, you see. I had to box up all my open food and—"

He held up his hand and waved her away. "Never mind. Please, just go."

"You are rude, sir." She turned heel and walked while letting out a long, silent exhale. She counted down ten hotel doors and stopped at number 117. Her head down. She fumbled in her purse as if looking for her room key. She took a chance and glanced sideways back toward the Z car.

The man forgot all about her, buying into the last-second termite legend she fed him. She was a fall leaf on the sidewalk underfoot, innocuous. And not so delicate.

He reached back into his car and brought out a small suitcase with pink and yellow flowers on the sides, along with a grocery bag. A box of sugary cereal peeked out the top, one with a leprechaun jumping in the air, clicking his heels, a halo of multi-colored marshmallow shapes floating around his head.

The man didn't look around and headed right to a hotel door. Used a key and entered.

When he disappeared inside, she kept her eyes on the door, quickly stepped backward far enough to count the rooms in between. Then walked that way, counting off the rooms until she came to the one he went in; 105.

At least she hoped it was the right room.

She hurried, got in the Gremlin, and backed up. Took a spot at the far end of the lot, mixing in with other parked cars. Cars several levels up on the socio-economic scale from the derelicts at The Capri.

Now her stomach really growled. Time ticked by, two Marlboros worth.

Out popped Ida's dad.

Without Ida.

He got back in the Z car and took off. This time, the Z car's engine roared as he moved through the gears. She tried her best to stay with him.

He's driving angry, E. Stay back. Don't get close ta this turd. I gotta bad vibe about him. And you know about my bad vibes. When I had that last one, I came home early for lunch and found Earl all up in my bed with Mabel. Up-the-street-Mabel of all people. You remember what I tolt ya. I taught 'em both a hard lesson with a little 12-gauge shotgun therapy. So, you watch this guy. I'm gettin' that same kinda vibe. Think it's about time for some more shotgun therapy.

They continued east back toward San Bernardino. Three times, the Z car caught yellow lights, didn't stop, and zoomed right on through. She had no choice, came up to those intersections, looked both ways, girded herself, and busted the red, holding her breath. Her arm pits turned wet from the continued stress.

And each time Imogene busted a light Ange screeched, *Eeeeee.*

Even so, after seven or eight miles, Imogene lost him. Darkness settled in like an unwanted cousin who came to visit and stayed. She drove a widening grid pattern to try and pick him up, not holding out too much hope.

Come on, quit actin' like a big buffoon. You know exactly where this turd got off to. Kick it in gear and get after it. You cain't put the toothpaste back in the tube once you've stomped on it.

She cackled after saying the two most popular cliché's in *Peekaboo POTUS,* mocking Imogene.

"Dirty, lowdown witch."

Imogene pulled yet another U-turn and headed to James Humphries' house.

Five minutes later, she cruised by the address.

Ange was right, the yellow 240Z sat in Humphries' driveway. Both of them were in this thing, thick as thieves. How in the world could she extricate herself from this whole mess with her parole officer involved up to his nose? She was trapped with no way out. The same as a naked virgin on a bridal bed.

These were the puppet masters. The men responsible for killing Alan Goldblatt.

And Imogene wasn't going to let them get away with it.

Chapter Sixteen

Imogene parked directly in front of room 105 at the Holiday Inn on G Street. She didn't intend on being there long. With a burning Marlboro on her lips, purse on her arm, she straightened her dress and knocked on the door.

No answer.

Dern it. Imogene forced herself not to look around and knocked again.

No answer.

She put her face up close to the door. "Ida? It's me, honey. Imogene, your neighbor. I need to talk with you. Please open the door?"

From inside the room came a muffled voice, scared and unsure. "Imogene, the avocado lady? That Imogene?"

"That's me. Come on, hon, open the door. I need to talk with you."

"I…I'm not supposed to open the door for anyone, or I'll get the strap."

The strap? Who in their right mind would strap a pretty little girl? Take me to him, E. I'll show him exactly how the cow eats the cabbage. You know me, I'll do it, too.

"Ida?"

"Yes."

"What's my name?"

"Imogene."

"Right, I'm not just anyone. I'm Imogene, your neighbor, so what your daddy told you doesn't hold true in this case."

The door rattled as Ida unlocked the knob then unhooked the chain. The door opened a crack. A cute little eye peeked out. The door opened wider, a smile filling her face. "I'm so glad you stopped by. I'm terribly lonely. Please come in."

Imogene entered. The room looked as if a herd of zebras had trampled through. The place was an absolute mess. Joyce's room used to have a similar appearance, minus the smell of soured milk.

Imogene's eyes fell to a spill on the cheap carpet, the source of the odor. "I…ah spilt."

"I can see that. Don't you worry about it, the hotel expects a certain amount of spillage." Imogene smiled, shoved some rumpled blankets and a sheet aside, and sat. Time ticked loudly in her head. Ida's dad could walk in at any moment. Imogene stuck her hand in her purse around the stock to the .380 in case he did. Acutely aware guns belong nowhere near a child.

"Did my dad send you here to keep me company?"

Imogene hesitated for the briefest moment, not wanting to lie to a child who had already been through too much, a pawn in a dangerous game. Separated from her mom, on some wild pretense as yet unrevealed, and made to stay alone in a scary hotel room. Her mother, back at the house, had to be in the dark on her daughter's whereabouts and would be far beyond worried and into full frantic. She, too, was fed the "missing girl" story.

The father oughta be flogged.

Candy wrappers, half-eaten chocolate cupcakes, bags of cookies, and three different kinds of the most popular sugar cereals seen in TV ads littered the two double-beds, floor and nightstands. Her suitcase lay open with clothes intermingled with the scattered food. An eight-year-old child-bomb had exploded.

"To tell you the truth, I heard that you were staying here and thought it quite awful. I thought us women need ta stick together. I came to take you to my house to stay with me for a few days. If that's acceptable to you?"

Her eyes lit up with excitement. "Really? Will you make that hot dog sandwich you talked about with the vanilla shake?"

Imogene made that promise two weeks earlier when she asked the girl to mow and trim her lawn on Sundays.

Just as quick the light in her eyes extinguished.

Imogene held out her hand. "Come here. What's the matter?"

The clock in her head continued to tick. Unrelenting. With each second, each minute the odds increased of being discovered.

Ida came over and took Imogene's hand.

"I can't leave."

"Is it because of your father?"

Her chin crinkled, and her eyes filled with tears.

"Oh, I should've said this right off. I stopped by and asked your dad. He said it was okay for you to come stay with me." The lie an ugliness black enough to shade the light in the room.

She jumped up. "Really?"

"Of course. Come on now, hurry. Get your things together. I'm hungry and can't wait to get something to eat my own self."

Ida jumped into action, moving like a little weasel looking for an on-the-loose, motherless kit. She opened her flowered suitcase and piled in clothes and cupcakes and opened bags of candy until the top wouldn't close.

Imogene had to smile at the child's innocence. She put the Marlboro in her lips, squinted from the smoke in her eyes, and pushed down while Ida zipped the suitcase closed. When Ida dragged it off the bed, it fell to the floor, almost too heavy for her to wield. They headed for the little red Gremlin.

Outside, Imogene's eyes immediately went to the driveway illuminated by the orangish sodium vapor lights, sure that any second the yellow Z car would zoom in. Catch them in the headlights, their eyes wide with fear.

They got in the car, started up, and headed out.

Once on G Street en route to Hawthorne Avenue, Imogene let out a long breath. Ida sat with her back to the passenger door, looking at Imogene. Darkness had fallen, snatching away the safety daylight afforded. The passing streetlights made Ida's face a kaleidoscope of black and white images; a 1930s silent film.

The fleeting, unprotected innocence of youth.

A lump rose in Imogene's throat. "Hey, kid, can you promise me something?"

Ida stared and only nodded.

"Promise me you'll never get on the back of a boy's Husqvarna motorcycle. No matter what he says, don't do it. Can you promise me that?"

Ida only stared. After a long pause, she said, "My dad didn't say it was okay for you to come get me, did he?"

Imogene flicked the finished Marlboro out the window. In the side mirror, the red cherry tip tumbled in the darkness and flickered out. Nowadays, that was how quick a young girl lost her youth. She looked over at Ida. "No, he didn't."

They drove a couple more blocks. "Do you have a problem with that?"

"Not if you don't lie to me and tell the truth." Something canned that her mother probably said in a continual mantra to battle future moral turpitude.

Ida was smart far beyond her age. Weird kinda smart. Teachers had said that about Joyce, said she could be the first woman astronaut.

"I'm good with that. Can you wait until we're back at the house, sitting at the table, eating hot dog sandwiches and drinking creamy vanilla shakes?"

"Of course." She finally smiled, turned in her seat, and rolled down the window. Closed her eyes. The warm Southern California air blew in, ruffling her golden, baby fine curls. Her skin smooth and unblemished under the passing streetlights.

How could a father—even a stepfather—exploit such an innocent girl? Use her as a pawn in a heinous bank heist that had already claimed one life?

* * *

Ten minutes later, Imogene opened the door and let Ida enter the house at 744 East Hawthorne Street. Ida set her suitcase down and used her foot to paw at the edge of the cut-out carpet squares that exposed hardwood floor underneath. "What happened here?"

"Thought I'd try to play some indoor hopscotch."

Ida froze.

"What?" Imogene asked.

"I thought the rules were you wouldn't lie."

"You're absolutely right. I'm sorry. I spilt some stuff that wouldn't come

152

out. I thought it unsightly, so…hmm, I just cut out the spots."

She giggled at the truth. "And you thought this would be better?"

"Yeah, big mistake. Right?"

"You're not kiddin'." She pointed up at the portrait above the TV. "Is that your daughter?"

"Yes."

"She's beautiful. Where does she live now?"

"Come in the kitchen. Sit at the table and talk to me while I fix us something to eat. My stomach's growling and about to start eating its way out. If that happens, it'll get real ugly fast. Ruin the rest of the carpet for sure."

Ida tilted her head, closed her eyes, and laughed. Imogene couldn't recall the last time she'd experienced such unbridled innocence directed at a world that lurked on evil's dark edge.

Imogene sliced the hot dogs in half and put them in the black iron skillet under the blue gas flame on the stove. She took her red Marlboro box into the living room, tossed them on the table. Not wanting to smoke while preparing food.

That would be rude.

Next, she got out the blender, the ice cream, and milk.

The dogs sizzled and popped. The heavenly aroma made Imogene's stomach stand on its hind legs and bark. She blended the ice cream with some milk, poured the first one in a tall, fat glass, and tapped some nutmeg on top. She set it in front of Ida, who grabbed it and brought it to her mouth.

Imogene stayed busy preparing the bread slices with mayonnaise and mustard.

"What's this brown stuff on top of the milkshake, it's really good."

She looked over. "Top secret. Special ingredient."

Ida smiled, used the long-handled spoon, and dug out another creamy glob.

Imogene set the hot dog sandwich in front of Ida. She picked it up with both hands, the thick sandwich almost too big for her to handle, and took a big bite.

She ate all that crap back at the room and she can still go for that piece a ugly cookin'?

"That's not ugly cookin'."

With a full mouth, Ida shook her head and spoke around the food. "No, this isn't ugly cookin'. It's good cookin.'"

"There, you see. Outta the mouths of babes."

"I'm not a babe. I'm seven years old."

"You're not eight? I thought you were eight?"

"Nope. Not till December twentieth. I kinda got cheated a little. My birthday is too close to Christmas, so I don't get as many presents as I would if it were, say, in June. That's what Maggie down the street said."

Imogene took a Schlitz malt liquor from the fridge and sat down across the table from her guest. A plate with her own hot dog sandwich in front of her. For only a moment, she wrestled with the idea of drinking a beer in front of the child. But thought Ida had already dealt with much worse in her young life.

A beer with a hot dog sandwich, the only way to go. That was livin' high on the hog.

"You're not gonna have a milkshake?"

"Folks my age aren't allowed to have a milkshake after five at night. The milkshake police would be all over us. Like that." Imogene snapped her fingers.

Ida nodded, smiled, accepting the little fib as a truth. "We don't want that, now do we? Dern milkshake police.

"Ida, what did your dad tell you as to why he put you up in the hotel room?"

She broke eye contact and looked at the sandwich like it was the most important thing in the world. "He said…he said that some very bad men were after me and it was safer if I lived in the hotel for two days until it's all over."

Maybe her stepfather wasn't so bad after all.

"Until what's over?"

Ida shrugged and spooned another glob of thick vanilla milkshake in her mouth. She looked up at Imogene. "If my dad really didn't say it was okay to go with you, why am I here? What's going on?"

"We still telling each other the truth?"

She stopped the spoon with another load en route to her mouth. She nodded, this time with a bit of trepidation.

"I think your stepdad is involved in a crime and that it's better for you to stay with me until after the Fourth."

Tears suddenly welled in her eyes. "Am I gonna miss the parade and the picnic?"

"Yes. I'm sorry. There's just no way to get you there and keep you safe with all that's going on."

She nodded. A fat tear brimmed and rolled down her cheek. She picked up the sandwich and took a bite. A small one this time, one used as cover for heated emotions. She spoke around the bite.

That tear liked to rip Imogene's heart out.

"What's going to happen at the parade?"

She didn't want to bring a small child into the robbery conspiracy where one person was already dead. But she had promised not to lie.

"There's gonna be a bank robbery."

She didn't freeze or react at all. She took another bite, this time a larger one. "A bank robbery at a parade?"

"It's complicated."

"Is my dad robbing the bank?"

"I don't know. If I had to guess, I'd say no. But I do think he's somehow involved."

She nodded again and kept chewing, her eyes defused, her mind munching on this new information.

Imogene lost her appetite after revealing such candid, ugly information to a child. She took a bite of the sandwich anyway. And another after her taste buds kicked in and flooded her mouth with saliva. Her stomach growled like an alley cat on the prowl, demanding more.

"Has your dad been acting…odd lately?"

She nodded. "He's mean all the time now. He was never mean before. Gets angry at the least little thing. He was always so nice."

Buttload of stress, robbin' a bank. I'd be surprised if he didn't have himself a peptic ulcer the size of Road Island.

There wasn't any way to tell that Ange had said "Road" instead of "Rhode." Imogene just saw the word that way up on the big screen in her mind. Same with "peptic." Ange didn't keep words like that loose in her back pocket. Those kinds of clues shook Imogene to the core. Made her think about how she stood on the razor edge of insanity. About to fall off into the dark abyss.

Imogene came out of her trance to find Ida standing in front of her, looking into Imogene's eyes. She held the big milkshake glass with both hands and sported a white mustache of ice cream. "You okay? I was talking to you, but you went somewhere. Like maybe to another planet. That's what mom says when I'm watching the boob tube. That's what she calls it. She says I just zone out and go someplace else."

E, ask her if her planet's in the shadow of Pluto. Go on, ask her. I wanna see her reaction. Hey, maybe she's really Thelma's kid and no one knows it. Huh? Has to be. I know it's true. Whatta think? Am I right? Tell me I'm right.

"You're way off the mark."

"About what?"

"Not you."

"Hmm. Are you crazy? Some of the kids say you're Lizzy Borden's great, great grandma, and that you have a hole in your floor where you bury kids underneath the house."

The carpet. That's why she froze and toed the exposed hardwood floor. Looking for a trapdoor.

"If that's the case, why aren't you scared?"

She shrugged and yawned. Set the milkshake glass on the table half empty. "Don't know. I probably should be I guess. I think you're too nice to be a killer. I'm tired. Is it okay if I go to bed now?"

Imogene couldn't help it and laughed a little. "Sure, hon. Come on, I'll show you to your bed."

The kid had grit.

She followed Imogene into Wayne's bedroom. No one had slept there for the last twelve years. Not since before Imogene accidentally mistook him for an intruder and shot him in the head. Her life had never been the same after that. Fate took an ugly hand, sent her down a path in an entirely different universe, one parallel to the world where she used to live.

Imogene pulled the sheet and blanket back. "Here you go. Don't sleep in your clothes and try not to mess up the room too much."

Ida set her suitcase down that she'd picked up going through the living room. She kicked off her white sandals, pulled her dress off over her head, and climbed up on the bed.

Imogene tucked her in and wanted in the worst way to kiss her on the forehead. But under the circumstances, that would've been improper. Right?

For a moment, she stood there and stared down at her.

Ida had closed her eyes and opened them to half-mast as the sandman took hold of her ankle and tried to tug her down into slumber's safe haven. "Imogene?"

"Yeah, Sweetie?"

"You don't have any axes, do you?"

"Fifteen or twenty out in the garage. I keep 'em honed to a sharp edge in case I talk a silly little girl into coming to stay with me. Why?"

"Thought it would be something like that." Her words trailed off as her eyes closed the rest of the way. She hadn't even registered what Imogene had said.

"Good night, Ida." She leaned down and kissed her forehead. Did it anyway.

Ida's arm snaked out from underneath the blankets, encircled Imogene's neck, and pulled her down into a hug. A good, strong one.

Imogene wanted to stay there forever.

A lump the size of Road Island rose in her throat as she fought back an audible sob.

She stayed bent over until the pain in her back threatened to take her to her knees. She eased the door partially closed and retreated to the divan where she smoked a couple of Marlboros, dozed off and on, dreaming of when Joyce was Ida's age.

The happiest Imogene had been in twelve years.

Chapter Seventeen

Nine o'clock the next morning, Imogene sat in the Gremlin in the driveway with Ida in the passenger seat. Imogene didn't know what to do with Ida. A seven-year-old couldn't be left at the house alone. Imogene couldn't take her to the pawn shop, not with all that was going on. And on top of all else, Ida was officially a missing person.

In recent memory, Imogene had never been so torn. If given the option, she'd stay home with Ida, close the curtains, bar the doors, and let the world continue to spin. Let time fix the unfixable at the bank and pawn shop.

But to ignore those issues would only make things worse. The cops, The Boss and his thug-uglies, and even the puppet masters would come looking for her and place Ida in even greater jeopardy.

Imogene stayed up half the night working the problem, trying to suss it out. Did it without Ange. She was off galivanting somewhere. No help at all, the selfish witch.

The whole untenable situation came down to a game of chess. If Imogene moved her Queen, all the others would move their Rooks to head her off. Checkmate. She had to think two or three moves ahead of the other players. Only she didn't have enough information. Tomorrow was the Fourth, the picnic and parade. Imogene only needed to wait thirty hours, and whatever was gonna happen would be over.

Yeah. She'd be back in the joint if she didn't make a move. The right move. It'd take three or four right moves to extricate herself and her friends.

Ida was reported missing as far as the cops were concerned. If she suddenly reappeared, she couldn't just disappear again. The cops would ask too many questions of her stepfather. If her stepfather made Ida disappear again, it would put him in a serious crack.

Imogene made up her mind about what to do.

Until she realized one component she had not considered.

What if Ida's stepfather wasn't hiding her in the hotel as a lever? A lever to get Luke Short, Ida's mother's brother, to break into the safe at The Bank of the West? The bank across the street from the pawn shop. What if the stepfather was nothing more than a puppet like the rest of them, and the real puppet masters had threatened the stepfather with harming Ida?

How deep did the conspiracy go? A bottomless sinkhole that dropped out from under everyone's feet.

How could she drop Ida off at her mom's if that placed Ida in more danger?

Round and round she went.

Imogene started the Gremlin. "Change of plan. You're going to hang with me today. What do you think about that?"

Ida smiled, one that warmed Imogene's heart. For a fleeting second, she thought of what it would be like to keep Ida as her own. As a daughter. Well, a granddaughter. Just take off, abscond from parole, leave the state, and start over. She'd done it before. She had the money, the check from the publisher for *Peekaboo POTUS*. The one in the glove box. She needed to deposit that check. Those funds would give her that much more wiggle room if she did have to take it on the lam.

But that thought was terribly selfish. She couldn't deprive Ida of her mother.

Imogene forgot all about Ida's mother, her feelings. The crushed emotions over her sweet daughter gone missing without a trace. Imogene would've been devastated if it had happened to Joyce.

"Aw heck, Little Girl, I gotta take you home."

But how would Imogene do that without triggering a police response that would drag parole into it?

"No, thank you, I want to stay with you today. I don't wanna go home."

Again, Imogene was torn. What to do.

"Okay, how about breakfast? Then we'll decide. Pancakes with strawberries always makes things a little brighter, don't they?"

"I'll take waffles with whipped cream, please."

Imogene started the Gremlin and backed out. "For a little squirt, you sure know your mind."

"I'm not a little squirt, I'm eight. Well, almost eight."

"Yes, you are. And going on eleven."

Ten minutes later, they pulled into the rear parking lot of The Iron Skillet that sat across the street from the pawn shop. They took a booth next to the window to take in the happenings of her cohorts.

City employees moved in slow motion, still setting up the parade route, picnic tables, banners, and blocking off the parking spots on Euclid. Hourly employees with no incentive to "kick it in gear and get after it." The parade route went a mile up Euclid.

Through the long front window of the pawn shop, Suz, Luke Short, and Thelma again stood at the counter helping a throng of customers. All her friends, mindless of what was in store for them. They had no idea the mob and the cops had been brought into the fray.

What an absolute mess.

Two more people entered the pawn shop while she watched.

That business was a goldmine.

The waffle came piled high with whipped cream, and Ida dug in. Imogene slid from the booth and headed to the Ladies. In the hall that led to the restroom, she picked up the thick phone book attached with a chain to the pay phone on the wall. Imogene found Ida's home number, dropped a dime, and dialed.

A harried woman answered. "Yes? Who is this?"

"You don't know me, and I won't give you my name. I—"

"Why? Who are you? What do you want? Do you have my daughter? Do you know where she is?"

"Calm down. I called to tell you, your daughter's fine. She—"

"Where is she? Who is this? Tell me. Where's my daughter? Where's Ida?"

"Listen to me or I'll hang up. I'll bring Ida home tomorrow after the parade. She's fine. Nothing's happened to her. She's in good hands."

Imogene imagined the frantic mom clutching the phone, tears streaking her face as she paced the distance of the phone cord allowed.

Imogene was again torn. Torn right down the middle.

The poor woman. Imogene only prolonged her distress. How would Imogene handle a similar phone call if this had happened to Joyce?

"Please. Please bring her back. I'll give you anything."

Don't let this broad cloud your thinking. Ask her. Ask her while you got her on the phone. She said she'll do anything. Go on, ask her. She'll give up all the answers. The reasons why. She knows. She has to be in on it.

Imogene put her hand over the receiver and spoke to Ange. "Oh, now you choose to show up. Where were you last night when I needed you?" She took her hand off the receiver. "This is going to sound like a crazy question."

The woman's tone shifted as if she ground her teeth when she spoke, anger taking hold. "Ask. Go ahead and ask. I'll tell you anything you wanna know. Just give…me…my…daughter back. You…you freaking witch."

Imogene gripped the phone till her knuckles turned white, her breath coming fast. A witch? Nobody called her a witch. Especially when she was doing a good deed.

"For your information. I was the one who *rescued* your daughter. She was… she was caught up in some heinous crapola. And I saved her."

"What?"

"That's right, now call me a freakin' witch again." Imogene hung up the phone.

She stood there and seethed. Her body shook like a diabetic in need of orange juice fortified with sugar.

Why did the simple name-calling get her goat? Somehow, she'd shed her prison skin.

She dropped another dime into the pay phone and dialed the number.

"Hello." Ida's mom said, "I'm so sorry. I didn't mean to call you that. Can I talk to my daughter? Please, can I talk to Ida?"

"What does your husband do for a living?"

"We have money if that's what you're asking. We can pay. How much. How much do you want?"

"I don't want your money. I only stepped in because I care about Ida. She's fine. She's safe. She's scarfing down waffles as we speak. Please answer the question."

Her voice caught as she took a deep breath. "Thank you. She loves waffles. And with whipped cream. She has to have them with whipped cream."

"The question?"

"Oh...ah. He works for a large corporation. A big conglomerate that acquires real estate for large commercial projects."

Her words came out canned like something she spit out to friends and family when they asked about her husband's monotonous employment description.

"Is this corporation local?"

Imogene wasn't even sure why she asked that question. Things just weren't making sense. The more information, the better chance of solving the puzzle. Find out who was behind it all and tell JB, let the cops deal with it.

Ida's stepfather being a puppet master no longer made any sense.

"No. It's based in China. His company puts together the deal, builds out the commercial project, sells it, then moves on to the next one."

Through the restaurant, over the top of the patrons, out the long window, and across the street, a black and white police car pulled up and stopped in the same place as before. Parked in between two road maintenance signs that indicated Euclid was closed for tomorrow's parade. The tall captain with red hair and mustache got out and sauntered, bold and brassy, into the Joseph Columbus for Mayor storefront campaign office. An office two doors down from the pawn shop—the jewelry store sandwiched in between.

She could only hope the puppet masters considered in their plans the captain's capricious visits right across the street from the bank. Then she remembered that the cops now knew about the bank robbery. So what did it matter? They would stake it out tomorrow. Maybe even sooner. She needed to get some names to feed JB or he'd shut the whole thing down before it got started and throw her hips back in the joint.

Ida's mother asked in a conspiratorial whisper. "What's your name?"

Imogene hesitated. "I can't—"

"Why did you ask about my husband?"

"What's his name?"

"Donald Ho. Why did you ask about him?"

"You don't have to believe me, but your husband was the one who took your daughter. He put her up in a hotel room. That's where I found her."

After that revelation, Imogene expected a huge intake of breath. Instead, there came a long pause. An epic silence.

"I do believe you. And I'm glad you rescued my daughter. Thank you."

It's a trap, E. The cops are at the house with her listening in. They're whispering in her ear, telling her what to say. Don't you dare fall for it. I'm tellin' ya true. They only need ta keep you on the phone for ten to fifteen minutes. That's what it takes ta get the tap. Hang up and run. Run for your life, E.

This time, Ange made a lot of sense.

Hang up, they're tracin' the call. She's jus' keepin' ya on the phone. The Flyin' Hat Squad's gonna come stormin' inta this place any second. They're gonna stick a big ol' gauge up where the sun don't shine and yell at ya ta GET DOWN. GET DOWN.

"You don't have ta yell. I'm standin' right here."

"What?" Ida's mom asked over the phone.

Imogene asked. "Why did you say you believed me? Are you just agreeing with anything I say, so I'll give your daughter back?"

"My husband's been acting strange. And…and when Ida went missing, I…well, I just didn't think he cared enough about it. He seemed almost stoic. Like an automaton devoid of emotion. Now you tell me he put her up in a hotel. It makes perfect sense that he's somehow involved in something. Please tell me where you are. Let me come get my daughter."

"The Iron Skillet on Euclid just south of D Street."

"Thank you. Thank you so very much. I'll be there in less than ten minutes. Wait for me. Please wait for me."

Click.

Now you gone an' dun it. That big ol' Flyin' Hat squad will come swingin' in like gangbusters ta take down your big ol' clown ass. You'll be back here with me in C-block 'fore dinner. We're havin' rubber pork chops and canned apple sauce tonight. Your favorite. See ya here, chickee-baby.

Imogene returned to the table, sat, and watched Ida finish her waffles. The little girl could really put away the food. Had to be in a growth spurt.

Imogene watched out the restaurant window and waited to see what would happen. She placed a major bet on humanity and prayed it wouldn't come up snake eyes.

Chapter Eighteen

An hour later, Imogene drove down the back alley, parked, and turned off the Gremlin. She sat and stared straight ahead at the rear of the businesses: the pawn shop, the jewelry store, and the big red, white, and blue banner above the back entrance to the campaign headquarters, Joe Co for Mayor Nov. 1974. The doors all along the back of the complex sported black wrought iron security gates. Thick. Heavy. Foreboding. All had little white and red signs tacked to the wall announcing the premises were protected by *Double A Security Systems.*

Ange guffawed. *You'd think they could afford Triple A, huh, E. Get it, Triple A?*

She smoked a Marlboro and tried to relax. Her nerves on edge, handing out body chitters like Halloween candy.

Ima, Ida's mom, turned out to be a great lady. Imogene trusted her and hoped it was reciprocal. Ima agreed to take Ida home, pack a few things, and get out of town for two days. Take the Greyhound to their uncle Herman's in Barstow.

Not even for a full two days. It would only take thirty hours more and it'd be all over.

No. Now twenty-seven hours. Ten in the morning until the following day, one in the afternoon. When the bank closed. Sure, twenty-seven hours? After ten years in the joint she could do that kinda time standin' on her head.

You're a fool, E. I tolt ya. Ya cain't trust no one but yourself. I tolt ya and tolt ya. That smelly-assed woman's gonna go to the cops as soon as she feels the danger's over and you ain't watchin' her. Sure as God made little green apples she's goin' ta the cops.

"That woman wasn't smelly."

That's what you took from that. Girl, you're headed for a fall. A gargantuan fall, you don't pull that head outta your patooty and start payin' attention ta me.

Ange, while in CIW, never used words like "gargantuan." Nor "patooty." She tended toward the vulgar and instead of patooty she'd have gone right to "ass," or worse. In the two years out on parole, Imogene had tried to scrub those vulgarities from her vocabulary. She would have to accept that Ange was gradually receding into memory, soon to disappear altogether.

She started her car, backed up, drove down the long, long alley until it dumped out on Holt Boulevard, where she made a right. She caught the green signal, traversed the biggest intersection in the city of West Valley, crossing Euclid, and made another right into the alley on the west side. She drove north and parked behind The Bank of the West, took the check from the glovebox, and went inside. This wasn't her branch, but she needed more information. Information was king. She needed to see inside this bank, be able to visualize it. Get a feel for it. Imagine how it would go down the next day.

And also deposit the check.

The bank didn't hold back on the air conditioning. It instantly dried the sweat beaded on her forehead and made her shiver from sweat-soaked hair that rested on her nape.

She scanned the interior. Ten teller windows, eight of them open, servicing twenty or twenty-five customers. Banks were always busier at the first of every month.

Out on the floor, eight desks with prim and proper employees helped other customers with banking needs. A single security guard, a white-haired old man with a widow-maker holster, one that held an antique .38, stood over by the Euclid Street entrance. Someone, if the need arose, Imogene could strongarm and take away his gun.

On the other side of the teller counter, the wall housed the humongous safe. One large enough to drive the Gremlin into. The thick round door was open and off to the side a stainless-steel gate barred entrance. That vault door, two feet thick, looked intimidating. Made it impossible to imagine the timid Luke Short could overcome something so formidable to get to the money inside. They would have to hit the bank before that safe door clanged shut. But that precision-made door wouldn't clang, would not so much as whisper.

At the customer self-service desk, she filled out the deposit slip for one hundred and fifty thousand, the first installment from the publisher for *Peekaboo POTUS*. One-fifty upon acceptance of the manuscript, one-fifty when the content edits were turned in, and two hundred when the book hit the shelves. More money than she'd ever seen in her life.

But it did her no good at all if Humphries tossed her butt back into C-block.

E, did you ever try that money trap I thought up? Huh? You open a new account with a bank that doesn't know ya. Once you do, they give you a temporary checkbook without your name on it until your regular checks come in the mail. Before you walk outta the bank, you tear out your deposit slips in the back of the temp, the ones with just your new account number on 'em, and mix 'em in with the deposit slips on the customer service desk. Then, when regular folks come in to make their deposit, they inadvertently grab one of yours, and voila, instant money trap. Whatta think, E. You think it'd work?

Imogene looked down at the deposit slip she'd just picked up from the customer service desk. Dern you, Ange. There wasn't any way to tell if it was a money-trap slip that someone else left behind. She whispered under her breath, "Thanks for nothin', friend."

Ange had said "voila" and "inadvertently." More evidence of Imogene's best friend fading, disappearing forever. The thought caused a lump to rise in her throat. She dearly loved Ange.

Maybe Imogene would visit a shrink with some of that hundred and fifty K, ask if there was something that could be done to keep Ange around.

She got in one of the four lines waiting for a teller, her mind working on the most important problem at hand: how to slip out from under the puppet masters, the mob, and the cops all at the same time. The problem beyond insurmountable. She had hoped a solution would present itself by now, but that wasn't happening. Instead, the knot around her neck tightened a little more with each passing hour. Her eyes took in the entire place, casing the joint.

She identified the cologne a half-second before he appeared next to her in line and bumped his shoulder into hers.

JB.

Of course, he'd stake out the bank the day before.

He snatched the check and deposit slip from her hand. He looked at the check. His mouth sagged open in shock. He grabbed her under the arm and jerked her out of the line. He quick-walked her out the back door, her feet having a difficult time keeping up. His fingers digging into her arm, sure to leave bruises the following day. Abusive flatfoot.

And yet all she could think about was the .380 in the purse that hung from her arm. A big fat parole violation. Humphries, her parole officer who was also wrapped up in the conspiracy, would violate her parole in a hot second.

JB yanked open the back door to the Iron Skillet and tugged her inside.

Not ten minutes earlier, Imogene had left Ida in her mother's care sitting in the booth next to the front window. Mom hugging and crying. Imogene could only hope they finished breakfast and already left for the Greyhound and Uncle Herman in Barstow.

He guided her to the only booth open on the south wall and gave a little shove. She flopped down. No way to treat an old woman. She slid around to a spot where JB couldn't see if the two girls were still there in the same booth by the window. She tried not to look for fear JB would catch her gaze. But not looking is like not thinking about a pink rhino when told not to think about a pink rhino. Her eyes, all on their own, stole a quick glance.

Ima still sat next to Ida, who talked nonstop, eating a second plate of waffles and whipped cream. Imogene had left a twenty on the table. Enough for six plates of waffles.

From Ima's surprised expression, Ima had spotted Imogene and JB coming in through the back. Earlier, they had agreed not to tell the police anything until after the Fourth. Imogene had also promised, if at all possible, to protect her husband, Donald, from committing a crime. She still loved him, but stashing Ida in a hotel and not saying anything about it caused a severe rift in their relationship.

She'd get over it, but would need some time. Something of similar severity had happened with Wayne. Time, the potion that healed all emotional trials and tribulations. Well, most all.

Poor little Ida had been involved. Used as a pawn.

On second thought, forget giving the relationship some time, she'd chunk him up-side the head with the black kitchen skillet and kick him in the butt all the way out the front door.

JB slapped the *Peekaboo POTUS* check down on the table. "What the hell is this?"

"It says right there. It's from the publisher Delacorte. You interviewed John Catskill not two weeks ago. The check's in my name, for crying out loud. Aren't you supposed to be a detective?"

"Don't push me, Taylor. I'm this close to grappling you up and turning you over to your parole agent."

"Huh?" He was the Puppet Master, what would he think of that?

"What's the 'Huh' for?"

"Humphries is a part of this whole mess."

JB sat back in the booth, stunned. "A parole agent's going to rob the bank?"

The same waitress, Marla, wearing a tan and brown uniform who served Imogene earlier, came over with a pad in hand. "You're back. Can't get enough of our home-style cookin', huh?"

JB waved her off. He wanted to continue the interrogation, and based on his demeanor and expression, it had not gone the way he expected. Not in the least.

Imogene said, "I'll have the Monte Cristo sandwich with the home fries and a chocolate malt. My boyfriend's buying."

JB scowled and said nothing, opting to let the order go so the woman would scat.

Off to the side, Ima and Ida slid out of the booth over by the window and surreptitiously tried to leave.

Marla stuck the yellow number 2 pencil behind her ear and started to walk away.

Imogene needed a distraction to keep JB busy. "Excuse me?"

Marla turned back.

"Do you have any nutmeg in the back you could sprinkle on the chocolate malt?"

"That does sound luscious. I'll ask the chef." She shot her a genuine smile.

Chef, my achin' ass. In this greasy spoon? You and me, we know better. The chef is the same dude who takes out the trash and mops the floor. The chef, hah. Ange cackled loud enough the entire restaurant should've stopped and looked over.

But they didn't.

Ima and Ida almost made it to the front door. But Ida stopped at the tall jaw-breaker dispenser with the colorful balls visible through the glass. "Mom, can I? Can I, please?"

Imogene watched JB's eyes. He looked up and dismissed the common mom and daughter contact, and looked back at Imogene.

A half-second later, "Hey?" He turned, pointed a thick index at Imogene. "Stay right there. Don't you move an inch." He slid out. Ima held Ida's hand, gently tugging her along to the front door.

"Hey? Hey. Hold it right there, you two."

Ima and Ida froze. He hurried over.

JB talked animatedly while waving his hands for emphasis. Angry. Imogene didn't blame him; the situation did look bad. Real bad in fact.

Ima could only nod and hold onto Ida's hand, her face a rictus of fear. He pointed over at Imogene, still talking, the restaurant's ambient noise too loud for her to hear. Ida's expression turned angry. She kicked JB's leg. He jumped and grabbed his shin, scooching backward.

Imogene took the cigarettes out of her purse, bumped out a Marlboro, and lit up. Her hands shook from fear, nicotine, and an empty stomach.

"Hun?" Marla appeared. "You're sitting in the 'no smoking' area. You'll have to move to the counter or over by that wall. See where all those others are smoking?"

No smoking area? What's this world comin' to, huh, E? Pretty soon the good people who smoke won't be allowed inside atall. That'll be a world I won't live ta see. Bet on it. Huh, E? Tell me that ain't the livin' truth.

Imogene waved Marla off, ignored Ange, and continued to stare at the massive screw-up unfolding over by the front door. She puff, puff, puffed that Marlboro, burning it twice the usual speed. White segmented clouds rose like desperate smoke signals to no one at all.

"Hon?"

She shifted her gaze and glared at Marla. Marla harrumphed and moved on.

JB had put two and two together and got five. Imogene's random drop-by on Bonnie Brae when Ida was reported missing, and now finding Imogene at the same restaurant when Ida was officially recovered. It looked bad by anyone's way of thinking.

He got behind Ima and ushered them both over to the booth. "Slide in."

Ida again kicked him in the shin. He hopped backward out of range. "I said stop that."

"You leave Imogene alone. She's my friend." She looked at Imogene. "I didn't tell him about the twenty sharpened axes in your—" Her hand flew up to her mouth.

JB nudged the two girls into the booth. Imogene said nothing and puff, puff, puffed her Marlboro. The white cloud of smoke floated to the ceiling, smoothing out in an even fog bank.

JB sat at the booth edge, trapping Ima and Ida between him and Imogene. "What's going on, Taylor? How are you involved in this missing child incident? I knew there was something to you just dropping by on Bonnie Brae. This somehow related to the—" He caught himself. He didn't want to give away the bank job if Ida and her mom weren't involved. "—ain't it?"

Marla returned with the Monte Cristo sandwich on a platter with a slew of home fries and set it in front of Imogene, along with the chocolate malt sans nutmeg. Imogene held the Marlboro in one hand and with the other picked up the one side of sandwich and took a bite. She needed time to think. The sandwich, the only available diversion.

"Taylor, you really know how to push my buttons. Answer me. Don't play your silly games."

Ida scooted close to the table, picked up the catsup bottle, and poured some on one end of the platter. She dipped a home fry and ate it.

Ima said, "Ida, that's rude. It's poor manners."

Imogene said. "These two got nothin' to do with what's going on. Let 'em go, and I'll finish telling you about the parole agent thing. If you continue to harass my two friends, I won't say another word. You can figure it out on your own."

Ima watched Imogene, then shifted to JB.

He again pointed his finger. "You don't get to run your game on me. This is my operation."

She stared at him and took another bite, the Monte Cristo savory and luscious.

He held her gaze a moment longer and took out a spiral pocket notepad. Opened it and held his pen ready. "For the report," he said to Ima, "where did you find her?"

Ida put another home fry in her mouth. "For the report?" she said, "I'm sitting right here."

Imogene smiled. Before Ima could answer, Imogene said, "Ida spent the night at a friend's house. There was a miscommunication. That's all. Don't make a federal case out of it."

"What's the friend's name and address?"

This time, Ida spoke before Imogene could work up the second half of the poorly formulated lie.

"I stayed over at my friend Imogene's house at 744 East Hawthorne, so there."

JB's jaw locked as he ground his teeth in frustration. He stood. "You two get out of here. I'll be talking to you later."

Ida and Ima fled.

At the front door, Ida tugged on Ima's hand as they passed the jawbreaker machine. Ima pulled Ida along and out the door.

Imogene took a sip of chocolate malt. Her nerves settled in. She decided on the tale to be told. One lie begets another lie until the entire fabric becomes one big sham. JB was too smart to eat a sham of that proportion.

"Talk, Taylor, and I better like what I hear."

"Like I said, there's a parole component to this thing, and I'm not sure how it all fits. Tomorrow, when you scoop everyone up at the bank, hopefully, it'll become clear." As long as he didn't scoop up her along with Suz and Luke. She hadn't yet figured out how to keep that from happening.

"No, I'm not gonna swallow that woof-cookie. You tell me right now how this Humphries is involved."

Imogene nodded, her mind traveling a hundred miles an hour.

Woof-cookie? Haven't heard that one in a month of Sundays. Toss him one anyway. Tell him...no...put it all off on the mob like you did before. The Boss and his thugs will be at the bank tomorrow to scoop up the bank robbers, the robbers you made up. They plan to torture and kill 'em for daring to hit a mob bank. Lay it all off on them. There. Now you owe me big.

"Okay, look. The mob's orchestrating this robbery, but they're not directly involved. They're...they're the puppet masters. These crooks are blackmailing everyone involved, making *them* rob the bank."

JB sat back and stared at her, working this new piece to the puzzle to see if he would accept it as true.

Imogene continued on. "Humphries is the parole connection. There are two other parolees involved who are on his caseload. They're told if they don't help, they'll be sent back to the Q to serve out the rest of their terms. That's a lot of years. A lot of leverage."

"Two *others*? Are you saying you're one of these parolees?"

She ignored his question. "One of them is a guy named Luke Short."

JB started to write the name in his notebook. "Hey, that's the name of a famous western writer."

"You can read?"

He didn't flip his lid. Instead, he let a creepy little grin slither out. One that scared the heck outta Imogene.

Imogene said, "Okay, look, Humphries...or...or whoever these puppet masters are, give out monikers, so no one knows anyone. They can't identify anyone or track anyone back to these organizers. This whole thing is ingenious, and once you bust it wide open, you'll find it's gone on before. They're gonna make you a captain outta this. You wait and see if they don't."

That shouldn't have worked, but it did. He stared at her as his mind absorbed this new information.

Imogene doubled down. "Don't shoot yourself in the foot, making something outta me being in the bank a little while ago. Or with my friend Ida and Ima, being in a restaurant right next to the bank. It's just a coincidence. And not really even a coincidence, this is a small town, remember. Do yourself a favor, wait till it all plays out tomorrow. You'll see. And look at it this way, you can always come back on me. I'm not going anywhere."

She took a ten out of her coin purse and set it under the platter edge. He watched her every move. She reached over, took the *Peekaboo POTUS* check from his shirt pocket. She slid out of the booth, picked up the other half of the Monte Cristo. "Now I have to deposit this in the bank before some nefarious person waylays me. Lord knows the cops won't protect me."

"Imogene, I'd feel sorry for the poor slob who tries to put the arm on you."

Chapter Nineteen

Twenty minutes later, after making the deposit, she drove around the back alley and parked behind the pawn shop. Stood at the back door knocking until her knuckle ached, the skin red. Angry. She finally scanned the ground. Bent over, back cracking, and grabbed an empty Thunderbird bottle with thick green glass. The favored brand choice of the disenfranchised street folk addicted to the fortified wine. She banged hard on the metal frame to the barred gate just short of breaking the bottle.

Until Luke Short peeked out.

He opened the heavy door all the way.

She took hold of his corduroy cowboy vest and yanked him outside, not wanting to deal with Thelma. The gray-white locks at his nape fluttered.

She'd had enough crazy for one morning and had to get some answers. "You been over to the bank yet to check it out?"

"You gotta do something," he said. "We can't go through with this. I can't go back to the Q. I just cain't. I think I'm jus' gonna run for it."

His emotions rose and fell like a rollercoaster on the Long Beach Pike.

Imogene empathized with him, she didn't wanna go back to that small, smelly cage with walls that never stopped closing in. An optical illusion that smothered and forced all the air from the cell. From her lungs.

That was the main motivation driving the whole mess, fear and loathing. The problem was they just couldn't sit on their hands. If they wanted out they would have to make it happen.

"Don't be a fool. You can't outrun a warrant put in NCIC. That's a nationwide system. And more important you can't outrun—"

She almost said, "the mob." But Luke didn't know about the mob's involvement nor the cops who, a day early, were at that very moment set up all the around the bank. Waiting. Guns loaded. Trigger fingers itching for a gunsel to come into range ta blast heck out of him.

Imogene smiled as the solution abruptly popped into her head. The mob and the cops watching the same location. A financial institution. That was tantamount to lighting a match while gassing up your car. One little spark and Sayonara, baby. Turn the lights off on your way out.

Now she just needed the spark, that catalyst to make it work. To get the two frogs to jump at the same time. But there wasn't any scenario that didn't involve Imogene and Luke going over to the bank to light it all off.

Luke re-engaged her with his eyes, almost as if he grew a spine. "Something's not right, and you know it. You spotted it yesterday. I'm a yegg, not a gun thug. I don't rob banks. I burglarize them. There's a distinct difference. If they brought me in to peel a safe, it's not gonna happen over there. I'm telling ya right now. That bank has to have nothing short of a beast, a huge Mosler 9000 or better."

"I just came from there. It's a Mosler model GM 12000. It's written in raised letters right over the top of the vault door as if they're proud of it."

"Ah, man. That's it then. We're through. They have every right to be proud of it. I've worked with the smaller boxes, never anything like that bad boy. No way. I can maybe take on a Mosler eight or nine hundred, even a T-1000. Maybe. But when you get up into the jumbo's...well, I don't have a clue how to even start getting into one of those babies. That's what makes this whole thing so crazy. And...and banks don't have that much money in them to begin with. Not for all this rigmarole, the hoops they're jumping through. For what? That bank'll only have enough to service the everyday transactions. The walk-ins and the businessmen."

Luke had turned pure professional, talking from experience, using larger words than usual as he thought out each important point. His country hick accent gone.

"How much will be in that vault?"

"I've heard the talk in the Q. Jus' the talk, 'cause I've never been in on that big of a job. On good days, a standard bank might have…might have anywhere from fifty to two hunnert thousand."

"That's it?"

Twenty minutes ago, when she stepped up to the teller's window to deposit the check from the book deal, the teller looked at the check, then up at Imogene like she had three heads. As if the teller had never seen a check for a hundred and fifty thousand dollars before. "Excuse me, I have to have my supervisor handle this transaction."

How embarrassing, standing there with everyone looking at her while she waited for the manager to come to the window.

Up walked a fussy little man in a three-piece black suit with gray pinstripes, a white shirt, and black bow tie. Working at a bank wasn't the same as attending a funeral for cripe's sake, but he apparently couldn't see the difference. He looked across the counter at her through coke-bottle glasses.

He reminded her of a favorite episode in The Twilight Zone where the clerk ate his lunch in the vault. One day, he came out after lunch, and everyone in the world was dead except him. He loved to read and stacked books on the library steps five feet tall. He named each stack after the month in which he'd read them. Then he tripped, broke those thick glasses, blinding him. A huge ironic death sentence.

This little man with one curl on the top of his near-bald pate said, "Ms. Taylor, may I please see two forms of identification?" Said it like she was some kind of criminal. The nerve.

She showed him her driver's license. "That's all I got. You wanna hold the check for five or six days, I'm okay with that. I got no use for the money right now."

She had a nice laminated card issued by state parole that she was by rule mandated to show any cop who contacted her.

Yeah, show the manager that, and he *would* call the cops on her.

"It'll be ten days and we will confirm with the bank of origin."

"Well, I hope you do."

Now she was glad the bank would get robbed the next day.

"You won't be able to draw on these funds until it clears."

"Look, little man. Did you check my account, my current balance?"

The clerk, standing by, showed him the index card she'd pulled from the file. Showed him the $20,000 balance. "Oh, I'm sorry, Mrs. Taylor. You understand how we can't be too careful nowadays. There are conmen and crooks everywhere we turn." He pasted on a fake smile reserved for special customers, one he must've practiced at home.

"Do I look like some kinda crook to you?"

"No. No, of course not."

"It's too late now. I'm considering taking my business to a place where a well-heeled patron is treated with respect."

"Ahhm." He cleared his throat, frustrated. "No need for that, we'll take care of you here." He turned to the teller. "Please flag Ms. Taylor's account as VIP."

"Yes, sir."

VIP, my achin' ass a hunnert and fifty should at least get you the toaster, or whatever they give to the folks for opening a new account. Markin' your file with VIP, tell this shyster to kiss your big white bottom and let's blow this pop stand.

"Please just credit my account and call me when the funds clear."

If she wanted to run, ten days later wouldn't do her any good.

* * *

Now standing in the back alley cowboy-convict Luke Short said, "Yeah, that's all. Two hunnert K at best. Not enough dough to justify this caper."

"But what if—"

She again caught herself before she said, "What if it's a mob-run bank?"

That question answered itself; hundreds of thousands, maybe even a cool million. Heck, the budget for the whole city of West Valley last year was *$633,915. 58.* For a whole dern city. This, according to The Daily Report. A million was huge money.

"What if it's what?" He asked.

"What if they want us to go after the safety deposit boxes? Who knows what's in those, right? Unreported income, cash money, gems, gold bars, and the like."

"Now that would make more sense. It could also explain why they want you and Suz involved. That's a lot of work punchin' out all those safety locks. Yeah. Yeah, that celebration parade would cause a big distraction for something like that." He shook his head. "But we still gotta get into the vault to get ta those boxes." His expression shifted, a gleam reentered his eyes, "Hey, speaking of Suz, does she have a beau?"

She gave him a friendly shove. "Don't even think about it, you dirty old man."

Scared half-outta his wits over the bank job, he could still think about man's prime directive, women.

He gave her a crooked little smile.

She said it again with more vehemence. "I'm tellin' you right now, don't even think about it."

"You gonna stand in the way if I give it the ol' Gene Autry try? You know, The Singin' Cowboy?"

"Suz can take care of herself. She'll be nice when she lets you down easy. As long as you don't try something lewd. You do try something like that she'll put a hurt on ya."

"So, you don't think she'll—"

Tired of the conversation, she pulled the door open and entered. She walked over and sat on the couch in the makeshift apartment. She lit a Marlboro, needing quiet time to think of a solution to the main problem: how to get the cops and the mob together. Then ignite 'em like a lit match to gasoline. Do it tomorrow during the parade. Do it before one o'clock when the bank job was due to go down. But most important, do it without the crew from the pawn shop—her friends—making the trek across the boulevard to rob that dern bank.

The mob, the cops, everyone involved across the street will be on edge. Throw guns inta the mix and all it'll take is…yeah…one of those big firecrackers. One strategically placed to set off the entire cataclysmic event.

Dangerous men shooting dangerous men.

Yeah, something like a cherry bomb. No, a cluster of cherry bombs. That just might do it.

Yep, kick it in gear and get 'er done, E. It's a good plan, but I won't put money on it. Odds are you're gonna take a lead pill. You play with fire you get your big butt shot off. Rules of the jungle, Babe. Rules of the jungle.

"I'm not gonna tell ya again, I don't have no big butt."

She thought on it a bit more. Naw. These weren't children. They're grown men on two different varsity teams.

Sworn enemies.

Even if it did work, the puppet masters still had to be dealt with. But if everything lights off and goes to guns, the puppet masters would logically just melt into the background. Go back where they came from, nobody the wiser. That's what made this caper so perfect for them. No skin in the game.

Luke Short had followed Imogene into the studio apartment section of the pawnshop. He took up a nice guitar with the pawn ticket hanging from the neck and strummed a song. Not half-bad for a faux singin' cowboy. He sat on the couch arm, his leg up on the coffee table, his black cowboy boot right there, not two feet away. The boot that carried the authentic Italian stiletto.

A ruckus rose from the customer area. Loud voices growing louder headed their way.

From the warehouse section, out popped four people. Suz and Thelma trailing The Boss, and of all people, Erv. Erv moved like he hadn't been shot in his leg while standing in Imogene's living room.

Ya gotta watch that Maury. That's The Boss's name by the way. He knew where to shoot Erv. All muscle no bone so as not to dee-bill-a-tate him. Keep him in the action. But also teach him a painful lesson. Maury's a dangerous son of a buck. E. You watch him with all three eyes, the two in the front and the one in the back. I'm not kiddin.'

Suz spoke over everyone else. "Oh, E, I didn't know you were here. I tried to keep them out front, but they insisted on talking with you. They walked right on back like they own the place. I told them you weren't here. You sure made a monkey's uncle out of me."

"That's all right, I'll talk to 'em. Please, go back ta the front and cover the counter. I'll be out shortly and tell ya what's going on."

"E?"

"Please, Suz."

Luke Short quit strumming when the flood of folks pushed into the small space. "I'll go with you, Suz." He shot her a sappy grin.

The dern fool.

His puppy love crush masked the danger right in front of him. Couldn't he see the type of men standing not three feet away?

Or maybe Luke was smarter than everyone thought. Maybe he did instantly recognize the situation and purposely played the fool. Appear nonthreatening in order to slink out.

Suz looked from Imogene to Luke. Her expression shifted from concern to someone greatly disturbed, someone who had just stepped in a warm pile of dog do. "Come on, Mom, let's go out front."

"No, I wanna stay here where all the action is. You don't know Imogene like I know her. Anything can happen." She looked at Imogene. "By the way, I caught a taxi cab home from A&W. Thank you very much, leaving me hanging. You gonna shoot one of these A-holes in the foot?"

"Mom. Now. I'm not going to ask nicely again."

"Humph, you didn't ask nicely that time. I'm not some slab of meat you can just order around. I'm the woman who sprang you from my loins."

Sprang? Really, E? The woman never ceases to amaze. Am I right? Did she "sprang" from that purple planet in the shadow of Pluto? Heh heh, heh. Ange's cackle added to the already heavy load on Imogene's nerves that threatened to spark and misfire. Shut her down altogether by turning her into a babbling idiot.

The Boss nodded. "Doll, you better take a walk, or I'll have my man *take* you for a walk. If you know what I mean?"

Imogene looked to Luke to see if he'd now stand up to the new threat, rise as a knight errant defending his fair maiden.

Luke's glare flashed for a second. Then he turned his eyes down. A subservient puppy bowing to the alpha dog in the room.

Indignant, Thelma jumped to her feet and advanced. Ready to go to war. "Try it, Buster Brown, and see where it gets ya. You don't know who you're talkin' to. Why I'm—"

Erv came between her and The Boss. Suz grabbed Thelma's wrist and jerked her along. "Mom. Mom. Come on."

That suddenly explained why Suz still stuck around even though Thelma had escaped from the puppet masters. Thelma refused to leave the pawn shop. She wanted to play the dangerous game, and Suz had to stay to look out for her mom.

Luke, Suz, and Thelma left the room, their footsteps receding to the front.

The Boss held up his hand and moved his fingers toward himself. "Now give. The names of who's movin' against us. Tomorrow's the day, and right now we got butkus. I'm thinkin' we got took and you just yanked our chain ta save your own skin."

"And you said you'd come into the pawn shop and act like any other customer. This isn't it. You barreling in here like some kinda thug."

He raised his voice. "I said no such thing. I'm not gonna tell ya again. Give or I'm gonna have Erv slap ya around. I don't care if you are an old broad."

Imogene remained silent, puffed, and glared at him, pushing him right to the edge of violence.

He left her no choice.

She started talking. She gave him a detailed description of JB and John Johnson.

The Boss looked over at Erv. "You got all that? You recognize either of them?"

"Yeah, I got it. And no. It could be anybody."

He looked back at Imogene. "Now tell me who they work for."

"How am I supposed to know? I was over at the bank today checking it out. I saw the first guy I described. He was casing the place."

The Boss rushed her, taking three quick steps. "He what? Today? Why didn't you tell me he was going to case it today? We coulda finished this thing before that big mess goes down ta-marra. With the parade and all. Thousands of people stickin' their noses in *my* business."

"How was I ta know he'd be there?"

Erv said, "Did you hear this guy you described? Did he say anything? Does he have an accent?"

"Hmm."

She couldn't think fast enough, her mind a blank slate.

New Jersey. Jus' tell 'em Jersey.

"Now that you mention it, he did sound…sound like—"

"What?" The Boss said.

"Jersey. I think he sounded like he was from Jersey."

Even under the direct threat of death, Imogene could not tell a Jersey accent from Boston, Scotland or for that matter anyone else from the big melting pot of the world, New York.

The Boss rushed over, stood close to Erv. Looked up into his face. "See, I tolt ya it was Tomasi's crew. They're makin' a move against us. I gotta call Vegas. They're gonna hit our bank. We need more help. More guns."

"We don't know that for sure. I think maybe we should jus' hold off. Don't you? Imogene said there's only two of 'em. We don't wanna look like a couple of chuckleheads."

"Whatta ya talkin' about?"

"We act like we're Chicken Little and yell the sky's fallen. Everyone rushes over here, and it's only two gunsels from Jersey. Think about it. They'll think we can't handle two." He held up two fingers.

"First off, you don't talk to me like I'm some kinda cannoli. Second, would you try a bank job like this with just two torpedoes? No. I'm callin'. Where's your phone?"

"Boss," Erv said, "it's not a good idea to call from here. We need a pay phone."

Imogene said. "There's one over in the Iron Skillet across the street. That's where I saw the first guy having breakfast. And then right after at the bank."

A partial truth. She'd just reversed the order. She realized that she'd turned The Boss into a gun, and her words pulled back the hammer. The sights aimed at poor ol' JB.

But that was JB's job to take risks. Right?

The Boss turned heel and headed out. Erv said, "Thanks, Imogene. You've helped us out a lot."

"Yeah, I may have just got someone killed."

Erv stopped, his back stiffened. He turned. He looked sad and shrugged. "The players in this game know the risks. Their poor choices are not for you to deal with. It's on them." He turned and hobbled out. He only put on a show, ate the pain when The Boss could see. Erv had more on the ball than his superior, who was far from superior. Maybe fate would swing Erv's way and leave The Boss' job open, needing to be filled.

Only fate was an evil temptress who never let the bones roll and pop up sevens.

Imogene waited until the Marlboro burned down. She got up, went to the phone, and called the number JB had given her. The one she'd memorized. On the other end of the line, the person who answered took down the detailed information; the physical descriptions, cars, and clothing of The Boss and Erv. Information to be passed on to JB and John Johnson.

If this was just a big game, she had to make the sides even. Level the playing field. Right?

She felt bad about giving up Erv. But JB had also started out nice and had flipped on her. Turned mean. Erv was cut from that same bolt of cloth. Wasn't he?

She lit another Marlboro, giving up all hope of keeping track of the cigarette count. After tomorrow, she'd restart the two-pack-a-day limit.

She told Suz she was leaving, that she needed to rest up for all of tomorrow's fireworks.

On Independence Day.

Chapter Twenty

The next morning, ten o'clock on the dot, Imogene parked the Gremlin at the back of the pawn shop. Before she left the previous evening, she took the store key from Luke. He didn't like it but didn't give any lip about why she didn't take Suz's key. Afraid it might tarnish his Singin' Cowboy image in front of a prospective girlfriend.

She walked right through to the front, stood, and stared out the long plate-glass window, the sun blindingly bright. Hundreds of folks already on the wide grass boulevard had set up their lawn chairs at the curb's edge, holding a spot for the parade. Others staked out their chosen picnic tables up and down the long, wide grass center, spreading red-and-white checked table cloths and napkins. Setting down casseroles, buckets of chicken, whole watermelons, and stacks of corn on the cob. Someone brought a battery-powered stereo, turned it up loud, playing show tunes. By their tables, others stuck in the grass narrow, wooden dowels with American and State flags, on this, the most patriotic day of the year. Young kids and dads threw footballs, baseballs, flung Frisbees, and little girls worked their hips slinging Hula Hoops.

Normal folks unaware of the doom and gloom headed their way later in the afternoon. A shootout that would originate right across that center boulevard at the innocuous Bank of the West.

The last two days in the run-up to that moment, she had not let herself think about how it would feel to leave the pawn shop, cross through all those nice folks. Cross the other half of the asphalt boulevard and enter the bank about to be closed for the holiday. What it would be like to chunk the security guard over the head and take his gun. Scare hell outta of all the other employees. Herd them into the back while Luke began to work on…on what?

How had life come to this? How could someone expect a woman like Imogene getting on in years to pull off a violent robbery? It just didn't make any sense.

Too much had been left to the unknown. Even if she wore a mask, it didn't matter. Without question, someone would recognize her.

Maybe Luke was right, taking it on the lam might've been the only sane thing to do.

The thought of pulling a gun on those nice people churned her stomach the same as eating a slew of bad oysters. It made her want to throw up. She puffed on the fifth cigarette of the day.

Jagged nerves kept her from eating breakfast. Her dresses fit looser just from the last two weeks' activities. Heck of a diet, murder, and mayhem. Gave M&Ms a whole different meaning.

She opened her purse and, for the fifth time that morning, checked on the six cherry bombs left over from the Fourth celebrated twelve years earlier, when Wayne was still alive. In that happier time, they closed off both ends of Hawthorne and put on their own block party. Everyone showed up, including Bernard Lowery, the neighbor/killer, now dead. Suz and her father, now deceased. Mrs. Weaver, whose testimony would later sink Imogene in court and precipitate a ten-year stint in Chino. And of course, Wayne, the love of her life.

Back then, Suz couldn't have been more than twelve or thirteen. Good times. Good memories.

And now all this mess.

At what age would that dern Mr. Fate, that son of a buck, go looking for another victim to harass? Allow Imogene to just live out her life sitting on the divan, staring out the front window. Doing nothing but watching the world pass while smoking her dern Marlboros?

Her mind skittered back to the present, to the problem at hand. Do cherry bombs fade in their potency? Do they eventually turn into duds? Twelve years is a long time.

A big box Dentco truck rumbled up in front of the pawn shop. Luke jumped out and moved the "no parking" barricades. Suz, plainly visible through the windshield, drove the truck in front of the pawn shop, blocking anyone's view to the inside. The truck cast a long, depressing shadow over a once sunny-bright day that illuminated the perfect picture of pure Americana. The happy people at play.

Now that Imogene stood at the window, seeing the layout of the caper, the truck in front of the pawn shop, the crowd, the bank's location—none of it made any sense. Once the parade began, the truck would be stuck without a way out. So why have it out front?

Stupid?

Or was it cunning?

Flip a coin. She opted for the latter.

They could only wait for the phone call with the final puzzle piece, the final directions on how to commit this heinous crime. By then, it would be too late to make an evasive move. They'd be trapped.

As if they weren't already.

Suz got out and met Luke in front of the truck. Luke tinkered with the hood, trying to open it. Hank, the nice uniformed cop, suddenly appeared. She forgot he said he was working an overtime slot, standing in front of Joe Co's campaign office.

What an absolute mess.

The Puppet Masters had missed too many details.

What did they care? It wasn't their butts on the line—decades of their lives in the joint hanging over their heads.

Imogene hurried out before Luke could panic, pull his stiletto, and gut poor Hank, who was nothing more than a kid who wanted to play cops and robbers.

Imogene caught up just as Hank said, "You have to move this hulk. You can't park here. There's a parade for cripe's sake."

Luke did look panicked. From behind, Imogene put a consoling hand on Hank's shoulder. He didn't flinch or jump away like a veteran cop would. He turned. "Oh, hey, Imogene." He turned back, "I was just telling these folks they can't park here. And if they don't move it, I gotta call for a tow."

Imogene nodded to Luke, who then turned back to the truck, snaked his hand inside the grill to again search for the hood latch. She said to Hank, "It's okay, it's just overheated. It does this periodically. We'll have it out of here long before the parade starts."

Hank lost his smile; his expression turned to consternation. He'd yet to earn that suspicious and mean-boned attitude all cops needed to survive on the street.

She gently gripped his shoulder. "You never did come back for that gun in the showcase."

"I know, but I don't have the money yet. It's not payday until next Friday. We only get paid every other Friday."

"We're friends. Come on in. I'll let you take it now. You can pay for it later."

He looked around, checking for his sergeant, who had far more important matters to deal with than watching after a rookie standing a go-nowhere fixed post. Security for a political favor. Wasted manpower. Nothing was going to happen to Joe Co's precious campaign office.

"Naw, I don't think that would be—"

She let her hand slide down his arm to his hand and tugged him along. "Come on, it'll be fine. It's really a nice gun. You have great taste."

He checked up and down the sidewalk one more time and relented, going along. She caught Luke's eye and nodded. He nodded back just as he found the latch to the big cabover truck and lifted the long, wide hood.

Back inside the pawn shop, Hank made a beeline to the counter, a kid going after a peppermint stick in a five-and-dime.

Just as the phone on the counter rang.

"Hey, what happened to the glass?"

Ring.

Imogene said, "What do you think happened?"

Thelma stood on the other side of the counter, watching the boy in blue.

He shrugged and pointed. "You mean the atmospheric conditions again?"

"Yep, happened yesterday."

"That's the funniest thing. Never ever heard of that happening anywhere, and now it's gone and happened two days in a row. I'm gonna go back to my high school. I know the science teacher, Mr. Reeves, he's a friend. Maybe he can help? Give us some ideas to keep this from happening again."

"Why, thank you, Hank. That would help out a lot."

He stopped at the counter and stared down at the prize he must've been dreaming about. As manners dictated, he stood by and waited.

Ring.

Thelma, with a quixotic expression, said, "Atmospheric conditions? Imogene, I thought that you were the one who—"

"Thelma, get the phone before it drives me half outta my mind."

Imogene reached in, picked up the gun, and handed it to Hank. He accepted it with the reverence of a sacred artifact, one recently dug up from the tomb of Tutankhamun.

Thelma picked up the phone mid-ring, muttering, "Half outta your mind, Baby, that ship has sailed. Hello, this is Alan Goldblatt's pawn shop, how may I help you? Yes. Just one moment please? Who may I ask is calling? Oh, sure." She put the phone to her shoulder. "Imogene, it's for you."

Imogene muttered under her breath as fear gripped her. "Sweet baby Jesus."

Only one person knew she would be in the store.

She gulped and hoped that fear didn't translate to furtive movements. "Who is it?"

"He said to just tell you it's your boss."

The Puppet Master.

Calling with instructions on how to rob the bank.

Imogene hurried over and took the phone. "Hello?"

"What the hell's that moving van doing parked in front of the pawn shop? Get it moved now!"

The sharp, curt words said with anger took her back a step.

"It's what you wanted us to—" The voice tickled her memory and locked in a second before she said too much.

JB.

He'd told Thelma he was Imogene's boss. She liked him less and less for the games he liked to play.

She looked to see if Hank caught on. Hank saw nothing around him except that dern gun. Men and their guns would eventually bring the world to its knees.

Imogene said into the phone, "I believe what you are referring to comes under your bailiwick, not mine. I run a pawn shop, sir. Not the city's parking control division. Please restrict further calls to this establishment to more important topics. It's the Fourth of July after all. Thank you and good-bye." She hung up.

Hank came out of his worshipful gaze when he heard, 'city's parking division.' "Who was that?"

"Don't you fret. It was some citizen looking for an unjust favor. He wanted to park behind the pawn shop and walk around to the parade. Asked if the city would cite his car?"

He nodded and hesitated, not sure he wanted to believe her. For some reason, Imogene's credibility had taken a hit with Hank. Not good at ten thirty in the morning, a mere one and a half hours before the whole shebang lit off.

The phone rang again. JB didn't care for the way she talked down to him and called back to chastise her. She grabbed up the phone. "I said, I'm busy with important matters, and to please—"

"Get a pen and paper. Write down these instructions."

"Oh, sweet baby Jesus."

The puppet master.

This time for real.

And while a cop stood not two feet away. "Ah, could you please call back in fifteen minutes? I'm sort of—"

"I chose you for your cool head under fire. You can deal with the cop standing at the counter and at the same time take down this information."

He didn't sound like parole agent Humphries, not in the least. But stress tended to blur and even obscure all five senses.

This time she didn't put her hand over the phone and said to Hank, "Dear, I have to take this. We'll work out the details later. I promise. Go on now, you better get back to your post before your supervisor comes by. Take that gun with you." She shot him a smile that felt fake even to her.

His face lit up with a huge smile. "Thank you, Imo—I mean Mrs. Taylor. I can't tell you how much I appreciate this. I'll get you the money…well, some of it…on payday."

"You're welcome, now run along."

He stood in the same place, feet glued to the spot, as he continued to fondle the gun. A child with a favorite Christmas toy. He opened the carriage, spun the wheel, and jerked his wrist, snapping it shut.

Bad for a gun, but a popular move used by good guys and bad on TV. Pop culture ruined a lot of things, created bad habits.

On the phone, the man started with the directions. "In the back room—the storage area. Go to bin number 459, all the items you'll need are in two canvas bags. They're tagged with a pawn ticket. You'll see them. Pull them both out. Lay the contents out on the floor. Get familiar with 'em. I'll call back in thirty minutes. Be ready to get started on this little project. Lock the front door, put out the Closed sign. Then Luke and Suz, get their minds right. You understand?"

He said nothing of Thelma. He didn't know she was in the store. Maybe she could use that error because they didn't make many.

Hank still stood in the same place. "Imogene…would you mind…I mean, could I trouble you for a box of shells? A gun's worthless if you don't have any bullets for it."

She hung up without saying goodbye. "Sure." She turned, scanned the wall of boxed ammo, chose one, and handed it to him.

"Thanks." He held up the box. "Put it on my bill. I *am* paying for it. I won't take no for an answer."

"Of course, you are. Now off with you. We have to lock up. We have a picnic table across the street reserved for us. My mouth is watering already for some of that hand-cranked ice cream with some nutmeg sprinkled on top. Thelma, please lock the door behind him."

"Me? Why me? I'm not a dern doorman."

She's Queen of a kingdom that lives on a small planet in the shadow of Pluto. How dare you give her menial chores. Ange let fly a cackle after the jab, one that sounded too much like the Wicked Witch of the West in the movie, *The Wizard of Oz.*

Imogene wasn't in the mood to laugh along. She waited while Hank followed the muttering Thelma to the door. He went out. She locked it. "Now come on, all of you. That phone call was the one we've been dreading."

Suz and Luke both looked pale. Thelma gave a little hop and a whoop. "Boy, this is gonna be a kick in the pants."

While walking to the back, Imogene replayed the phone conversation in her head. Examining each word.

Dats right. He talked like he knew everyone in the store. He's watching your ass. So, don't do anything stupid. Think girl. You cain't go through wit this. It's pure unadulterated suicide. Go back ta the front, pull that Winchester shotgun down off the rack. Load it wit double ought buck. Then sit down in the corner somewhere in the shadows and jus' wait. You don't do what he asks, he'll be comin' fast ta take care of bitness. Dat's when you show him the mouth a dat gauge. How it can bark fire. Spew hot lead. It's the only smart move, E. To do what he says will only lead to hate and discontent. Trust me on this, I'm tellin' ya true.

Ange had one thing right for sure, the man on the phone had an eye on the pawn shop. But from where? He also had to be close to a phone.

Imogene turned down the first long row of floor-to-ceiling shelving. Moved around two ladders on rollers. Then made the turn at the end counting down to the fourth row. At the end of four in bin 459 sat two large green canvas bags, zippered closed. Her fate, sitting there waiting for her, no different than a bear trap locked open ready to snap shut.

Snap her head right off her shoulders.

Chapter Twenty-One

L uke said, "We need more light." He scurried off on the pretense of finding a lamp. Imogene gave fifty-fifty odds he'd return at all. She bent over, took hold of the top canvas bag, and tugged. Her back tweaked, and pain shot up her spine to her neck and into her head. "Augh." She stood.

A seventy-five-year-old woman robbing a bank? Not in her wildest dreams.

"Don't be silly, E." Suz said, "Step outta the way, let me do that." She dragged out the canvas bag, squatted, and unzipped the long zipper.

The sides fell open.

In the dim light, the contents stunned Imogene. She didn't really know what to expect but thought maybe a couple of Tommy guns, some shotguns, pistols, and masks. What else would you use to rob a bank?

Instead, three sledgehammers, a huge electric saw and drill, and three sets of work gloves and goggles. Her hand on her back pushing in at the pain, she stepped aside to confirm they had the right bin. Yep, *459.* Then she questioned if she even heard that number correctly over the phone. That maybe her mind, under all the constant stress, had whispered a different number in her ear. Naw. She wasn't even close to being that cuckoo.

Now we're talkin'. A puzzler for sure. What's your guess, E? We gonna go in the side of the bank wall? Let me tell ya, nothing here is as it seems. Not one dern thing. But I'm all in. I'm stickin' around jus' to see what happens next. For my money, we're all gonna get in the back a that big truck, back up to the side a that bank and make like Heckle and Jeckle. Go ta town knockin' down the buildin' all the while that dern parade marches by big as you please.

Those two magpies crack me up. You know what I'm sayin' here, E. You and me are gonna be Heckle and Jeckle.

"You're not goin' nowhere."

Suz, still squatting by the tools, looked up. "What?"

"Nothing. The stuff in that bag doesn't make one bit of sense."

Luke returned with a long-necked, three-foot-tall living room lamp with a pawn tag hanging from it and dragging a long extension electrical cord. Gold fringe hung from the bottom edge of the lampshade.

Imogene said, "Thanks for coming back."

He stopped and pulled his chest back with his neck, looking at her queer. "Where'd ya think I'd be goin'?" He didn't wait for an answer. The light from the lamp illuminated the canvas bag and its contents. He squatted next to Suz, his leg touching hers, and said, "What the heck is all this?" He again didn't wait for an answer, pulled the second bag off the bin shelf, and unzipped it. "Well, I'll be dawg gone."

Imogene peered over his head, looking down. "What? What's in the bag?"

He feigned falling to the side into Suz, putting a hand on her leg, the other on her shoulder. A cheesy perv trick that dropped him down in Imogene's book.

Suz shoved him. "Stop it. Just stop it."

"Take it easy. I fell over, that's all." He looked up at Imogene, his eyes pleading innocence. She believed him and instantly felt bad for prejudging him.

"Quit it, you two. Luke, tell me what you see in that bag. From what I can tell, it's all tools."

"Yep, it's everything I need to peel a safe. But not one of those jumbos like we talked about across the street. These are the kinda tools I've used before on smaller safes."

The phone rang in the other room, in the customer section. Imogene checked her watch, only ten minutes had passed. She hurried and made it to the counter out of breath. She put her hand to her chest and breathed, wanting to be cool, calm, and collected while talking to the punk on the other end of the line.

Suz, Luke, and Thelma crowded in.

Imogene picked up the phone.

"Do exactly, and I mean exactly, as I say. Any deviation and I'll call the police down on you. Do you understand?"

"You call the police down on us, and you lose as well. So, don't toss out idle threats. You have us hooked on the line. Let's just get on with it. I'm tired of living under your thumb. I wanna be done with all of this mess."

"Then pay close attention, and you can walk away in two hours."

"We all agreed we're not gonna kill anyone for ya."

"Don't be ridiculous. If you do exactly what I say, no one will even know what happened until Monday. You don't screw up, no one will even know you ignorant plebes were even involved."

"Don't be ridiculous. You already killed poor old Mr. Goldblatt."

Suz, Luke, and Thelma had moved in even closer, putting their heads up toward the phone receiver. Imogene allowed it, their butts were on the firing line just like hers.

The man on the other end paused. Then spoke in a calmer tone. "That little…ah…blivit couldn't be avoided."

Thelma whispered, "Plebe, blivit, this guy thinks he's some kinda Scrabble champion."

He considered killing Alan Goldblatt in a fiery crash nothing more than a blivit. It was a human life wasted for no reason.

He continued. "Send someone out to move the truck up exactly 96 feet, no more and no less. 96 feet. The rest I will tell Luke Short and only Luke Short. You and Suz need not listen. Hand the phone to Luke."

Imogene gripped the phone until her hand blanched white. She didn't want to be left out of the final directions; there was too much at risk. She nodded to Luke, moved the phone closer to him, but kept her ear close. "Here's Luke."

"I know you're listening. I can see everything. I know everything before you even think about it. Now do as I say."

"No one's going to get hurt?"

"If I hang up this phone, all of you will get ten years minimum in a high-security prison. That's no joke. I'm not blustering. It's a fact."

She handed Luke the phone and moved away. Luke said, "I'm here. Go ahead." He listened intently, nodding at no one.

Imogene looked around for any way the puppet master could be watching. The only possible way was out the front window, but the truck blocked anyone from the street seeing in. She didn't believe for a minute that he could see them, know what they were doing every second. He was using simple manipulation and logic. Of course, everyone would listen in on the phone call. That wasn't a big leap of logic.

She said, "Suz, could you please pull the truck forward ninety-six feet? I'd do it, but I don't think I could handle a truck that size."

Imogene *could* drive that truck. During picking season, she helped Wayne with their groves up in LaVerne and could drive even larger trucks. But she wanted to stay close to Luke. Once he got off the phone, things would start popping.

She also needed time to think about all the sudden changes. Changes that happened so quickly, her mind started to spin at all the possible implications. The main one: they were not using guns to rob the bank. That alone took a heavy chunk of pressure off her shoulders. She could almost breathe freely again.

Thelma said to Suz, "I'll go with you."

They both started for the front door.

"No, wait." They froze. Imogene moved to them and lowered her voice so the person on the phone couldn't hear.

She whispered. "Thelma, I don't want you to go outside. In fact, I don't want you to even go by the window or out in the customer area once that truck moves. He doesn't know you're here, and we're going to keep it that way."

Suz looked at her strangely, "Why?"

"I'm not sure right now, but information is power, and right now that guy on the phone has most of it in his back pocket. We have to start playing a better game."

Suz nodded. "That makes a lot of sense. I think."

Imogene didn't have time to explain it to her.

Thelma said. "All right, I'll play along. I love games."

"Thelma, please go in the back out of sight, and I'll be right there."

"I'm gonna be like some kinda sleeper agent, right? This is exciting. The most fun I've had since the Gaylans attempted overthrow of my kingdom."

Suz looked at her mother, her expression open and easy to read, pure distress over her concern for Thelma.

"Suz, move the truck and we'll meet you in the back room when you're finished."

Suz, wallowing in the funk over her mom, said, "Huh? What?"

"The truck?"

"Oh, got it."

Thelma headed to the back, and Suz to the front door. As soon as Thelma disappeared in the back, Imogene quietly said, "Suz?"

She turned and met Imogene halfway.

Luke still held the phone to his ear, not speaking a word and nodding as if the heinous criminal on the other end could see him.

Imogene turned back to Suz, who now looked anxious, waiting for Imogene to say something.

Suz's open expression, her innocence made it even more difficult to say what needed to be said.

"I'm sorry, I've been…I've been selfish."

"What are you talking about?"

"You don't need to be here. You don't need to risk going to prison. As soon as we found your mom, I should've insisted you run, fast and far. Get away from this entire mess. I…I just needed you here. You're a huge crutch that—"

Suz gave up a sad smile and put her hand on Imogene's arm. "E, you're my best friend. I would never, ever leave you hung out. No matter how bad this thing get, I'm with you to the end."

A large lump rose in Imogene's throat, and tears filled her eyes. The last time she cried was twelve years ago, the first two weeks in CIW, Chino

Institute for Women. When Ange took her in hand, told her how tears in that new environment drew predators like moths to a flame. Tears opened you up to a shank in the gut. Imogene had lived by that edict for too long.

After those two weeks, Imogene thought she'd never cry again, that mechanism permanently broken. Sadly, the now revived emotion made Imogene feel alive, something else she had given up and didn't realize how dearly she missed it.

More importantly, she never had a best friend.

Not since high school, and that was sixty-odd years ago. An eon. A memory tarnished with rust and difficult to conjure.

Suz spotted the welling tears. "Ah, E." She moved in and hugged her.

Imogene glommed on to her, a lifeboat in a churning sea of fear and anxiety.

Suz whispered, "E, you're the grandmother I never had."

Now, Imogene cried in earnest and didn't care if it did make her vulnerable.

Suz started to quiver as her own tears took hold.

Finally, Imogene broke the clench, sniffled, and looked Suz in the eyes, seeing a strength they both needed. "You better get the truck moved before that bastard on the phone—"

She turned. Luke had hung up and disappeared in the back.

Suz headed for the front door. Imogene watched her. No matter what Suz said, it was horribly selfish not to push her away, to send her running for the hills. Imogene would find some way to make it up to her.

She turned and headed for the back to check on Luke. She found him and Thelma in the warehouse section at the north wall, taking all the pawned property off the shelves and tossing it willy-nilly behind them. Almost frantic as if they'd both lost their heads.

"What's going on?"

Luke didn't turn or slow in his rush to unload the shelves. "Can't tell you. Not yet. Orders. Give me a hand."

Imogene didn't even try to decipher the why in regard to their idiotic behavior. "Thelma?"

She stopped, looked up, still on her knees where she'd been sweeping the items aside from the bottom shelves.

"Please come in the other room, I have a special assignment for you."

"Bull pucky. I'm not gonna miss out on one minute a this. Find yourself another brainless pogue."

Ange cackled again. *Did you just hear that? Does she even know what she said? She called herself a mindless boob. She knows, E. It's no big secret. With each passing second, this gal just grows larger than life. I don't think she's annoying anymore. She's jus' plain fun.*

"Thelma," Imogene said harshly. "This will be more exciting than clearing off shelves. In fact, it's a little dangerous."

She stood, quick and easy. Far too spry for a woman her age. "Really? No, wait. You're just gaslighting this old gal like you did at the A&W. No, sir, I'm not gonna fall for it this time."

Imogene took her purse off her shoulder and opened the clasp. "All right. I'll have Suz handle it. But you're gonna kick yourself when you find out what you missed." She stuck her hand in her purse to further bolster the mystique, not believing such a juvenile ploy would work on her.

She came forward, going up on tiptoes, trying to see in the purse. "Whatta ya got in there?"

Luke never slowed, he picked up a drill and foraged around in the canvas bag sorting through the loose drill bits, preparing for the job at hand. The bank across the street with the impenetrable Mosler GM 12000. The drill had to be for the safety deposit boxes.

One side of her mind wandered off on its own, plucking at a possible solution, the why in what Luke was doing. That idea tickled and threatened to bubble up. But she had to focus on getting Thelma to do a difficult task. First, torn on whether Thelma was even capable; and second, what would happen if the plan went awry? If Thelma got hurt? How would Imogene forgive herself. Worse, how would she explain it to Suz?

No other options existed.

None.

Imogene took from her purse the faded red and round cherry bombs, held all six them out in two cupped hands.

Thelma's eyes grew large when she saw them.

On her Gulliver's Travels planet, those cherry bombs are the same as Fat Man and Little Boy. Enough destructive power to blow the crap outta of those little fellas. That's what she's thinkin', E. You can see it in her eyes. She wants to blow the crap outta something. Obliterate it. Get even for that little escapade in the airplane toilet when she danced with a lifeboat. Man, I can't tell ya how loony that sounds.

Thelma didn't take her eyes off the explosives designed for celebrations, the mere possession a straight felony in California. If caught with them, Imogene would go back to the joint for another twelve years before she'd come back up for parole. A virtual life sentence.

She handed them to Thelma, then took a Zippo lighter from her purse and held it out.

Thelma looked at the bombs in her hand, then up at the lighter. She licked her lips the same as a lion about to munch a bold hyena that wandered too close. Getting her mind right for the heady action of a Bond girl. The taste of violence. The blood.

This was a bad idea. A real bad idea.

But what choice did she have?

"Listen to me." Imogene moved her head to the side to catch Thelma's eyes.

"Yes. Yes. I'm right here."

The electric drill whined in the background, an audible annoyance, a mosquito looking for blood.

The drill going? What the—

The light in the room brightened as the truck out front moved north ninety-six feet as requested.

Thelma said, "Tell me. Please tell me what you want me to do with these lovelies. I'm gonna pee myself if you don't tell me right now."

"I'm trusting you on this."

"You know you can. I'm your faithful servant. Please command me."

She handed her the Zippo. Thelma's body gave a little shiver.

"I want you to go out the back door. Down the alley to Holt. Go right, that's west. Cross the first side of the boulevard into the wide grass area. Cross that grass to the other side and—" The second part of the plan festered and bubbled up as she spoke. In her head, Imogene witnessed Thelma doing the deed. And at the same time, worried that a county coroner might later describe it as 'death by misadventure.' "Then you climb up into one of those old pepper trees."

"Yeah. Yeah, then what?"

"Wait until one o'clock. This is important. It has to be one o'clock exactly, you understand?"

"Yeah. Yeah. You want me ta light all of these and throw them down on the parade. Right? Is that right?"

"No. The parade will only be on the northbound side of the boulevard. I want you to toss them as hard as you can out in the southbound boulevard. Get them as close to the other side of the street as you can. Right in front of the bank."

"Well, that doesn't sound very exciting."

"Stay up in the tree after you throw them."

"Why?"

"All hell's gonna break loose and you're going to have a bird's-eye view."

"Oh, yeah? You really think so? Now we're cookin' with gas. I'm with ya. You can depend on me."

Imogene had Thelma by the arm, guiding her to the back door. She opened it. Thelma tried to step out in a rush to fulfill her secret mission.

Imogene took her by the arm and pulled her back. "Tell me. Repeat what I just said."

She had to get Thelma on her way before Suz came back from moving the truck. Guilt, the same as if a dark cloud rolled in, now covered Imogene's world. Friends didn't deceive friends. Nor did they put their friend's mother in harm's way.

"Climb a pepper tree. Wait until one o'clock, then toss these sweet, sweet little babies into the street. And watch all the fun." Her voice rose in a crescendo, the same as Imogene imagined it would if this woman were having hot, spicy relations with a man.

This was a bad idea. A very bad idea.

Down past the apartment and warehouse area, out in front of the pawn shop, the front door opened and closed. Suz coming back.

"If you see me, Luke, and Suz coming your way, don't wave or say hi. Your only job is to light and throw those cherry bombs exactly at—"

"I know. I know. One o'clock, now leave go of me."

Imogene let go of Thelma's arm and couldn't help thinking it was like pushing away a drowning Titanic survivor clinging to their lifeboat, shoving her away so she didn't capsize the other survivors.

What had the world come to? Her character, Bessie Gottschalk, would never rely on a nutty woman like Thelma. Depend on her to save the nation by being the one chosen to assassinate a sitting president. In that thought, in that microsecond, Imogene caught a glimpse of herself as if in an out-of-body experience. Metaphorically, she was leaning a little too close to the flame of insanity and was about to burn to a crisp.

Imogene closed and locked the door. She closed her eyes and put her forehead against the door, fighting back the regret.

Just as the phone out front rang.

That would be the puppet master.

Had he seen Thelma leave out the back?

Chapter Twenty-Two

Imogene hurried to the phone in the customer area and met Suz at the counter. Suz knew the importance of any phone call and stood close, waiting. Imogene snatched it up, the guilt over what she'd just done rising up and trying to choke off her air. "Hello?"

"Well done with the truck. Now, you two are to help Luke with whatever he tells you to do."

Out front, Hank peered in the window and tapped on the glass door with a key, his other hand up close to his face, shading out the bright Fourth of July sunlight.

Imogene ducked down. Suz came around the counter and did the same.

Imogene said into the phone. "There is a very young and ambitious police officer at the front door, and he's—"

From the back came a loud bang.

A second later, another.

Suz put her hand to her chest. "Oh, dear Lord."

The puppet master said, "Don't worry about that dumb cop. When you don't come out to talk, he'll come to the correct conclusion and busy himself towing the truck."

Imogene put the phone to her shoulder. "He knows about Hank standing out front and accounted for it far in advance. That's what the truck was for in the first place: a diversion. How did he know Hank would be there?"

Now they both squatted down below the counter, ducking from view. Suz whispered, "It could only mean the cops are involved. This whole situation just keeps getting worse."

Another loud bang.

The small, tinny voice on the phone yelled. Imogene put the phone back to her ear. He said, "I'm still here and I can hear you talking. Don't ever do that again. Now listen to me. Ignore the cop out front and get your big butts in the back with Luke. Do it right now. We only have the time it takes to tow that truck to get past phase one and into phase two."

BANG.

Phase one and phase two, the jerk thought he was directing an episode of *Mission Impossible.*

Imogene hung up without saying goodbye and hurried to the noise. Hurried to help Luke in whatever he had going on. Suz stayed right behind her.

Imogene turned down the aisle.

Down at the end, Luke swung the big sledge into the 2x4 stud that stood behind the demolished drywall. The wall that separated the pawn shop from the...*jewelry store.*

She froze, her mouth dropped open as the significance sank in.

She'd made a terrible mistake.

An absolutely awful mistake.

She had assumed it was the bank and never asked herself what else could it be? Investigations 101 never get tunnel vision on anything. Always stay loose and take in every possibility.

She had literally screwed everything up from top to bottom. All the ramifications spun through her mind at high speed. The two mob guys, the cops.

She muttered, "Sweet baby Jesus." Then, lower, she whispered, "Thelma." She spun and hurried. Tried to run but her old body said, "nothin' doin', Sister," citing an Old Age clause in the human race union contract that represented human bodies. To wit: "No ex-con after eating prison food for ten years and smoking two packs of Marlboros a day can make said body perform a feat a healthy sixty-five-year-old would have difficulty accomplishing."

Her gait must've looked like a wounded emu running from a hungry native on Thanksgiving.

Hah. E, you broke the golden rule, never assume. You just made an ass outta you and me. She again let loose with that awful, wicked witch cackle.

Imogene made it to the front and stood by the glass window that ran the length of the store. Off to the right, almost too far to see from that angle, Hank stood with his clipboard by the Dentco truck. He'd given up knocking. Fearing repercussions from his sergeant, he stood by the huge Dentco truck, filling out a tow sheet. He had to be thinking that maybe—possibly the tow truck could arrive before the parade started at one o'clock, keeping him outta the grease for dereliction of duty.

Doing exactly what had been planned for him. Just like all the rest of them.

Imogene put her hands up against the glass, her eyes scanning the hundreds of people across the street enjoying the holiday.

She looked for Thelma.

No need to worry.

Thelma would screw it up. She could never follow such complicated directions. Not and get them right. Something shiny, like a bright bauble, would distract her, and she'd forget all about her mission. Sure, that's exactly what would happen.

Her eyes stopped. Across the entire boulevard by the north side of the bank, JB and John Johnson stood together, trying to act nonchalant in their suits and ties. Suits and ties on a day with the mercury standing tall, reaching just past one hundred. They wanted to be dressed for the newspaper photos sure to come after they bagged a couple of bank robbers. The poor, ignorant fools.

Imogene looked south from them and down along the front of the bank. She spotted a car parked on the wrong side of the street on the south side of the bank. Just west of the front edge. The two clods thought the uniformed cops would never bother them for a red curb violation. Being too busy with the parade. JB, John Johnson, Maury, The Boss, and Erv were no more than two hundred feet apart. Her plan with the cherry bombs would've worked. A quick, down-and-dirty idea that had struck right outta the blue. And now the scheme was all for naught.

What a mess.

Too many citizens clustered together, celebrating the Fourth. A gunfight would've gotten someone killed. Maybe even multiple someones.

To the left and down past Holt, the parade queued up. The few floats, cheesy in their construction, the school marching bands, high school kids all, the Shriners in their tall red fezzes sitting in their little cars, and a flatbed with the previous year's homecoming kings and queens from both of the city's high schools. With more participants stretching down the boulevard.

In the lead vehicle, a convertible, the mayor Jo Co—Joseph Columbus—sat with his wife Marge. He wore a bright and gaudy red, white, and blue striped suit. Atop his head sat a straw boater that shaded a flat pie-pan face with a rich man's bloat.

She looked the other way up the boulevard. Ten picnic tables north of Holt, not far from the front of the pawn shop, she caught sight of two people. Her eyes, all on their own, locked onto them as if these two carried some importance.

Two people that, when her eyes reengaged with her mind, caused her heart to skip several beats. Flutter and threaten to quit altogether.

Little Ida and her mom had joined a group of folks sitting on the curb waiting for the parade to start. Both within easy range of pistol and shotgun fire.

"Sweet baby bald-headed Jesus."

"What?" Suz asked. They now stood shoulder to shoulder in front of the long pawn shop window.

It couldn't get any worse.

Then it did.

An entire family, fifty or sixty folks, all at once, moved. The herd parted from the rest of the crowd. For a brief second, before the crowd surged again, she spotted Thelma climbing a pepper tree. Doing exactly what was asked of her. Of course, she would. This time. How could a woman of sixty-five climb like a monkey? Sometimes life just wasn't fair.

Quit crying in your Wheaties and do something. Kick it in gear and get after it. You can't put the toothpaste back in the tube once you've stomped on it.

Now Ange mocked her, and Imogene didn't like it one dern bit. She tried to put Ange out of her mind and focus. Focus

All the action was no longer at the bank. No robbery after all. And yet she had set in play something far worse than a bank robbery.

Not knowing what to look for, Suz asked again. "What's going on?" She had yet to see her mom, or Ida and Ima out front in the surging throngs of gaiety. Out in the bright July sun, frolicking, eating wonderful food. That was the way life was supposed to be.

The phone rang.

Imogene spun and hurried to the phone. Short of running out the front door screaming, she could do nothing to stop what she had inadvertently set in motion. All of those poor people are victims of Imogene's ignorance. Hundreds of unknowing glee-filled people, and among them three friends she cared about.

She picked up the phone. Before she could speak, the man on the other end yelled, "What the hell were you doing at the front window? You'll ruin everything. Stay back from there. Get the hell inta the back. Go help Luke. I'm not gonna tell ya again. This is your last warning."

"Shut up."

Suz had her head up close, listening. She pulled back and looked at Imogene, her mouth going to a little "o" then a smile. She put her ear back to the phone.

Imogene didn't know where the "Shut up" came from. Though she knew those words had actually come from her mouth.

"What did you just say?" he asked.

"I know where you are," she said. "And…I know who you are."

"Is that right?" He hesitated as if he looked around to see if Imogene did actually know his location. He said, "I'm tired of this game you're playing. And I'm tired of you not following directions. Trust me when I say you can do nothing to stop what I have set in motion. I have contingency plans. Backup plans for backup plans. Do. Your. Job." He hung up.

Imogene looked at the phone for a second before hanging up. She reached into the showcase with the broken counter glass and picked up a little automatic. She turned, found the corresponding bullets and loaded it.

"Oh no, E. We're not resorting to violence. Not again. Please don't do this."

"This is just in case someone gets froggy. That's all. You know, just to brandish it around a little, scare 'em."

Suz smiled and suppressed a smirk at Imogene's gun moll imitation. Humor, the best poultice for fear and loathing. "Do you really know who it is and where he is?"

"Of course not, but he tried to play that bluffing game on us, so I turned the tables. This time, giving him something to think about. Let him sweat a little."

Bang. The noise again from the back.

Imogene nodded, "Come on, we gotta help Luke. We can't let him do all the work by himself. That wouldn't be right."

They went into the back and found Luke stepping through into the jewelry store. He stuck his head back through the hole. "Here, hand me that bag, the one right there. Then bring that second big hammer through. Don't forget the gloves and goggles."

Suz did as he asked.

Imogene followed her through, ducking, careful not to snag her dress on the jagged edges, the hole wide enough with two studs knocked down. She came out of the Mad Hatters rabbit hole and into a posh jewelry store. The air was laden with lilac and a faint scent of burnt metal, a place where well-heeled people shopped. The deep, plush baby-blue carpet muffled their footfalls. All the showcases stood open and empty, the jewelry put away in two tall safes in the back room. Strong, ominous safes. Both with double doors and dual handles. Each had one combination dial. Beautiful calligraphy letters covered the front with gold scrolls above and below the writing: "Mort Stein Quality Jewelry." The two safes, Mosler T-1100s, had to have enough precious gems inside to make the incursion of the business worthwhile for the puppet master and his other unseen henchmen.

Imogene had never seen such workmanship in a safe and ran her hand along the perfect seams, the steel cool and impenetrable. They would never breach these babies. Not in a couple of hours. Not in a couple of days.

Bang.

She startled and jumped.

Over at the next wall, on the other side of the business, Luke again swung the nine-pound sledge and struck the wall. He looked over his shoulder, "Come on, grab up that other sledge. We're running outta time." From the wide and open archway that led to the back office, he nodded toward the front of the business entrance. On the other side of the long glass window, not unlike the one in the pawn shop, a tow truck clanged and rattled, hooking up the big Dentco truck. Hank, the baby-faced cop, stood by supervising.

Imogene hurried over, picked up the sledge, the weight too great. The handle slid through her arthritic hands. Luke struck another blow. And another. Turning a little frantic with the speed of the blows. Sweat beaded on his forehead and ran into his eyes. He was a tough-as-leather cowboy after all.

"Put those leather gloves on and pull off this drywall. I'm not kidding, we gotta move."

Imogene and Suz leapt into action, clearing away the drywall, pulling it free, and tossing it in a pile as he smashed through it. The next swing, he struck an exposed 2x4, shattering it.

He looked up through the archway to the front of the store and suddenly ducked. Imogene and Suz followed suit, their reaction more an inborn instinct carried forward through eons from the time before the dinosaurs roamed the earth.

Imogene and Suz squatted behind an elegant oak desk.

E, man wasn't around during the time of the dinosaurs. A fallacy put forth by books of fiction and bourgeois movies. They want ya ta believe because it's exciting. Stories filled with conflict, danger, and high adventure. Hey, why is this soda shop cowboy burrowing into Jo Co's political office? You stop long enough from cryin' in your Wheaties to ask yourself that huuuge question?

Imogene brought her eyes up above the desktop to peep at the front. To see what had spooked Luke, the soda shop cowboy. She immediately ducked back. Hank stood at the window with both hands up to his face, trying to peer in. He must've heard that last whack when Luke shattered the first stud. All three of them huddled down behind the oak desk, now covered in a fine white dust. Gypsum powder from the drywall. She looked up. That same dust hung in a cloud over their heads. Clearly visible.

Luke uttered a harsh whisper. "Is he gone?"

Imogene said, "Just give him a minute."

"We don't gotta minute."

Imogene said, "What're we doing bustin' into the mayor's campaign office? This is nuts."

Suz grabbed a hold of Imogene's arm. "He's doing what? The mayor's office?"

"The both of ya, keep your voices down." The soda shop cowboy said.

"Don't you dare shush me," Suz said in a harsh whisper to match his. "Now answer the question."

He shrugged. "I'm doin' exactly what that guy on the phone told me ta do. Doin' it ta the letter. So I can get my skinny hips outta here and not get thrown back in the can. But I gotta tell ya, I never hit a box before, not in broad daylight. Not like this. Not with a parade fixin' to light off out front. Not with a uniformed patrol copper guardin' the door. This is gawd dern crazy. And Bunny, I don't mind sayin' I'm scared half outta my wits"

Suz lunged at him with a clenched fist. "Call me bunny again. Go on. I dare ya."

Imogene got in between them. "Luke's right. Let's do our job and get the heck outta here."

Maybe if they were lucky, they could get what the puppet masters wanted out of the mayor's political office before one o'clock. Before the parade started. Then she could just go out the front door over to Thelma and stop her. Tell her ta climb down outta that tree, say it like Thelma was some kind of weird idjit for shimming up there in the first place. Maybe she should do that anyway. Forget all of this mess. Stop Thelma. Then take it on the lam. Run for the hills.

Suz helped Imogene to her feet. They backed up, watching the front window, afraid Hank might return and stick his face up to the glass.

They found Luke using his cowboy boot to kick in the drywall. He finally stood back, breathing hard. "These studs are sixteen inches on center. That gives us thirty-two inches ta crawl through. It'll have ta do. We can't risk that blue belly coming back to the window if I gotta club down another stud. Come on. Grab that second bag. Let's get this thing done."

Imogene looked over her shoulder at the expensive grandfather clock that stood along the south wall. Twelve-thirty-five. Twenty-five minutes until Thelma lights the fuses and tosses the cherry bombs. Twenty-five minutes until those bombs start a gunfight in the middle of a Fourth of July parade.

Luke slipped through the opening without any problem. Suz dragged the second bag over and pushed while Luke pulled it through. She slipped through easier than Luke. Imogene approached and turned sideways. "Geeze-a-loo, this isn't gonna work. Too many hot dog sandwiches and vanilla malts."

Suz stood on the other side, "Come on, you can do it."

Luke said, "You can do it. Squeeze."

Imogene wanted to sock him. Squeeze, her achin' butt. She sucked in her stomach and tried to fit through. "You go ahead." Her too-large bosom became the biggest obstacle. Dern boobs.

I took down plenty of studs in my time. That was before they shoved me inta that beaver farm and forced me to change teams. Am I tellin' it true, E. Am I? The cackle again.

Imogene had to smile at that one.

Luke and Suz disappeared from view. Getting after it. They were not going to do this without her.

No way.

She brought an arm up across her bosom and pressed down while sucking in her stomach. She started going through and got stuck. "Oh, geeze-aloo." Her claustrophobia instantly kicked in. She brought both hands up, put them against the wood "2x4" and pushed. The wood creaked. Pressure filled her face and surged behind her eyes. She pushed harder.

Crack

She fell to the dirty linoleum floor on the other side. From that angle, she could see Luke and Suz working on a safe the size of an easy chair.

Ah, no. There wasn't enough time. Not to break into a safe and get away clean. Not do it before that whole mess out front blew up like Nagasaki.

Chapter Twenty-Three

Luke leaned into a huge drill, the bit digging into the single door on the left side of the dial. Steel curled and fell to the floor. Smoke came from the hole and rose into the air as if escaping the penetrating violence created by the bit.

The steel screeched over the whine of the drill.

Imogene stood by and lit a Marlboro, her nerves a wreck. "How long?"

Luke, with googles on, didn't look back. "An hour, maybe forty minutes. Unless I get lucky and find the mechanism early with these exploratory holes."

"Then you need to get lucky."

This time he stopped and looked, the googles making him a cartoon character; Atom Ant. "Why? The guy on the phone said I had until the parade goes by. Hour and a half—two hours."

"If you don't want the world to come crashing down on all our heads you got twenty-five minutes. Trust me on this."

"I'm sorry, Imogene. On my best day, I couldn't—"

"Then kick it in gear and get after it."

He nodded, pulled down the googles, and wiped sweat from his eyes. He pulled them back into place and did get after it.

Suz sidled over. "What's going on, E?"

Imogene stared at her. No way could she tell Suz about Thelma. Or the cops and the mob.

"It's a mess," she said. "I really screwed the pooch on this whole thing. Made things ten times worse by believing I could out-think these…these—"

"A-holes?"

"Yes."

Suz's sympathetic eyes burned a hole right through her faster that Luke's drill could cut through steel.

"Tell me. It can't be that bad."

"Oh, it's bad." Imogene took the Marlboro box from her purse and started to bump one out and realized she had one already burning suspended between her fingers.

Suz put her hand on Imogene's arm, stared, and said nothing, the silence killing her.

Time ticked on, not slowing one wit. Time, fate's evil mistress. The two of them worked hand in hand to ruin the world.

Sweat beaded on Imogene's forehead and ran into her eyes.

"Okay, okay, I'll tell you. You already know about the mob guys out there across the street."

"Yeah, we're over here, though, and they're over there. What's going on, E? We're best friends. You can tell me anything."

The phone rang in Joe Co.'s campaign office. They both jumped.

Imogene picked up the phone, thinking it couldn't be anyone else besides the puppet master.

"You two idjits were standing in that archway to the office in plain view of the street. Now you're in *the* office in plain view of the front window. What's the matter with you? You wanna get caught? That cop takes two steps to the left and looks in. It's all over for all of ya'll. Now get back. Get back before you ruin everything."

Imogene said, "I had to answer the phone, didn't I?" She wasn't that dumb but wanted to stick the knife in a little deeper, share with him some more of that teeth-cutting stress.

"Get back. Get back outta that display area and further back in the office. Do it now."

Imogene's head whipped around. Her mind, all on its own, had been reviewing the facts from the last few days. Doing it on a continuous loop. The people involved, the locations, the things she'd set in motion. Going over it again and again.

When a cog suddenly locked into a gear. From the desk where the phone sat, she looked out the window.

In that instant, she put it all together.

Of course. What a fool she'd been. What an absolute Gawd dern fool she'd been.

She said into the phone, "We've got three holes drilled. We'll be through here in twenty or thirty minutes." She'd made all of that up. "We're getting off the phone now and going further back in the office."

"Wait. I already told Luke, but I wanna be clear. When you get the locked valise that's inside the safe, do not open it. Take it back through to the pawn shop, use the ladder and put it up in the bin on the top shelf. Bin number 487. Then leave through the back door of the pawnshop. Leave the area as fast as you can. Then you're done."

Out front, Hank moved in front of Joe Co's office but didn't look in, his full attention on the thousands of folks out on the boulevard from Holt, north, running the many blocks of the parade route.

"Fine. But we're done for good. You will not use us again."

"Get down. He's right there. Can't you see him?"

Imogene hung up the phone and said to no one. "No, but I can see you. She knelt down behind the desk, dragged the phone with her to the floor, and dialed a number from memory. A second number JB had given her to call if something changed after twelve in the afternoon. She wiped the sweat from her eyes while it rang on the other end.

The drill in the back room whined.

Suz knelt next to her. "Who are you calling?"

"The police."

Suz's hand moved quick as a snake and pushed down the receiver, ending the call. "Are you crazy? We're in the office of the city mayor, breaking into his safe. After…after we broke into a jewelry store. For cripes sake, E."

Imogene stared at her. "Are we friends or not?"

Without hesitation, Suz pulled her hand from the phone. Imogene dialed the number again. This time a gal picked up on the first ring and said, "Hello."

This was a "cold phone." Imogene had read about them while in the joint. Some cops called it the Hello phone because big letters taped to the phone read "HELLO," meaning don't pick it up and say, "Police Department, how can I help you?" A phone used strictly for undercover operations. JB and Johnson were on an undercover bank robbery surveillance.

"Listen carefully. My name is Imogene, and I have dire information that needs to get to JB."

"Yes, he told me about you. What information do you want me to relay?"

Imogene, sitting on her butt now, stared into Suz's eyes as she said into the phone. "Tell JB, the man who is running the bank robbery, the man responsible for this whole mess, is at this minute talking on the pay phone in The Iron Skillet. If JB moves fast, he can grab him and maybe shut this whole thing down."

Suz's eyes grew wide and her mouth dropped open.

The woman was a hundred percent professional. Cool, calm and collected. "What does this man look like?"

Imogene described his physical attributes while watching Suz's expression. Suz didn't tumble to who Imogene described. But Suz did know him.

The woman on the Hello phone said, "I'll get this information to JB."

Before she could hang up, Imogene said, "How long. How long will it take to get the information to him?"

"Ten minutes. I have to send another undercover to tell him. JB doesn't have a radio. Do you have eyes on this man? If he moves, can you call me back?"

"Ten minutes? Are you crazy? The parade's about ta start."

"Call me back if he moves." And she was gone.

Imogene beat the phone on the desk. "Dern you. Dern you." She crawled on her hands and knees into the back room, knees screaming in pain. Suz crawled after her, talking in a harsh whisper, "You called the police? Really? Oh, my Gawd, E."

Imogene struggled to her feet using the doorframe and hurried over to Luke. "How much longer?"

He didn't turn around and said over his shoulder—over the whine of the drill, "I got lucky. One of my exploratory holes found what I needed. I'm drilling the last hole right now. Then I can get to the gears. Ten-fifteen minutes, max."

Imogene hurried to the hole in the wall.

Suz, behind her, said, "Where are we going? Talk to me, E. Did you really call the police on this whole operation?"

"We can't look out that window in the mayor's political campaign office, Hank will see us." She ignored the part about the police.

The stud she'd broken made it easier to slip back into the jewelry store. She hurried to the front window with Suz close at her heels.

Imogene couldn't see over all the people who clustered in surging crowds. She backed up, moved a desk chair out, stood on it. Suz helped to balance her as she stepped up onto the desktop.

"E, what are you doing? You're gonna fall and break your neck."

Now, over the heads of the picnickers, Imogene could see JB and John Johnson standing alone at the north side of the bank in their suits and ties like a couple of country rubes.

Suz climbed up next to her. "What are we looking at?"

"That root-beer brown car parked on Holt just south of the bank. That's the two mob guys."

"Okay, we knew they would be here."

"See those two men in suits and ties by the north corner of the bank, they're cops."

"Ah, no, E. You did call the cops on the mob guys. Didn't you know that would cause a horrible confrontation? And during a parade ta boot? With all those people, dear Lord."

"I was pushed into a corner with no way out. I had to give the cops something or I'd be on my way back to Chino right now. I know it's bad, but I wasn't goin' back. It's horribly selfish and—"

She put her hand on Imogene's shoulder and gently rubbed. "It's okay. With any luck, those two won't even know the two mob guys are there."

"Except for one other little thing." Imogene didn't want to tell her about Thelma up in the pepper tree with six cherry bombs.

"Except for what? What did you do, E?"

From the other room, Luke yelled, "I got it. I'm through, I'm tripping the gears now."

A yellow Volkswagen Beetle pulled up to the curb close to JB and John Johnson. The driver leaned over the seat and rolled the passenger window down.

"Good," Imogene whispered. "That's good. It's all going to work out. Go. Go catch that little rat bastard in The Iron Skillet."

She glanced at the grandfather clock. Seven minutes to one. Seven minutes before—

Off to the left, down Euclid past Holt, the parade started moving north. The lead car with the mayor honked. Jo Co and his wife were already waving before they even made it across Holt to all the people in the center of the boulevard.

Imogene teetered, almost falling. "No. No. No, they're early. They're seven minutes early."

Suz shrugged. "Or that clock's slow. Those old grandfathers are notoriously inaccurate."

Back in front of the bank, JB leaned down, his hands on the yellow VW's windowsill, talking to the driver. He suddenly stood and looked all around. He spoke rapidly to Johnson.

"No. No. No. The both of you have to go. You both have to go to the Iron Skillet."

JB reached inside his suit coat, pulled a big pistol from a hidden shoulder holster, and took off running north toward the restaurant. Made several long steps.

A loud explosion went off in front of the bank.

The first cherry bomb.

Chapter Twenty-Four

Imogene and Suz stood on the desk as Luke popped out of the mayor's political office carrying a fat brown leather valise. "Got it, let's roll."

Imogene didn't see Luke directly and caught his image from a wall mirror in her peripheral vision. She couldn't take her eyes off the actors in the violent play unfolding in front of the bank.

The second cherry bomb went off.

All the people in the crowd shifted and froze as one entity, their faces snapping round toward the threat. Mothers grabbed up their small children and ran headlong in the opposite direction.

A palatable collective fear rose and hovered over the crowd. Wide eyes and quick, furtive movements, the same as trapped animals with nowhere to flee.

The parade came north, the mayor's convertible about to pass in front of the jewelry store. At the sharp crack of the second cherry bomb, the mayor startled even more this time. He rolled off the back of the car. He fell face-first into the street with an unheard smack, his nose, mouth, and eyebrows mashed into the searing asphalt. Marge started to scream, her beehive hairdo wobbling as she scrambled down to help his honor.

The explosion didn't sound startling to the marching band, not with all the racket in their ears from the brass and drums. They continued the march around the stopped convertible, the car a large rock in the stream, and they the water.

Simultaneously, Erv and The Boss exited their root-beer brown sedan, guns in hand.

"No. No. No." Standing up on the desk, the blood left Imogene's head, and she swooned. Suz wrapped an arm around her waist and held on. Now they both teetered atop their perch.

John Johnson was closer to the two bank robbers who ran toward him with their guns drawn. He drew his from under his suitcoat and stepped from the curbside to the middle of the sidewalk, going into a shooter's stance; feet spread, the gun in two hands pointed at the threat.

Gunfire from both sides erupted. BAM. BAM. BAM.

The crowd surged more violently and fled from danger, shifting into an out-of-control mob. Their screams, the loudest over the gunshots, and even the band that wouldn't stop moving in unison or playing the Star-Spangled Banner.

Amidst the chaos, Ima grabbed up Ida and, thinking fast, dove under a picnic table to ride out the tornado of humanity that trampled those who fell. The out-of-control mob knocked over chairs and card tables in their selfish rush to survive.

The safe haven picnic table jostled and threatened to turn over.

John Johnson crumpled to the sidewalk, struck by hot, flying lead that slapped into his body. JB spun around, his mouth open in a silent scream. He charged, firing, running to his downed partner.

The Boss ran toward the two bank robbers who'd dared hit a mob bank and suddenly flipped backward, a perfect halo of red mist blasted from his forehead. A bullet from JB's gun finds its mark.

Erv spun on his heel as he took one to the shoulder.

JB and Erv's guns both clicked empty, their fingers doing a silent dance on the triggers, the firearms no longer kicking or belching flames.

Erv looked at his downed boss, saw the futility of trying to drag a dead man back to the car. He turned and fled with a widening blood patch on his shoulder. He made it to the brown sedan, started up, and tried to flee.

But the parade had stopped and bunched up in the intersection. The largest intersection in West Valley is now made small by all the floats, cars, and marching bands.

He honked and honked.

Foot patrol cops who'd been patrolling the parade surrounded the root-beer brown sedan. Erv put his hands up.

Hank suddenly appeared across the street in front of the bank and helped JB pull John Johnson into the yellow VW bug. JB yanked the driver out, got in, and sped down the alley between the Iron Skillet and the bank, the only egress available.

Hank stood in the same place, his face pale, his eyes on his bloodied hands. Life had pivoted and left him behind. He pulled from his waistband the gun Imogene had given him. He looked at it as if it were a horrific artifact used in a slaughter of the innocent.

"Hey! Hey!" Luke yelled. "Come on down from there. Let's get the hell outta here."

He helped them down off the desk. Imogene's legs wouldn't work like they were supposed to. They wobbled and, with each step, threatened to throw her to the floor.

Suz and Luke helped Imogene get through to the other side of the wall and into the pawn shop. As Imogene went through the gap, her mouth all on its own whispered. "Thelma? What about Thelma? What about Ida and Ima?"

Suz stopped and looked around. "Where's Mom? Where'd she get off to?"

Imogene said, "We gotta find her. There's nothing but mayhem out there, and she's in the middle of it."

Suz looked distressed for a second. "No, she must've gone home. She'll be all right. Come on, let's go."

Guilt all but smothered Imogene, keeping her from telling Suz how Thelma had been the one to light off all the pain and pandemonium out front.

Luke stalled in their headlong flight and started to climb one of the ladders next to the wall of shelves.

Imogene said, "What are you doing, you dern fool. We have ta go."

"The guy on the phone told me to put this valise in—"

"Are you serious? Get down from there. We're keeping that thing. It's the only leverage we got. Come on."

Luke's expression shifted to confusion. Suz said. "You heard Imogene.

We're taking that bag with us. Now come on."

He hesitated a moment more and shrugged. "What the heck?" He followed them out into the back parking lot, where some random parade goers had taken refuge from the chaos out front.

Luke put the heavy valise in the bed of his red Ford pickup truck. All three of them squeezed into the front seat.

Luke took off, driving wild. Crazy. Imogene reached over and put her hand on his, patted it. "Slow down, Kid. We got away. It's over. It's all over."

He nodded. Tears filled his eyes and ran down his nut-brown leathery cheeks.

Chapter Twenty-Five

Imogene sat on her divan, looking out the front picture window, waiting for the car to arrive. Waiting for fate to come calling, her nerves stretched to the limit, her hand in between the cushions wrapped around the loaded gun she'd taken the day before from the counter display case in the pawn shop. Not much doubt remained that in fifteen minutes, at nine o'clock, she'd once again use the tool of violence in her own living room.

She had called Humphries and told him if his puppet master wanted the valise with the cool million all in used fifties, he had to be at her house at nine o'clock straight up.

Not one minute before, not one minute after.

Humphries half-mumbled his assent, not nearly the arrogant lout from her prior meetings in his office. The Fourth of July caper had not gone their way. Once the swath of mayhem that swept through the city's pride and joy event was investigated, the trail had better than even odds of ending up at his doorstep. The shoe now rested on the other foot. He and his puppet master had to take it on the lam. Imogene didn't feel sorry for them. They had a million dollars to dab their tears.

Humphries, her parole officer, would come to the meeting as muscle.

And with Imogene in possession of a handgun, a huge parole violation. The least of her worries. Staying alive now topped that list.

The entire situation was untenable. One way or another, she'd end up back in prison.

Unless JB could pull her cookies outta the fire. If she could, by chance, corral the evil men en route to her house.

That left a whole lot up to JB.

Next door, Suz's VW bug, solid red with big round black spots, pulled up and parked.

Imogene muttered to no one, "Ah, what the heck, Suz. You were supposed to stay over at your boyfriend's house till ten. You promised, dern you."

Imogene watched, taking shallow breaths as she hoped Suz would change her mind.

"Don't come over here. Don't you do it."

Suz got out of the ladybug car, stood by the open door, and looked at Imogene's house. She looked down at her watch, checking the time.

"That's right. That's right, get back in the car and go. Come back in an hour." Imogene looked up at the clock on the wall. Five minutes had passed. Ten minutes until Humphries and his puppet master arrived.

Suz made up her mind. She closed the car door and headed over.

"Ah, dern you."

Imogene lit another Marlboro and fidgeted. She couldn't take much more stress before she just exploded.

Take a breath, Big Gal, you got this. You're Imogene Taylor, Queen of Beaver Town. Queen of C-block. You slew more beaver tail than Lewis and Clark. Heh, heh, heh.

"Not funny. You're not helping the situation by jibber-jabbering and lying ta boot. And for the record, I never…well, you just keep those kinda lurid thoughts to yourself. Or…or we won't be friends anymore. I value my reputation even if you don't value yours."

Suz crossed the grass and mounted the two concrete steps up to the concrete porch. Imogene would've met her at the door and turned her away, but she didn't want to leave her perch. And more importantly, the gun. The Grim Reaper's number one tool used most often to pry souls loose from their bodies. Like abalone from the rocks.

Suz opened the screen door and bounded in the same as if the day before a major disaster had not befallen their quiet bedroom community.

For the young, a good night's sleep had the absolute ability to rejuvenate and tuck away ugly memories. Suz's cup was always half full. Gawd bless her.

She moved over and sat in Wayne's easy chair.

Imogene immediately said, "You have to leave. Please, get yourself up and leave right now."

Suz ignored her. With her leg stretched out, her foot scraped the exposed wood in the closest square where the gold high-low carpet had been excised by Luke on his first visit. A visit that now seemed eons in the past, reaching back to the time of the pharaohs of Egypt.

Suz looked up, her eyes leaving the marred floor. "Hard to believe it was only two weeks ago that whole mess…I mean…" She swallowed hard as emotions of what she experienced hit her hard.

"Suz, I'm asking you as a friend, to please leave. Get up right now, walk out the door, and…Ah, go get me a coffee and donuts. Please? I'm hungry and a little hungover. I drank too many Schlitz Malt liquor last night. Please, Suz."

She shook her head. "No. You're my friend. I know you, and by the way you're acting something's about to happen. I'm going to be here for you when it does."

Imogene didn't want to get tough, but it was for Suz's own good. "That right? You think you can handle something like what happened right here two weeks ago? In this room? The gunplay? The loud bangs that clogged your ears? All the blood?" Imogene clapped her hands together. "Bang. Bang. Bang." She hated doing it to her friend, but it was for her own good.

Suz squirmed in the chair, uncomfortable. The images of the past swooped back in on her. Her body was begging her to stand and flee. She fought it. "It's about that million dollars in the valise, isn't it? I thought that last night we agreed to call the police and turn it all over to them. Let them handle it. We agreed that kind of money can only lead to sorrow and…and even death. I figured something was up when you said not to come over 'til noon. What's going on, E?"

The night before, all three of them sat at the kitchen table and counted the contents from the valise. All of them on edge, afraid the puppet master would barge in at any moment, kill them all, and make off with the loot.

But Ange had whispered loud and true in Imogene's ear. What she said this time made perfect sense. The Puppet Master wanted the valise deposited high up on the shelf. He intended on coming for it later after all the dust settled. After all the hoopla from the burglary of the campaign office wore down.

Only the Puppet Master never expected the melee that occurred with the shooting, the mass hysteria of the people fleeing in a stampede, the mayor falling out of his convertible, the ambulances, the fire trucks, all the cop cars.

What a Gawd awful mess.

In the early edition that morning, over Imogene's first cuppa Joe and Marlboro, The Daily Report listed the score. The damages, the people hurt—43 transported, 13 hospitalized. And one dead mobster shot and killed by "two vigilant Johnny-on-the-spot detectives." One of those detectives "took a bullet in the line of duty and is expected to make a full recovery." The paper went on to say, "The two gunsels, east coast mob transplants, thought they would use the cover of the parade to rob the bank. They didn't account for West Valley's finest being on the job. Truly a day that would live in infamy."

Imogene hoped the truth would never come out.

Ange was right, the Puppet Master would've had to wait a week or more before trying to break into the pawn shop to retrieve the valise on the top shelf in bin 487.

If Imogene and her team had actually put it there.

The night before, after they'd counted the money and the others left, Imogene couldn't wait any longer for the hammer to fall. Her nerves wouldn't allow it. She called Humphries and asked for the meeting at her home, ten o'clock sharp.

Also, the night before, Luke said he was through. He couldn't take it anymore. Said he was running. Said, "I'll drop you a postcard from Timbuktu," tipped his cowboy hat, kissed Suz on the cheek, hurried out to his red Ford truck, and fled California to parts unknown.

The foolish man. His parole tail would eventually catch up and yank him back. You couldn't run from the long arm of the law.

Back in the living room, Imogene hoped Suz would've had her fill of violence as well and lay low for a couple of days. But no, here she sat about to ruin everything.

Don't look now, E, time to put on your big girl panties. Check out the front curb.

Imogene's head whipped around and looked out the window. Ange was wrong this time, the front curb was empty.

She looked up at the clock on the wall, seven minutes till. Looked back outside just as a black Grand Marquis pulled to the curb. She muttered to Ange. "How did you do that? How did you know?"

"E, what are you talking about?" Suz stood and took a couple of steps to get an angle on the front window. "Oh no. No, no, no. Come on, E, we gotta run. Come on, let's beat it out the back door. How did this happen? Not again. Please, not again."

"Go. Take those young legs and get the heck outta here. I'll stay here and stall 'em. Go."

Suz took three long steps heading for the kitchen, ready to flee to the safety of the backyard.

But stopped.

She slowly turned around. "You set this whole thing up, didn't you? Them comin' here? Ah, E, you don't have some kinda death wish, do you?"

The three men came across the front lawn, Humphries in his black denim pants, white long-sleeved shirt, and a ballcap pulled down over the top of his eyes. The other man, one shorter than Humphries, The Puppet Master, walked a step ahead of Humphries. He wore black slacks, slick and shiny in the morning sun, a white shirt, and a hooded sweatshirt with the hood up. He walked with his chin down, obscuring his face, forever the enigma.

Trailing the two of them was Donald, Ida's stepfather. He looked like a puppy with his tail between his legs.

"Quick, go into the kitchen and be quiet. Go. Go."

For a second, Suz looked confused in her indecision. Finally, she fled into the kitchen just as the screen door opened and in stepped Humphries.

Chapter Twenty-Six

Humphries came in and stood over one of the cutout patches in the carpet. Right where two weeks earlier, a dead man had fallen and bled.

The enigma entered, passed Humphries, and sat in Wayne's easy chair.

Donald Ho came in and stood by the television underneath Joyce's portrait, Joyce looking down upon all of them. Donald Ho was nervous as a cat, standing in one place, stepping from side to side, going nowhere fast.

In the kitchen, Suz tried to be quiet as a mouse, but her heavy, quick breathing carried a faint echo off the linoleum floor. Did the thugs hear it? Would Suz be safe after everything lit off in the living room? Imogene could only hope her best friend stayed safe.

I'm your best friend. You seem to keep forgetting that. I'm right here with you in harm's way. We're both gonna get our asses shot off. You can't cheat the Reaper, not two times in a row. Your number's up for sure, E. Bend over and kiss that fat bottom of yours goodbye, and I'll see ya on the other side. Heh, heh, heh.

All the attention in the room focused on the man sitting in Wayne's chair.

After seconds ticked by and he had made his point—he was the grandmaster in control of all—he pulled back the hood from his sweatshirt. His eyes watched Imogene's, waiting for surprised recognition.

But Imogene had figured it all out the day before, moments before the Fourth of July extravaganza turned into a packed, three-ring circus after the lions escaped from their cages.

The diminutive Alan Goldblatt.

The owner of the West Valley Pawn Shop.

The man who orchestrated the whole shebang.

The living room was dead silent except for the breathing in the kitchen.

Quiet as a mausoleum, I'd say. Wouldn't you, E? Let's get this party started. Get it over with. I want some waffles with whipped cream.

Alan Goldblatt said, "I'm disappointed. I thought you'd be more…well, shocked."

Imogene took a long drag off the Marlboro to hide the stark fear that threatened her bladder's continence. She blew out the stream of smoke. "I knew it was you all along."

He sat forward to the edge of his seat. "You did not. You thought I burnt up in the car like everyone else. It was a stroke of genius."

"Well, the cat's outta the bag now, genius."

"Just get my money. We have places to be."

"Just hold your horses. I know you can't possibly let me continue breathin' after I give you the money." She nodded toward Humphries and Donald Ho, who hadn't said one word.

"That right?" Goldblatt said, "Why don't you enlighten me? It's your word against mine…and theirs too, of course."

"See how he just slipped. You two are worm food as soon as he gets a chance. Don't turn your backs to this low-down snake in the grass."

Goldblatt waved his hand as if unconcerned, but his eyes said otherwise. "You guys can see what she's trying to do. She's trying to turn us against each other. But what she doesn't know is that neither one of you has a spine, or you wouldn't be in this situation."

His eyes flared. "Now get me my money!"

"I will. You have my word, you'll get what's coming to you. Just tell me about the money. How did you know it would be there?"

He sat back, smug. "In a million years, you'd never figure out how this whole thing played out."

"Let's say I guess it right. Will you take your money and leave?"

"Who's to say I'm going to do anything otherwise?"

"Don't try and pull the wool over the eyes of these two clods. As soon as you have the money, you're gonna gun 'em both and lay the gun at my feet.

Blame the whole shebang on me. The perfect crime after what happened here two weeks ago. In the exact same place you three are right now."

History repeats itself. I woulda never guessed it would've so soon. Am I right, E? Tell me true. I'm right?

Alan Goldblatt allowed a little grin to slither out. "That right? Do tell? Why would I do that?"

"Because of the felony murder rule."

He lost his grin.

Humphries let his hand ease under his shirt to where he had to have his gun. Being a parole agent, he had to catch the meaning of what she'd said. Donald Ho, wringing his hands, took one half step forward. "What does she mean? What's she saying?"

Imogene said, "When someone dies during the commission of a felony, the felony murder rule applies. Everyone involved is guilty of murder. That means Goldblatt and you two clods."

"Is that true, Alan?" Donald Ho said, his voice more of a squeak.

Goldblatt, miffed, held up his hand to silence his minions. "Quiet." He never took his eyes off her. "Tell me the rest. You have your deal. You guess the rest of it, I'll let you walk."

The man thrived on information, intelligence. It helped make informed decisions. The reason why he was still out and about and not already locked up.

Imogene let her hand ease down between the cushions of the couch to the pistol's stock. She took another long drag and let it out.

Just as she heard the back door in the kitchen ease open. A little creak no one who hadn't lived in the house for twenty-five years would've noticed. Suz had slipped out the back. Good for her. She'd run next door to her house to call the cops. Imogene could breathe a lot easier now.

But this would all be over before the cops could get there.

"You better start talking or Humphries here is going to start by shooting you in the foot, then the leg, then the knee, then…well, you get the idea."

Imogene nodded. "It's all about the West Valley Motor Speedway."

Goldblatt's mouth sagged open.

"The million dollars is bribe money to the mayor. You were somehow involved, and part of that money was supposed to go to you. Donald Ho works for the Chinese company building the speedway. They paid the bribe money to get the plans approved through the city council. That's why Donald's here."

Goldblatt recovered quickly, the evil grin returning. He clapped. "Very good. But for bonus points, tell me, who burned up in the car outside the Stuft Shirt restaurant?"

It's Ocalas Razor. Tell 'em. This one's easy as pie.

"If I had to guess, I'd say it's kinda obvious. It's Occam's Razor."

"Ha." Goldblatt smiled. "Go on."

"The simplest explanation is preferable to one that is more complex."

"And?"

"I would guess you used an obstinate city councilman who didn't want the speedway. Burnt him to a crisp so he could never be identified. Took care of his dental records, I imagine. That leaves you still dead and free as a bird. And that would also mean you probably bought up a lot of property surrounding the speedway. That's why you needed the councilman out of the way. You have plenty of money. But you took the valise filled with cash because you couldn't allow the mayor to pull one over on you. Your ego's as large as this house."

Goldblatt sat back in his chair. He took out a cigarette case, extracted a narrow brown cigarro, tapped the tip against the case. "You got a match?"

Ange jumped in, said, *How about my butt and your face?*

Humphries said, "Is all that true?"

Goldblatt's head whipped around. He glared at Humphries. "Of course it's all true. If you two bumbling idiots had half the brains this old broad has, we wouldn't be sitting here now waiting for her to produce the money." He turned back to face Imogene. As he did, he pulled a gun from his waistband.

Donald Ho couldn't see the move. He'd had enough and made for the front door.

Goldblatt pivoted and shot him in the back. The gun booming in the small living room.

The living room with the portrait of Joyce looking down, judging. Always judging.

Donald Ho fell to the floor.

Imogene's hand moved in slow motion. Too slow. Goldblatt whipped around and pointed the gun at her. He grinned. His finger tightened on the trigger. He no longer cared about the million dollars. Or he thought she had it hidden somewhere in the house.

Bang.

A gun went off.

Chapter Twenty-Seven

Imogene jumped in her seat. She lived a whole life in half a second.

The gunshot came from the left, the doorway to the kitchen. Gun smoke billowed over her, acrid and bitter.

Goldblatt took the bullet to the shoulder. His gun hand sagged. The gun fell to the floor.

Humphries pulled his gun.

Luke Short stepped from the kitchen into the living room, a gun leveled at Humphries. "FBI, don't you do it."

Humphries dropped the gun and went to his knees, his face in his hands.

Luke Short yelled. "Suz, make the call."

In the kitchen, Suz picked up the phone and dialed. The sedate sounds had a calming effect. Just before Donald started to moan.

Luke Short didn't look at Imogene and kept his eyes on Humphries and Goldblatt.

Sirens filled the air.

How had they gotten there so soon? Luke Short must've queued them up down the street, and they had only waited for the phone call.

In seconds, blue suits swarmed around the house. They came in through both back door and front, guns drawn, eyes wide, ready for action.

They grappled up Humphries and Goldblatt, handcuffed them, escorted them out to waiting cop cars. Paramedics scooped up Donald and trundled him off to the hospital.

The loud din dissipated all at once.

Imogene's house returned to normal. But what was normal? This was the new normal, and Imogene didn't like it one bit.

Suz came out of the kitchen where she'd been huddling, hugging herself. Luke put his arm around her, escorted her to the chair. He knelt next to her and held her hand. "It's okay. It's all over."

Through all of it, Imogene had not moved one inch. It had happened all around her.

Finally, Ange returned. *Pfft. FBI. I knew it all along.*

"You did not. I'm not a fool, and I won't believe that for one second."

Luke and Suz broke eye contact with each other and looked over at her as if she were a full-blown loon.

"Would one of you please bring me a Schlitz from the refrigerator. My nerves are like to tear me apart."

Suz smiled, got up, and headed for the kitchen.

Luke smiled at Imogene. Didn't say a word. He pulled his long stiletto from his boot, got down on one knee, and cut out a new square of gold high-low carpet, the place where Donald had bled.

Acknowledgments

This project would not have happened without the great assistance from Shawn and Deb; thank you.

About the Author

During his career in law enforcement, best-selling author David Putnam has worked in narcotics, violent crimes, criminal intelligence, hostage rescue, SWAT, and internal affairs, to name just a few. He is the recipient of many awards and commendations for heroism. He has three book series: The Bruno Johnson series, The Dave Beckett series, and the Imogene Taylor series. *Imogene's Grand Fiasco* is the second book in the series after *The Blind Devotion of Imogene*.

AUTHOR WEBSITE:

wwDavidPutnambooks.com

SOCIAL MEDIA HANDLES:

David@DavidPutnamBooks.com

Facebook.com/DavidPutnamBooks

Instagram.com/DavidPutnamBooks

Goodreads.com/ DavidPutnam

Also by David Putnam

The Bruno Johnson Series:
The Disposables (2014)
The Replacements (2014)
The Squandered (2016)
The Vanquished (2017)
The Innocents (2018)
The Reckless (2019)
The Heartless (2020)
The Ruthless (2021)
The Sinister (2022)
The Scorned (2023)
The Diabolical (2024)

The Dave Beckett Series:
A Fearsome Moonlight Black
A Lonesome Blood Red Sun

The Imogene Taylor Series:
The Blind Devotion of Imogene
Imogene's Grand Fiasco